"About last night—" Laura began.

Quinn cut her off. "Forget about last night."

"But I want to thank you. It was very kind of you to—"

"I wasn't trying to be kind."

"Oh, no?" she challenged. "Then why did you come to me and offer to stay until I went to sleep?"

His hard gray gaze moved suggestively to the swell of her breasts. "Is it so surprising that I'd want to be in your bed?"

"Is that what you want me to believe?" Laura said, angering. She wouldn't allow him to ignore the genuine emotions behind his actions. "Why is it so hard for you to admit that you're capable of offering kindness, and that maybe you need someone to do the same for you?"

"I don't *need* anyone," Quinn said instantly.

"Fine. But you might want to ask yourself whether you're lying to me or to yourself." She spun away, intending to slam the door behind her, only to be caught by a strong hand. Quinn pulled her into his embrace, and his mouth was on hers before she could utter another word.

Dear Reader,

In past months I've used this page to tell you what we editors are doing to live up to the name Silhouette **Special Edition**:

> We've brought you the latest releases from authors you've made into stars; we've introduced new writers we hope you'll take to your heart. We've offered classic romantic plots; we've premiered innovative angles in storytelling. We've presented miniseries, sequels and spin-offs; we've reissued timeless favorites in Silhouette *Classics*. We've even updated our covers, striving to give you editions you can be proud to read, happy to own.

All these editorial efforts are aimed at making Silhouette **Special Edition** a consistently satisfying line of sophisticated, substantial, emotion-packed novels that will touch your heart and live on in your memory long after the last page is turned.

In coming months our authors will speak out from this page as well, sharing with you what's special to them about Silhouette **Special Edition**. I'd love to hear from *you*, too. In the past your letters have helped guide us in our editorial choices. How do you think we're doing now? Some time ago I made a promise on this page— that "each and every month, Silhouette **Special Edition** is dedicated to becoming more special than ever." Are we living up to that promise? What's special to *you* about Silhouette **Special Edition**? Share your feelings with us, and, who knows—maybe some day *your* name will appear on this page!

My very best wishes,

Leslie Kazanjian, Senior Editor
Silhouette Books
300 East 42nd Street
New York, N.Y. 10017

GINA FERRIS
Healing
Sympathy

Silhouette Special Edition

Published by Silhouette Books New York

America's Publisher of Contemporary Romance

For Sandra Canfield, with friendship, gratitude,
a little awe, and fond memories of a shared "first."

SILHOUETTE BOOKS
300 East 42nd St., New York, N.Y. 10017

ISBN: 0-373-09496-5

First Silhouette Books printing December 1988

Printed in the U.S.A.

GINA FERRIS

has lived her entire life within twenty miles of the Arkansas hospital where she was born and is a confirmed armchair traveler as a result. "I haven't had an exotic life," she admits, "but it has been a happy one, filled with love and encouragement—which is probably the reason I enjoy writing happily-ever-after romances."

Gina met her husband when he sat down beside her in her first college class at Arkansas State University, where she was studying journalism. "As foolishly romantic as it may sound," she says, "I knew by the end of that first class that he and I were special together." She began writing fiction when her second daughter was born four years ago, and sold her first book a year later, fulfilling a long-time dream. Gina Ferris also writes under the name Gina Wilkins.

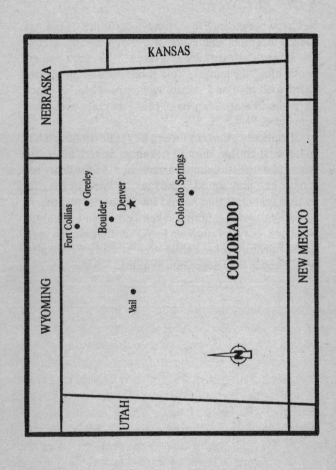

Chapter One

Though she had no intention of buying it, Laura Sutherland picked up the newest Quinn Gallagher novel and scanned the back cover. It had been at the top of the lists for weeks now. Rumor had it that it would be made into a movie, just like his first two novels, but she had no desire to read the grim epic. Gallagher's books were stark tales of crime and violence in which the weak and vulnerable were victims and the ruthless were dominant and usually victorious. Laura hadn't seen the one movie based on his work that had already been released, nor did she intend to see the one that was due for release in the next few weeks.

Wrinkling her nose, she replaced the book on the rack in front of her and moved three steps sideways to seriously consider the newest romance novels on the bookstore shelves. She had never been able to resist a happy ending.

"Did it look that bad?"

Laura turned her head to find a tall, lean man standing in the very spot where she'd been only moments before. A very attractive man, she noted automatically, even as she said, "I beg your pardon?"

"The Quinn Gallagher book. I wondered why you made that face. Like it smelled bad or something." The man didn't smile as he spoke but gazed steadily into her eyes as if he were sincerely interested in her answer.

Laura pushed a wisp of curly blond hair out of her face and smiled ruefully. "That pretty well sums up my feelings about it," she admitted. She waited for him to defend the book; after all, men usually liked that macho type of fiction.

Instead the man pursed his lips thoughtfully beneath his brown mustache and nodded once, briefly. "I see," he murmured. His gray eyes cut sideways to take in the array of romances in front of Laura. Lifting a copy of the book she now held in her hand, he began to read the blurb on the back. As he read, Laura watched him, making no effort to be discreet in her study. After all, he *had* approached her. If this was an attempted pickup, she reflected with a ripple of amusement, he was being awfully serious about it.

At first glance she'd thought him to be dark. At second, she realized the darkness had been something of an illusion. His hair, untouched by gray despite her guess that he was near forty, was rich brown at the roots but sun-lightened almost to blond around his face. It was heavy, luxurious hair, softly parted on the left and brushed back, though its very weight made it fall forward onto his forehead. She would have loved to run her hands through that hair, she mused fleetingly, curling her fingers more tightly around the book she'd chosen.

His eyebrows were brown, straight and divided by a vertical crease that gave him a perpetual frown. She'd always liked mustaches, and his was thick and silky-looking, parting in the center to reveal the interesting shape of his upper lip. She'd have called his mouth kissable had it shown the slightest appearance of a smile. She fancied that the illusion of darkness about him was an aura, a clue to his personality, then chided herself for her foolishness.

Even as his gunmetal-gray gaze turned back to meet hers, Laura found herself wondering if those lean, smooth cheeks ever creased with a grin. She couldn't quite picture him grinning.

"This is more your taste in reading?" he asked her, his voice still quietly pleasant despite his obvious distaste for the book in his strong-looking hands.

"Yes," she returned just as politely. "I love happy endings."

She thought the corner of his mouth flicked into a semblance of a smile as he replaced the novel on the shelf, but the movement was so fleeting that she could have been wrong. It surprised her how very much she suddenly wanted to see this man smile. "Um, do you like Quinn Gallagher's books?" she asked impulsively, suddenly not wanting him to walk away.

He tiled his head and gave the seemingly simple question grave consideration. "Sometimes," he answered finally.

"Sometimes?" she repeated, encouraging him to continue.

"Yeah. Sometimes." He did smile then—not a grin by any interpretation, but a slight movement that just touched the corners of his mouth, tilting his soft mustache invitingly. Her heart jerked at that faint softening of his expression. It had been a long time since she'd been quite this intrigued by a man.

He dipped his head in a gesture that suggested a bow. "I'll be seeing you," he said, and turned to walk away.

When? she wanted to call after him. Then she blinked and closed her mouth with an audible snap.

"What a strange man," she murmured, her eyes lingering on the width of his shoulders beneath his heavy, sheepskin-lined parka as he walked out the door of the bookstore and into the frigid winter air. And what a compelling man, she added silently, wondering if he'd actually meant that he'd be seeing her again or if the words had simply been a casual way of ending the impromptu conversation.

She couldn't stop thinking of him as she climbed behind the wheel of her car, the two books she'd chosen stapled into a paper bag and piled with other purchases in the back seat. Turning onto the long stretch of highway that would eventually take her home, she replayed the brief but somehow memorable encounter several times in her mind.

I'll be seeing you.

She shook her head. Of course she wouldn't see him again. Greeley, Colorado, wasn't that small a town. Chances were their paths wouldn't cross. The sigh that left her parted lips at the thought startled her. It had actually sounded regretful.

Her arms piled with packages, Laura stepped onto the long porch that ran the full length of her large, two-story frame house, her crepe-soled shoes making no sound on the painted boards. She paused to glance down at a ragged, three-legged gray cat contentedly washing his one back paw as he rested beside his best friend, a plump white duck named Doo. "Hello, Sabu. Sorry I can't scratch your ears just now, but as you can see, my hands are full. Catch you later, okay?"

Laura smiled as the cat meowed understandingly.

The front door opened before she reached it. "Hi, Laura. Did you remember that nail polish I asked for? And the magazines. Did you get the magazines?'' asked the obviously pregnant teenager standing in the doorway, a welcoming smile creasing her heart-shaped face.

"Yes, I remembered the nail polish and the magazines, Janet. I also refilled your vitamin prescription and made you an appointment with the doctor for next week.''

An elderly woman with a vague smile and kindly eyes appeared behind Janet. "Hello, dear. You're home late today, aren't you?''

"Yes, Mrs. Elliott. I had several things to do after work this afternoon. And I did some shopping. I found the color of yarn you wanted. Three skeins enough?''

"Oh, yes, lovely. Thank you, Laura.''

"I'll go get the rest of the bags,'' Janet offered.

"Careful, sweetie, some of them are heavy,'' Laura warned, setting her packages on the glossy cherry table in the foyer.

The teenager threw an impatient look over her shoulder as she stepped outside. "I can manage.''

Mrs. Elliott clucked and shook her head. Though Laura stood just five foot seven, the older woman came only to her shoulder. "She's so independent,'' Mrs. Elliott murmured, watching Janet for a moment before turning to rummage eagerly in the bags for the yarn Laura had brought her.

Laura plucked the package containing the romance novels from the pile on the table, pushing a mental image of the stranger with the luscious hair and penetrating eyes firmly out of her thoughts. "Where's—'' she began, only to be interrupted by a child's squeal.

"Aunt 'aura! Aunt 'aura!''

Laura held out her arms to catch the little body hurtling at her. She was promptly rewarded by a smacking, juicy kiss from a three-year-old imp with enormous blue eyes and a long, swinging blond braid. "Hi, Renee. Have you been a good girl today?"

Renee nodded vigorously.

Laura reached over to the table to pull out a coloring book and a box of crayons. "Then here's a present for you. These will replace the ones Sabu chewed up."

Clutching the gift in chubby fingers, Renee smiled broadly, exposing at least four dimples in her round face. "Thank you, Aunt 'aura."

"You're welcome, sweetheart. Where's your mommy?"

"Inna kitchen. I color now?"

"Yes, go color. I'll find your mommy."

Laura headed down a long hallway toward the kitchen. A delicious aroma emanated from the room, and she licked her lips greedily. She'd skipped lunch and she was starving. "That smells so good, Betty," she commented as she pushed through the swinging door. "What is it and when will it be ready?"

The woman standing at the stove was only five years older than Laura's twenty-seven, but looked at least ten years older. Shorter than Laura and a good ten pounds underweight, Betty Pritchard wore her dull brown hair in an unflattering ponytail. Her green eyes were shadowed and haunted, her unpainted cheeks pale, but a smile curved her thin lips as she looked at Laura. "Don't tell me you missed lunch again."

"I'm afraid so. Things got hectic at the hospital."

"How's the Johnson baby doing?"

"He seemed a little better today. His vital signs are stabilizing."

"Oh, that's good. And the Travanti twins?"

"The boy's up four ounces. The girl's still under three pounds, but she's much better than she was two weeks ago."

"You look tired. Why don't you go freshen up? Dinner will be ready in about fifteen minutes."

"Great. What would I do without you, Betty?" Laura said gratefully.

Betty shrugged one thin shoulder beneath her gray cotton blouse. "You'd just bring home another stray to do the cooking," she said matter-of-factly. "Now go on and let me finish up here."

"Yes, ma'am," Laura replied with assumed meekness.

Stepping into her bedroom, Laura finally shed the heavy quilted slate-blue coat she hadn't yet bothered to remove. Her room had been decorated as a woodland retreat, and that was how she viewed it as she closed the door behind her. Drawing strength from the rich browns and deep greens of the furniture and fabrics, the delicate floral wallpaper and the lovely oil landscapes, she mused that as much as she loved her assorted housemates, there was always a sense of relief in closing herself in her own room.

Here she could escape for a little while from the pressures of her job as head nurse in a neonatal intensive care nursery and the cheerful but noisy chatter of her eccentric makeshift "family." During the past few years Laura had continued her late father's longtime tradition of taking in people who had nowhere else to go, and she'd never regretted that decision, preferring to share her large home with people who needed her rather than live alone. Still, there were times when she cherished the silence of her room.

Shedding the blouse of her rumpled white uniform, she pulled out a soft sweater and a comfortable pair of jeans, planning to enjoy each of the fifteen minutes of solitude she would have until dinner was served.

But somehow she wasn't completely alone. Thoughts of a brooding, handsome stranger kept intruding on her privacy, and Laura found herself becoming annoyed with him.

Why wouldn't he go away and leave her alone? He'd been attractive, true, but her fascination with him wasn't entirely physical. There was something about his eyes—something that had drawn her. Something that wouldn't let her forget him.

Everyone was settled at the long table in the dining room when the doorbell rang. Having just finished saying the blessing, Laura lifted her head and frowned slightly at the sound. She really was hungry, she thought wistfully.

"Oh, dear, whoever could that be?" Mrs. Elliott murmured, her forehead creasing beneath the crimped gray-blue hair that almost exactly matched her eyes. "Have I forgotten that we're having guests?"

"We aren't expecting guests, Mrs. Elliott," Laura replied gently. She glanced at Betty, whose face had gone starkly white, making the dark circles under her frightened eyes stand out dramatically. "I'll see who it is, Betty. I'm sure it's nothing to worry about."

"No, of course not," Betty whispered, obviously not convinced.

"Want me to get it?" Janet volunteered.

"No, thanks." Laura shook her head in amused exasperation as she walked down the hallway to the front door. Unexpected visitors were a definite disruption of the normal household routine.

But she promptly forgot her housemates when she opened the door to find the odd stranger from the bookstore looking down at her with the same dispassionate gray gaze she'd tried so hard to forget.

"What are you doing here?" Laura asked blankly.

He gave her that funny little quirk of the mouth she already recognized as his only outward sign of amusement, then asked, "You are Laura Sutherland, aren't you?"

"Yes, I am. Who are you?" she asked in return, forgetting her manners in her surprise at seeing him again.

"Quinn Gallagher."

Laura exhaled in mild disgust. "Sure you are," she drawled sarcastically.

His mouth twitched again. "I am," he assured her quietly, reaching into the back pocket of his faded jeans for his wallet. He flipped it open to reveal a Florida driver's license.

"Oh, my God," Laura muttered weakly, staring at the name and photograph on the plastic card. "You really are Quinn Gallagher."

"I told you I was," he pointed out, returning the wallet to his pocket.

"Yes, I know you did," she answered impatiently. Honestly, didn't the man's expression ever change, aside from that infrequent and almost nonexistent smile of his? "What can I do for you, Mr. Gallagher?"

"I was told you have a guest cottage you might be willing to rent to me for a few weeks. Is that correct?"

"Who told you that?"

"Dr. Amos Webster. I understand he's a friend of yours."

"My godfather," Laura admitted slowly. "He lives in Florida."

"I know. I rent a room from him there. When I told him I was thinking of spending some time in Colorado, he suggested I look you up. You can call him to confirm," he added, slipping his hands into the front pockets of his jeans as if he had nothing better to do than to wait for her decision.

"I will." Acting on a sudden impulse, Laura moved aside to allow him to enter. "Have you had dinner, Mr. Gallagher? We were just about to eat. There's plenty of food, if you'd care to join us."

Quinn hesitated a moment, then walked slowly past her. "If you're sure it's not an imposition."

"Not at all," she answered graciously, struggling not to grin. They were suddenly being ridiculously polite, she mused wryly. She led him into the dining room where an interesting assortment of expressions met them—Betty's frightened, Renee's and Janet's curious, Mrs. Elliott's vaguely welcoming. "Everyone, this is Quinn Gallagher. He's joining us for dinner tonight." Then she rapidly introduced her housemates to Quinn.

As Betty went to get a plate for Quinn, Laura took his coat and invited him to be seated. The only empty chair was at the opposite end of the table from where Laura had been sitting—the place her father had occupied until his death just over a year ago. Quinn slid smoothly into the chair, nodding pleasantly to Janet as she smiled a cheery greeting. Renee, on his other side, stared at him in timid curiosity, but he didn't seem at all conscious of the child's attention. Laura deemed it safe to leave them for a few minutes while she made a quick call to Florida.

"Amos, this is Laura," she blurted as soon as she'd connected with her longtime friend and godfather. "Did you—"

"I take it Quinn has arrived?" the retired physician interrupted blandly.

"So you really did send him here." Laura shook her head in resignation. "Why, Amos?"

"He needs a place to stay for a few weeks," Amos replied, all innocence.

"He can afford a hotel or a resort cottage. Why did you send him here?" Laura repeated doggedly.

"Let's just say I'm sending you another stray, darlin'. He needs you."

Laura failed to hold back an incredulous laugh. "Oh, sure. Quinn Gallagher, the famous writer, the man with the iron face, needs help. I'm not buying this, Amos."

"Honey, you've already identified his problem. 'The man with the iron face has lost the ability to enjoy life. I'm counting on you to reeducate him."

"Why me?" Laura asked with a groan.

"Because no one enjoys life more than you do. That boy's a friend of mine, and he needs help. You're not going to turn him away, are you?"

"That *boy* has got to be forty years old."

"He's thirty-five," Amos replied brusquely.

Laura blinked. "Oh. He looks older."

"He's forgotten how to be young. Let him stay awhile, Laura. The cottage is still empty, isn't it?"

"You know it is. *I* keep you informed about what's going on in my life. You never told me about Quinn Gallagher."

"I distinctly remember telling you that I've been renting a room to a writer friend because it got kind of lonesome in this house of mine. You approved of the idea, as I recall."

"You never told me his name. Or anything at all about him."

"I had my reasons," her godfather answered obscurely. "So, girl, are you going to let him stay?"

She twisted the hem of her sweater, her face thoughtful. "Just what do you expect me to do for him, Amos?"

"You don't have to do anything special. I'm hoping that he'll benefit from the beauty of the area and your own lovely smile. You have smiled for him, haven't you, darlin'?"

"Not much," Laura muttered. "He doesn't exactly encourage it."

"Well, smile for him anyway."

Laura frowned suspiciously. "Amos?"

"Yes?"

"You're not trying your hand at matchmaking, are you? Believe me, I'm not interested."

"Matchmaking?" Amos repeated indignantly. "Of course not. I have better things to do with my time than arrange romance for a beautiful young woman who probably has to beat men off with a stick." Neither of them mentioned that it had been Amos who'd introduced her to Robbie, her former fiancé, or that he'd denied just as vehemently then that he'd been matchmaking.

Laura chuckled, looking around the empty study, pushing the bittersweet memories from her mind. Just where were those hordes of men, anyway?

"I just thought the clean Colorado air and your nice friends would be good for Quinn," Amos continued. "He's hurting, Laura, and I've never been able to see anyone in pain without trying to help. You know that."

"Yes, I know. Daddy was the same way," Laura replied fondly.

"And you're just like us," Amos answered knowingly. "He's a good man, honey. Don't turn him away."

How could she argue with that? Bowing to the inevitable, Laura assured Amos that she would allow Quinn the use of the guest cottage, though she made no promises that she could help the man with whatever problems he might have. She hung up the phone and dropped her face into her hands. How did she get herself into these things? she wondered despairingly. Then she squared her shoulders, lifted her chin and walked back to the dining room to welcome her new stray to the fold.

Laura was delighted—and secretly relieved—to see that Quinn's expression had actually changed. He looked bewildered. She could only imagine the kind of conversation that had gone on around him in her absence. "Gosh, this looks good," she said as she slipped into her seat and picked up her fork.

"Betty, this lasagna is delicious," she enthused, swallowing a welcome mouthful. She doubted that either Betty or Renee had spoken since Quinn had entered the room. They had good reason not to trust men and were always wary of strangers.

"I'm glad you like it," Betty murmured shyly. "Is yours cold? I'll pop it in the microwave for you if you like."

"No, thank you, it's fine. Can I get you anything, Mr. Gallagher?"

"No, thanks," he answered, swallowing the last bite of his dinner. "Did you call Amos?"

"Yes, I did. He confirmed that you're a friend of his. You're welcome to use the cottage for as long as you like."

"He's moving into the cottage?" Janet demanded. "How come?"

"He needs a place to stay," Laura answered, turning a quelling frown on the outspoken girl.

"Mr. Jacobson was such a nice man," Mrs. Elliott put in, looking soulfully at Quinn.

Since she seemed to be waiting for a reply, he slanted a questioning look toward Laura. "Mr. Jacobson lived in the cottage until a couple of months ago," she informed him.

"He was recovering from a broken heart," Janet added, wide, mischievous brown eyes directed toward Quinn. "His wife left him for another guy. You got a wife, Mr. Gallagher?"

"Janet," Laura interceded quickly, "back off."

"Just trying to be friendly," her young friend replied carelessly. "Didn't mean to pry, Mr. Gallagher."

"I don't have a wife," Quinn told her, his gaze drifting down to her noticeably protruding stomach before turning back to Laura. "Would it be possible for me to move in tonight?"

"Yes. I'll get you some fresh linens after dinner. The cottage doesn't have a washer and dryer, but you're welcome to use the ones here in the main house. You needn't knock every time you enter, either. Feel free to come in whenever you like. As for meals, the cottage has a kitchen, but you're welcome to eat with us. Breakfast is at seven, lunch at noon for those who are here, and dinner at—"

"I'll take care of my own meals," Quinn broke in.

Laura didn't think he'd actually meant to be rude, but he managed to be, anyway. "Fine," she answered a bit shortly, forgetting that Amos had asked her to smile at this exasperating man. What good would a smile do? she asked herself. The man was obviously hopelessly solemn.

After dinner Laura asked Quinn to wait for her in the den while she gathered linens and retrieved the key to the cottage. When she rejoined him in the large, warmly decorated room, she was astonished to find Renee sitting quietly on Quinn's knee. "She just crawled up there on her own," Betty whispered to Laura, looking perplexedly at her tiny daughter. "I don't understand it. She never goes to strangers—particularly men."

"I know," Laura replied. "Are children always attracted to you, Mr. Gallagher?" she asked, trying to make pleasant conversation.

"I like kids," he replied, holding the child with ease. "I guess they sense it."

"Mr. Gallagher needs to go to the cottage now, Renee. Go to Mommy."

Renee turned her huge blue eyes up to Laura somberly, her many dimples conspicuously absent. "Hurts," she said succinctly.

"What hurts, Renee?" Laura asked, thinking the child might be ill. "Your tummy?"

"Him." Renee patted Quinn's broad chest. "Hurts."

In a moment of blank silence the three adults stared at the uncannily perceptive toddler. "Yes, well, I'm sure he'll be just fine," Laura stammered, flustered. Hadn't Amos told her that Quinn was hurting? How could Renee sense anything behind that emotionless facade Quinn Gallagher wore like a suit of armor? Just what was it that was hurting this man?

Rather abruptly Quinn set the child on her feet and pushed himself out of the deep armchair. "Good night, Mrs. Pritchard," he said to Betty. "Good night, Renee." Without another glance at the little girl he turned on one heel and stalked out of the room, leaving Laura to follow as best she could with her arm load of towels and sheets.

Chapter Two

Quinn had no words of praise for the snug little guest cottage, though he didn't criticize, either. The cottage was clean and recently dusted, since Laura never knew when her next guest would appear. She gave Quinn a quick, unnecessary tour of the two rooms and tiny bath that made up his temporary home. He followed closely behind her as she walked, closer than necessary even in the small rooms, and Laura was much too aware of his proximity. His size. His unexpectedly graceful movements.

She turned abruptly to return to the safety of her own house, the hasty movement causing her to walk right into him. She hadn't realized he'd taken a step closer to look over her shoulder into the bathroom she'd just shown him.

Quinn's hands shot out to steady her, though she'd already regained her balance. "You okay?" he asked in his deep, quiet voice.

"Yes, I'm—fine," she replied, her shoulders somehow feeling the heat of his palms even through her thick coat and sweater. "I'm sorry. That was clumsy of me."

"No. I was standing too close." Still he didn't release her but stared down at her with those gray eyes that told her nothing yet somehow seemed to mirror his thoughts. If only she knew how to read him, she thought a bit wistfully, returning the bold look with what she hoped was equal impassivity.

He lifted one hand and stroked the line of her cheek with the back of his thumb. "Amos keeps your photograph on his mantel. Did you know that?"

"Yes," she answered, her voice a bit husky. "I've visited him in Florida. Before you moved in."

"He's very fond of you. He talks about you often."

She could almost feel Quinn's breath ruffling the curls on her forehead. She wasn't sure how long she could continue this conversation without stuttering. He was standing so close. She took a deep breath and made an effort to speak clearly. "I'm very fond of him, too. I've known him all my life."

"Your portrait doesn't do you justice. You're even more beautiful in person." Quinn stroked her jaw as he spoke, then frowned and stepped abruptly away from her.

Feeling as if she'd suddenly been dropped to earth with a thud, Laura blinked and turned toward the door, telling him to feel free to ask her if he needed anything.

"This is fine." Quinn walked with her to the door then hesitated. Sensing that he had something more to say, Laura paused. "Those people—do they all live with you?" he asked.

"Yes, they do. I have a large house—two bedrooms downstairs and four upstairs—so we have plenty of room. Why?"

"I was just curious. You, uh, you rent out rooms?"

"No. They're my friends. I don't charge them. Betty works for me as housekeeper and cook and she insists that room and board make up most of her salary, but she would be welcome to stay, regardless. I like her and I adore Renee. My housemates are all people who have nowhere else to go or need help for some reason, but I don't consider myself to be handing out charity. I love them, and they bring a great deal of pleasure into my life." Though she hadn't mentioned that she had a comfortable amount of money available for the care of her guests, Laura had otherwise answered him with complete honesty since she suspected that curiosity was not something Quinn expressed often. Healthy curiosity was good for him.

"I'll be paying rent while I'm here," Quinn informed her concisely. He reached for his wallet for the second time since he'd arrived. "How much?"

"We'll settle up tomorrow. And don't argue," Laura ordered, when he appeared ready to do just that. "I have no intention of doing you any favors, Mr. Gallagher. You obviously don't want any."

"That's right. I don't."

"Fine. Good night." Chin high, she stepped outside. Something made her turn just as he moved to close the door. "Oh, by the way. About what I said in the bookstore—"

"Don't apologize," he cut in, sounding bored. "I couldn't care less if you dislike my books."

"I wasn't going to apologize for expressing my opinion," Laura snapped, instantly annoyed. "I still don't like your books. However, I didn't mean to offend you."

"You didn't." With that, he closed the door in her face.

"What a strange man," Laura muttered for the second time that day. "Almost nice one minute and a real jerk the next, for no apparent reason. Oh, Amos, what have you done to me?"

Quinn shoved his fingers through his heavy hair to push it off his forehead as he looked impassively around the main room of the cottage. The long, narrow room served as kitchen and dining area at one end and living room at the other. A door directly in the center of the back wall led into the bedroom and small bathroom. The total area of his temporary home was perhaps eight hundred square feet. But then he didn't need much in the way of space.

He'd brought in his things from his aging Jeep: a portable computer that now sat in the center of the tiny round dining table and a canvas duffel bag that lay on the floor beside the bed in the other room. He didn't need much in the way of possessions, either.

Neither television nor radio were provided, but he wouldn't have turned them on if they had been. The books that served as his only form of entertainment—if such sober, heavy tomes could be considered as such—were stuffed somewhere deep in his duffel bag. They didn't interest him now.

He was tired. So damned tired. God only knew when he'd last gotten a full night's sleep. He tried to tell himself that sleep was another thing he didn't need, but his aching, weary body told him differently. Stripping off his white cotton shirt as he walked, he headed to the bedroom. Fifteen minutes later he had the bed made up, the thermostat set just high enough to dull the chill in the cottage and a patchwork quilt pulled to his ears as he lay naked on the narrow bed, striving for oblivion. His body needed it, his mind craved it, but sleep remained just out of reach, nibbling at the edges of his consciousness but refusing to swallow him.

He'd never seen skin quite like hers, he found himself thinking, not bothering to clarify in his mind whose skin he was contemplating. Nor felt skin as soft. Smooth as carved ivory, delicately tinted with shades of rose and peach, unmarred by line or blemish. The first time he'd seen her she'd worn a heavy quilted coat over a uniform of some type, later a thick sweater and a pair of jeans. All he'd seen of her skin had been her beautiful face, slender throat and long-fingered hands. He wondered if the rest of her body were as flawless.

He'd known who she was the moment he'd seen her in the bookstore. Quinn had been looking at the photograph on Amos's mantel for almost a year. There was no way he could have missed recognizing her.

He dreamed about her sometimes. He could never exactly remember what happened in those dreams, only that she had been in them. Not surprising, considering the hours he'd spent staring at the photograph of her. He could close his eyes even now and see that picture—Laura smiling brightly at the camera, her face surrounded by a halo of impossibly curly golden hair, her brown eyes seeming to dance with inner laughter. Something had drawn him to that silver-framed portrait again and again. He would stand in front of it for a long time, staring at it as he worked out plot twists in his mind, not seeing her and yet never unaware of her.

"Why do you do that?" Amos had asked him once, frowning thoughtfully at the younger man when he found him once again at the spot before the fireplace. "What is it about Laura's picture that draws you over there?"

Quinn had turned away from the mantel with a frown, looking blankly at the man whose house he'd shared for several months. "I don't know," he'd replied with a shrug. "Just habit." Never one to pry into things that didn't concern him, Amos had only nodded and changed the subject, leaving Quinn with a vague sense of relief that he hadn't been required to delve any deeper into his motivations.

This trip to Colorado had not been something he'd planned, exactly. He'd certainly never intended to meet the woman in the photograph. It was just that he'd been restless lately, unsettled. Sleeping even less than usual, finding it hard to concentrate on his writing. And the dreams—the bad ones that he could remember no more clearly than those containing Laura—were coming with more frequency.

Amos, always the perceptive one, had suggested that Quinn needed a change of scenery—a working vacation. It had been Amos who'd recommended Colorado.

"Why Colorado?" Quinn had asked.

"I spent two-thirds of my life in Colorado," Amos had answered, his round, creased face pleasant, his faded green eyes innocent of subterfuge. "There's nothing like the crisp, fresh winter air there to clear out the mustiness of a stale mind. Do you good."

"I don't need a vacation."

"Everyone needs a vacation sometimes. Consider it research for a possible new setting for your books. Your readers may be getting tired of New York or Miami or L.A. Surely there's a crime story to be written in Greeley. And the press would never find you tucked away in the mountains."

"I suppose you're also going to recommend a place to stay?"

"Of course. My goddaughter, Laura, lives in a large house on some ninety acres of wooded mountainside. Her nearest neighbor's a mile away. Greeley's about a thirty-minute drive east. She has a guest cottage that she rents out sometimes, and I happen to know it's empty just now. It's just what you need. You can take long walks, ski if you like, and write like you've never written before. Why don't you try it, boy?''

It always made Quinn uncomfortable when the older man called him boy. Made him feel like a favorite grandson. Quinn didn't want that familial feeling. He didn't want emotional ties. He chose to be alone, to keep himself emotionally apart from those around him, even those, like Amos, whom he could not help liking. Ever since he'd lost his mother, and then his brother, Quinn had made a deliberate effort to avoid that kind of gut-ripping pain again by keeping his emotions out of his few relationships with others. He'd been doing so for so long now that he doubted he had any genuine emotion left. Lately he'd begun to feel like a dead man inside—a machine that functioned as a body was supposed to function but that had lost whatever spark of soul or softness that would make him human. Even if he *had* wanted more than cool courtesy from his interactions with others—which he was sure he didn't—who could possibly love an unfeeling automaton?

Dragging the patchwork quilt with him, Quinn threw himself onto his other side and wondered just why Amos had wanted him to come here. Did the old man consider Quinn another stray in need of whatever the hell Laura offered to those she took in? If so, Amos was wrong. Even if Laura were interested in reforming Quinn or revitalizing him or whatever, she had said herself that those she helped gave her something in return—pleasure, assistance with cooking or cleaning, something. Quinn had nothing to offer.

Peace and solitude, Amos had promised him. Yeah, solitude. He would be sharing this retreat with a beautiful, perplexing woman, a visibly frightened mother and her unusual though oddly compelling daughter, a pregnant, smart-mouthed teenager and a dippy little old lady.

Strange how the only one of the bunch who made him the least bit uncomfortable was Laura.

Three a.m. found Quinn at his computer, wrapped in the patchwork quilt as he attacked the keyboard with his usual intense violence—he'd been through two keyboards in as many years. A cigarette smoldered in an ashtray at his elbow and occasionally he stopped writing to draw deeply on it, staring at the green symbols that made up the story he was telling.

His protagonist, a New York cop on the beat, had just come across a thirteen-year-old hooker who'd been beaten to a bloody pulp and left dead in a Dumpster. The cop sighed, glanced without emotion at the all-too-familiar corpse and called it in, regretting the fact that he'd probably be detained awhile at the scene. He was hungry. He thought of steak and eggs while he waited for homicide to arrive. Quinn would have shrugged off any suggestion that there was anything odd in the cop fantasizing about food while a dead child lay beside him. It was, after all, what Quinn himself would have done. Had in fact done, when the same situation had happened to him some six years earlier. He'd had to learn to react that way to keep himself sane after his first couple of years on the force when he'd torn himself up over every murder, every wasted young life. Most of the material in Quinn's books came from experience.

An hour later Quinn was back in bed, trying to add to the four hours' sleep he'd managed earlier. He was up again at six, having slept maybe forty-five minutes. He located a coffeepot and a canister of coffee in the partially stocked kitchen and set the brew on to perk. He had just lit another cigarette when he heard a car door slam outside. Mild curiosity took him to the window.

Laura was sitting in her idling car with the interior light on as she rummaged through something on the seat beside her. Quinn watched her until she snapped the interior light off and drove away. He glanced at his watch. Six-twenty. What was she doing leaving at this time on a Friday morning? It was barely light outside. He checked the house, surprised to see that most of the lights were on. An early-rising household, apparently. He turned away from the window, telling himself that he had no interest in his unorthodox neighbors.

He wondered where Laura had gone and when she'd be home.

The light was on in the cottage. Laura was surprised that he was up so early. Her household was always up at the crack of dawn, of course, but she didn't expect a man on vacation to keep those same odd hours. Could he be ill? Was that what Amos had meant when he'd said that Quinn was hurting? The nurse in her worried about that for a moment.

And then Laura frowned, realizing it wasn't the nurse who was worried. It was the woman.

No, she told herself forcefully. She wasn't taking on this man's problems. She had her hands full with her own and those of her housemates and patients. One more could well prove to be too much. Especially if he was a tall, gravely attractive man with gray eyes that held a world of suffering and a cool exterior that she suspected hid years of pain.

She would put him out of her mind today, she thought firmly. She wouldn't think of him again.

But she was thinking of him as she stowed her coat and purse in her locker and began her working day.

Quinn had been writing steadily for a couple of hours when he was disturbed by a knock on his door. He sighed impatiently, glared at the door, then rose reluctantly to his feet when the knock came again. He wasn't in the mood for visitors. But then he was rarely in the mood for visitors.

The teenage mother-to-be was standing on his doorstep, a foil-covered plate in her hands. He couldn't remember her name. "I brought you some breakfast," she told him with a broad, friendly smile. "We knew you didn't have much in the way of supplies yet, and we thought you might be hungry."

"I told Miss Sutherland that I would take care of my own meals."

The young woman's mobile mouth turned down in an exaggerated scowl. "My name is Janet, since you seem to have forgotten. Not very friendly, are you?"

"No, not particularly," he answered bluntly, hoping she'd take the hint and share it with her housemates.

"Tough luck. We'll be nice to you anyway. That's just the way we are." Her impudent grin told him she didn't take hints easily. "Now move it and let me bring in your breakfast."

Quinn was somewhat surprised when he did move. If Janet was equally surprised, she didn't show it, but breezed past him as if she'd been politely invited to enter. "I see you found the coffee," she commented. "Boy, that smells good. I'd almost kill for a cup of coffee, but Laura would be mad at me. She says caffeine's not good for the baby. Man, would you look at that computer. That's a beauty. What do you need a computer for? You an accountant or something?"

"A writer."

"Oh, yeah? Quinn Gallagher. Oh, you write those cop books! Laura doesn't like 'em, but I think they're great. I haven't actually read one, but I saw the movie *Under In-*

vestigation. I loved it when the cop who'd been thrown off the force blew the face off that guy who'd set him up to look like he was on the take!''

Wincing inwardly, Quinn abruptly changed the subject. "You going to put that plate down somewhere, or are you going to stand there and hold it all day?''

Janet grinned, and even Quinn was not immune to the sheer beauty of her toothy smile. She wasn't exactly pretty, but her smile lit up the unpainted face framed by bright red hair. She looked like a person who enjoyed each moment of every day, who'd been untouched by trouble or sorrow. Yet Quinn sensed that she'd been through hell and was grateful to have come out alive.

"Where do you want me to put it? Your table's covered with that computer and all those papers.''

"Just set it on the counter.''

Janet did as instructed, then pushed her hands into her pockets. "Don't bother begging me to stay and visit,'' she told him with assumed gravity. "I have things to do. You'd better eat your breakfast before it gets cold. Lunch will be ready at twelve. Unless you want someone—namely me—bringing you a plate again, you'd better show up. You're going to eat balanced meals while you're here whether you like it or not. It's the rule.''

She was almost out the door when Quinn stopped her. "Thanks for the breakfast.''

She turned another high-voltage smile over her shoulder. "You're welcome.''

"I didn't mean to snap your head off,'' Quinn heard himself saying. He rarely explained himself, yet he continued, "I'm not used to being interrupted while I'm working.''

"I'll keep that in mind," she answered with a surprising degree of understanding in her young face. "See you later, Quinn."

"See you later, Janet." He frowned as he watched her walk out. Something told him that Colorado wasn't going to be quite as peaceful as Amos had promised.

As noon approached, he began to think of Janet's invitation to join the others for lunch. He wondered if Laura would be there. He was relatively sure that she wouldn't. He wasted a few more minutes wondering why he cared. When he'd passed nearly half an hour without writing a word, he ground out a rather rude four-letter word, stood and reached for his jacket. It seemed he was gong to join the other oddballs for lunch, he thought, his lips twisting into a grim smile.

By the time the meal was completed, he hadn't changed his opinion of the group. Strangely likable, the lot of them, but oddballs nonetheless. Despite the fact that she was painfully polite to him and welcomed him shyly to the lunch table, Betty Pritchard continued to look at him as if she suspected him of carrying a concealed weapon and having full intentions of using it on her. The solemn, somewhat pitying looks in her small daughter's enormous, expressive blue eyes made him extremely uncomfortable. The looks Quinn received from Mrs. Elliott, on the other hand, could only be described as "measuring"—literally. He could almost see her adding the inches in her blue-haired head as she scanned his shoulders and the length of his arms. He didn't even want to know what was going through her mind, though he found himself remembering scenes from *Arsenic and Old Lace*.

Janet chattered incessantly, her small talk punctuated by the flip one-liners that Quinn already recognized as characteristic of her quick mind. By the time he'd finished his soup, he knew that Janet was seventeen years old, seven-and-a-half months' pregnant, studying for her GED and planning to go into nurses' aide training after the birth of her child. She never mentioned a family or made any reference to the father of her unborn child. Quinn wondered how she'd ended up living with Laura. Actually, he had a lot of questions about Laura. He found his eyes turning all too often to the chair at the end of the table where she'd sat the night before.

After lunch, Quinn remembered to thank Betty before he left in barely concealed haste. She brushed off his thanks without looking at him, and he wondered briefly how long it had been since she'd escaped her abusive husband. He recognized a battered wife when he saw one; he'd certainly seen enough of them in his former career. But Quinn didn't want to know her story. He didn't want to get close to these people.

Maybe he should leave Colorado. Obviously Laura's guest house was not going to be the best place to hole up and write. Unless he forced himself to be deliberately rude, he would continue to be interrupted by visits from his determinedly friendly neighbors. Quinn was quite capable of putting an end to the unwelcome overtures in just such a manner, but he found himself strangely reluctant to do so. He wasn't a man who went around kicking puppies, either, he reflected with a grim attempt at humor. Sitting on the plump, overstuffed sofa pushed against the far wall of the main room of his cottage, he crossed his feet on the inexpensive coffee table in front of him, staring darkly at the scuffed toes of his Western-style boots as he tried to come to a decision about whether to stay or pack up and head back to Florida.

Still lost in thought, Quinn reached into the breast pocket of his shirt and pulled out a cigarette. He'd just placed it between his lips when a small voice spoke from the doorway. "Aunt 'aura don't wike cig'rettes."

Quinn whipped his head around to see Renee, bundled in a thick pink snowsuit, standing in the open doorway as cold air swirled in around her.

You're getting slow, Gallagher, he told himself, even as he asked the child, "What are you doing?"

"Mommy said I could pway outside," Renee answered as if that explained her presence in his living room. She took a few steps forward, looking curiously at his computer. "What's that?"

Translating "pway" to "play," he answered mechanically, "A computer. Did your mother say you could come in here?" Something told him that Betty would be horrified.

"Dint say I couldn't," Renee replied logically. "What's a ca-co-puter?"

"You'd better go back outside," Quinn told her, trying not to sound too stern. "I don't think your mother would like you being in here."

"Okay. Come wif me. See my pwayhouse."

"No, I—uh—"

Renee turned her oversize cerulean eyes on him. "Pwease?"

Ah, hell. Who could say no to a little blue-eyed kid saying "pwease"? "Okay. But just for a couple of minutes," he said gruffly, reaching for his parka as he stood.

She dimpled in delight and reached for his hand. "I wike my pwayhouse," she informed him gravely. "Mommy and Aunt 'aura made it for me."

"Okay, kid. Show me your pwayhouse," Quinn drawled, swallowing her tiny hand with his big one as she tugged on his arm. *What the hell am I doing in this place?* he wondered, even as he closed the door behind him.

Chapter Three

Laura had to bite the inside of her lip to keep from grinning. She was looking at a man in need of rescue, she told herself. She really shouldn't be fighting the urge to laugh.

Quinn stood with his hands shoved deep in the pockets of his parka, a pained look on his attractive face as he stared down at the pink-suited urchin beside him. Renee dashed around his long legs, talking nonstop in her lisping, toddler dialect, showing him every toy she kept in the tiny gingerbread-style playhouse Laura and Betty had built from a kit ordered from the Sears catalog. A red-and-white striped swing set stood beside the playhouse. Obviously Quinn was understanding only about half of what he was being told, though he was making a noble effort to respond to Renee's conversation.

Laura almost wished he would do something rude and walk away. She already found him much too attractive. Now the discovery of this hidden streak of kindness beneath that cool exterior made him even more appealing. She had decided earlier that day—one of the many times she'd thought of him despite her decision not to—that she would allow him to stay in the guest cottage as long as he wished, but she would *not* get involved with him. She wasn't going to try to find out what the real Quinn Gallagher was like behind the facade. So why was she standing here melting inside just because he was being kind to Renee?

"Found yourself a friend?" she asked him, hoping to quell her quivering feminine senses with a dose of his rude, unencouraging conversation. She figured that being treated the way he'd treated her when they'd parted last night was better on overactive hormones than a cold shower.

Quinn's face showed little change of expression, but Laura thought she detected the faintest hint of relief in his gray eyes. "I was just leaving," he replied in the deep voice she found too intriguing. "I have work to do."

"But Quinn, I gots to show you my baby buggy," Renee protested, staring pleadingly up at him. Laura fought that grin again, understanding exactly what made Quinn reluctant to do anything that might hurt the child's feelings. She'd always thought that in twenty years or so, Renee's huge blue eyes were going to be downright dangerous.

"Mr. Gallagher said he has to work, Renee," she interceded gently. "He can see your baby buggy another time."

Renee exhaled deeply but nodded her acceptance. "Okay. You see it tomorrow, Quinn?"

"Maybe," her reluctant friend answered noncommittally. He seemed to be deliberately avoiding Laura's eyes.

"Shouldn't you be calling him Mr. Gallagher, honey?" Laura suggested.

"Him said I could say Quinn," Renee assured her. "I can't say Mr. Gaw—Mr. Gag—I can't say that."

Laura couldn't help smiling. "Oh, I see."

"I was going to say Uncle Quinn, but him din't wike that, too." Renee sighed soulfully.

There was no way Laura could respond to that without laughing aloud, so she sent Renee inside to find her mother and then turned to Quinn only when she was certain that she had her features sternly under control. "Well, Mr. Gallagher, are you finding the guest cottage satisfactory?"

He ran his fingers through the heavy fall of hair on his forehead and then shoved his hand back into his pocket. "Yes, it's fine," he replied briefly.

Laura dragged her eyes away from his luxurious hair, her fingers curling in the pockets of her quilted down coat. She'd heard of hands itching to touch something, but she'd never experienced the feeling herself. Until now. "Good," she managed to say quite normally. "Is there anything you need?"

"A little peace and quiet would be nice." The frown line between his brows creased in sharp relief. "Half your household decided to pay me a visit today."

"They're just trying to be friendly," Laura answered evenly. "They're very nice people."

"All I ask is to be left alone to work."

Laura heard the frost in her voice when she answered, "Fine. I'll tell them to leave you alone. Is there anything else, Mr. Gallagher?"

He released an impatient sigh. "Look, I'm not trying to cause trouble or to make anyone angry. But I'm a writer, and writers need time alone to work. I have deadlines to meet."

"I told you that I'll take care of it. Anything else?" she demanded, not at all mollified by his ungracious explanation.

"No, that's all."

"Then I'll see you later. I've just gotten home from work and I'd like to change before dinner." Laura spun on the crepe heel of one white oxford, determined to get away from him before he caused her to lose her temper.

"What do you do, anyway?" he asked unexpectedly. "Are you a doctor?"

"I'm a nurse," she replied.

His brow shot upward. "You support this entire household on a nurse's salary?"

"We manage," she answered encouragingly. She had no intention of explaining her finances to Quinn Gallagher.

"We still haven't discussed my rent."

"Seventy-five a week, utilities paid," Laura returned flatly. "You can pay me at the end of your first week."

Quinn blinked as if he'd expected her to argue about charging him. "That doesn't sound like much," he answered finally.

"Nevertheless, it's what I charge. Now I'm going in. If you want to join us for dinner, you may. If you want to lock yourself into the cottage and starve, go right ahead. I can assure you that no one will disturb you."

With that, she turned fully and marched away, furious with herself for losing her temper and speaking so rudely, but even more furious with him for his relentless unfriendliness.

Quinn watched her walk away, then pulled himself around to stalk briskly back to the cottage, where he fully intended to lock himself in and starve. In an uncharacteristic show of frustrated emotion, he slammed the door behind him as he entered.

Whatever Laura had told her housemates, it seemed to have worked. They left Quinn quite alone for the next week. Deciding rather quickly that starving to spite Laura was ridiculous, Quinn drove into Greeley for supplies the morning after their exchange of unpleasantries. The day after that, he worked for several hours and then took a long walk in the woods. Since then, the long afternoon walk had become part of his daily routine. He saw little of his unusual neighbors, though he made a point to speak with brisk politeness whenever he passed one of them on his daily outings. Not that his conscience was bothering him about brushing off their friendly overtures, he assured himself. He simply saw no reason to be boorish now that they were making an effort to give him the privacy he had requested. He refused to even consider the fact that he was just a bit lonely without Amos or anyone else to talk to.

The beauty of the area and the crisp, fragrant air was a panacea even to Quinn's hardened soul. He soaked in the scenery, the sounds of woodland wildlife and the pleasant, though cold, November weather with the appreciation of a man who'd spent a long time in a dark, musty prison.

He frowned when that thought crossed his mind on his seventh daily walk in the woods. He had hardly been in prison, he assured himself flatly. Hadn't he spent the last couple of years in sunny, scenic Florida? He finally decided that he was enjoying this particular walk so much because it had been so long since he'd been in a region of the country that actually experienced winter.

The smell of snow was thick in the air, though the few fat clouds were not ready to unload their icy burden. Watching the gray, more thickly clouded horizon, Quinn reflected that it had been a long time since he'd seen snow. Now that Laura's friends were leaving him alone to work, maybe he'd stay awhile longer.

Laura. Why did the thought of her cause a change in his respiration? He listened to his own quickened breathing with disgust, trying to clear his mind of the picture of her facing him with angry fire in her clear brown eyes, her chin lifted in regal temper as she'd informed him that he could starve for all she cared. He'd almost believed her. And he'd wanted her so much at that moment that he'd almost reached out and taken her.

"Damn," he muttered, pulling a cigarette out of a pocket and striking a match to it. He drew deeply, trying to use the taste of the tobacco to assuage a totally different kind of hunger. It didn't work.

His eyes followed a small gray squirrel up the trunk of a spruce, but Quinn was barely aware of doing so as he tried to deal with the uncomfortable aching brought on by his thoughts of Laura. He wanted her, but there was just one slight problem. The lady despised him.

With a muffled snort of self-disgust, Quinn threw his half-smoked cigarette on the ground and crushed it under his heel. "Stupid son of a bitch," he muttered, and though he was still watching the squirrel, he was talking to himself.

He turned and strode rapidly back through the woods toward the cottage. He supposed he'd better get back to work.

Laura leaned into the back of the Subaru and pulled one of the bags of groceries toward her. It was the one holding the canned goods, and it was heavy. Bending her knees a bit, she lifted it into her arms—only to have it immediately taken away.

"Let me get that for you."

It was the first complete sentence Quinn had spoken to her in almost a week, though they'd murmured greetings as they'd passed each other on the grounds. Somewhat surprised, Laura considered telling him that she could carry her own bags, but she resisted. He seemed to be making an effort to be friendly for a change; she really shouldn't discourage him. "Thank you," she said, lifting the other bag out of the car.

"Hi, Aunt 'aura," Renee chimed from her position at Quinn's heels. "Quinn pushed me."

Laura shot Quinn a teasingly reproving glance. "You pushed that child?" she demanded, though she knew exactly what Renee had meant.

"In the swing," he almost growled, seemingly embarrassed at being caught acting nice again.

"Him pushed me big. It was fun," Renee continued, skipping along beside him as they headed toward the house. Her flushed face, outlined by the close-fitting hood of her pink snowsuit, was liberally streaked with chocolate. "I had a cookie," she went on, as if that fact weren't quite obvious.

"So I see." Laura smiled a thank you to Quinn when he held the front door open for her. He was right behind her as she walked toward the kitchen with the groceries, Renee chattering along beside them.

"Hi, Betty," Laura called out as she entered the kitchen.

"Hello, Laura—oh, um, Mr. Gallagher," Betty stammered as she turned and caught sight of him. She began to twist her hands in her characteristically nervous gesture and then her eyes fell on her daughter. "Oh, Renee, you have chocolate all over you. Let's go wash your face."

"Okay." Renee threw her chubby padded arms around Quinn's leg and snuggled her cookie-smeared face into his jeans. "Thank you for pushing me, Quinn."

"Yeah." The look he threw Laura was humorously awkward. She bit the inside of her lip and turned to start unloading the groceries into their proper places.

She'd expected Quinn to walk out immediately behind Betty and Renee and was rather surprised when he seemed inclined to linger. He leaned against the counter, watching her, making her self-conscious of her movements. "Could I get you anything?" she offered almost shyly, slipping out of her jacket and draping it over the back of a kitchen chair.

He ran his gaze over her neat white uniform, then turned his eyes back to her face. "No, thanks."

Feeling as if he'd actually touched her, she had to repress a shiver. She turned back toward the refrigerator, sliding a carton of milk onto a shelf. "How's the book coming along?" she inquired, making a subtle reference to their conversation the week before, when he'd asked to be left alone to write.

"Fine."

"Good." So much for that, she thought with a sigh, shutting the refrigerator door and turning to look at him. He was still watching her, his gray eyes impenetrable, yet penetrating. She wondered what he was thinking. She certainly didn't expect his next words.

"Tell me about the people who live with you."

She tilted her head in question. "What do you want to know about them?"

"Where did they come from? How did you meet them?"

"What is this, research for a book?"

He shook his head, causing a heavy lock of hair to brush his forehead. "Research on you."

"Oh." She swallowed. "Mrs. Elliott was a nurse at the hospital where I work now. She worked a lot with my dad, who was a doctor, though she retired before he died two years ago. Her husband died not long after I lost my father. She has no other family and she was afraid to live alone. Her heart's not good. Though she seems healthy enough, her heart is slowly failing. When she goes, it will be quickly. I didn't want her last days to be spent in a nursing home, so I asked her if she wanted to come live with me. She's very sweet and she keeps an eye on all of us, sort of like a surrogate grandmother."

"And Janet? How did she end up here?" he asked without commenting on her summation of Mrs. Elliott's situation.

"I met her at the hospital five months ago. Her mother threw her out when she became pregnant and Janet had been living on the streets for several weeks before she passed out in a department store from lack of food. One of her nurses introduced her to me, knowing that I'd want to help, and I invited her to stay here until after the baby's born and she gets back on her feet. She's a loving, sweet-natured young woman, and I think she'll do quite well for herself with a little encouragement."

"What about the baby's father?"

Laura drew a deep breath, familiar anger twisting inside her. "Her mother's live-in boyfriend raped her. He, of course, claims that she came on to him, and the mother chooses to believe him. Janet refused to press charges. She couldn't deal with the ugliness. I'd like to see the bastard behind bars, but I agree that Janet isn't emotionally able to handle a trial at this point. I *will* see that he never lays a hand on her again. I've been awarded guardianship of her until she's eighteen." She managed a bit of a smile then. "The judge was a friend of Dad's," she admitted.

Quinn's expression never changed during the unpleasant explanation. Laura supposed he was used to such tales. Instead, he asked simply, "And Betty Pritchard? Battered wife?"

She nodded. "I guess that was easy enough to guess. The local women's shelter contacted me about her, since the director knew I was looking for a full-time housekeeper. Neither Mrs. Elliott nor Janet are physically capable of handling all the housework, and I really don't have time in addition to working full-time.''

"How do you support all these people?'' Quinn asked with a frown. Although he looked almost reluctant to continue the conversation, he seemed overcome by curiosity.

She didn't take offense at the personal question this time, though she knew she probably should. Despite his blunt, tactless tone, Quinn didn't seem to be prying, actually, as much as trying to understand.

"I don't fully support them all,'' she explained. "Mrs. Elliott has monthly retirement checks, and as I explained, Betty earns her salary. I also inherited a nice sum of money from my parents—not a fortune, but more than enough for my needs. I live on my salary and use the rest to help people when I can. It was something my father started years ago, and I've continued the tradition in his memory.''

"And because you like doing it,'' Quinn added perceptively.

She nodded. "That, too.''

"Will there be others?''

"Yes. As these move on, there will be others who need help. If I'm able, I'll help them.''

"And what about your own life? You give so much to all these people, but what do you give to Laura?''

"Friends,'' she answered immediately. "People to love, to love me. A family to fill the void left by the loss of my parents.''

"You could start your own family,'' he suggested carefully. "Husband, kids. Don't you want those things?''

She busied herself with opening a new roll of paper towels, thinking fleetingly of the family she should have had by now, the family that had been denied her by the senseless, violent death of the man she'd planned to marry. Aware that Quinn was expecting an answer, she phrased her words carefully. "Of course. Someday. But a man would have to be exceptionally tolerant and flexible to take on the rather unusual ready-made family that would be part of the package."

Before he could say anything in response, she turned the questioning to him. "Have you ever been married?"

"No."

"Ever come close?"

"Not even close," he answered with a shrug. "I was always too involved in the job to get too involved with a woman."

Whatever she might have said to that was cut off when Betty reentered the kitchen to start dinner. Laura invited Quinn to join them for the meal, but he declined, telling her he had a chapter he wanted to finish that evening. He didn't linger after that, merely nodding with distant politeness to Betty as he left.

"He seems to be trying to be a little friendlier," Betty commented when the door had closed firmly behind him.

"Yes," Laura agreed. "He seems to be trying." She wondered why.

Long after the rest of the household had fallen asleep that evening, Laura was still trying to sort out her own feelings about the man in her guest cottage. She couldn't stop thinking about their conversation earlier, wondering what had motivated his question. She didn't really think he was curious about her boarders; as he'd indicated, the question seemed to have come more from curiosity about Laura.

Could it be possible that her compelling interest in him was not entirely one-sided?

She was physically attracted to him. He could make her shiver with only a look. But her attraction to him was more than physical, and she was having a hard time deciding what exactly was involved. Something drew her to him. Something about the pain in his haunted gray eyes. And that funny little excuse for a smile. And the kindness he showed to Renee.

She stood by the window in her bedroom, staring across the moonlight-silvered yard to the cottage, where a light in the front window testified that Quinn, too, was still awake. She wondered when he slept. During the nine nights that had passed since his arrival, the lights in his cottage had rarely been out. She'd checked, though she hadn't really known why, each time she'd climbed out of bed to go to the bathroom or get a glass of water or for any of the other excuses that had given her an opportunity to look out her window and across the yard at odd hours.

She shivered and huddled deeper into her voluminous flannel nightgown. It was cold by the window, reminding her that the temperature outside had taken a sharp drop in the past few hours. A major snowstorm was predicted for sometime in the next few days. She hoped it would wait until after she finished her shift the next day. After that, she was on vacation for a week. She always took Thanksgiving week off, as well as the week of Christmas and one week during the summer. She chuckled a little, thinking of the reasons she habitually split her annual vacation time into thirds. She wasn't sure she could take her adopted "family" for three weeks all at once without the eight-hour-a-day release of her job.

Almost immediately her thoughts drifted back to Quinn. She wondered if she would be seeing more of him now that he'd made the effort to socialize a bit for the first time since they'd parted so coolly at Renee's "pwayhouse."

What was it about the man that fascinated her so?

Annoyed with herself for her unhealthy obsession with her temporary tenant, she started to turn away from the window, only to stop with a frown when the cottage door opened and Quinn stepped out. She wondered why he was going outside in the middle of a night when the temperature was in the single digits. He wasn't even wearing a hat and gloves, just jeans and his parka. Did he *want* a case of frostbite?

Then she realized that he was headed straight for her house and that he didn't look at all happy. He was moving with the sharp, jerky movements that meant he was irritated. Funny how she'd already started to memorize little things like that about him. Snatching up a fuzzy green robe, she belted it around her as she hurried down the hallway to the front door, intending to meet him before he could ring the bell and arouse her sleeping household.

Quinn looked a bit startled when the door opened before he could summon anyone, but the expression quickly faded into the inscrutable, emotionless mask that he usually assumed. "What are you doing?" Laura asked before he could speak, impulsively taking him by the hand and pulling him inside. "It's freezing out there."

"It's freezing in the cottage," he answered, jerking his chin toward the cottage as he pulled back from her touch with too apparent haste. "Heater's out. I looked at it, but it's not something I can fix."

Laura frowned in distress, his bad news pulling her thoughts away from the electric tingling that had coursed up her arm when she'd touched him. "Oh, I'm sorry. I don't know who I can call at two in the morning. You'll have to stay here in the main house until I can have it serviced tomorrow."

Quinn didn't look at all pleased.

Immediately on the defensive, Laura glared at him. "You obviously can't stay in the cottage with no heat," she told him decisively, tossing her hair back from her face in an impatient gesture.

"I don't want to put anyone out of their room," Quinn returned flatly.

"That won't be necessary." Despite her exasperation with his rudeness, Laura felt her lips quirk upward at the stubborn determination in Quinn's voice. He sounded almost like Renee when she announced that she wasn't going to take a nap.

Her smile faded at the expression that immediately darkened his gray eyes as he stared at her mouth. What was the fleeting emotion she'd read on his face? If she hadn't known better, she would have sworn it was desire. Ridiculous, she told herself as his eyes returned to hers.

"If you're offering to let me share your room, I accept," Quinn told her, his gritty voice carefully uninflected.

She swallowed. The last thing she would have expected from Quinn was a pass. Or *had* that been a pass? From this enigmatic man, it was hard to tell. Whatever it had been, she decided to treat it lightly. "That won't be necessary, either," she told him briskly, her voice a bit strained to her own ears. "There's an extra bedroom next to mine. Everyone else sleeps upstairs."

He nodded. If he were disappointed that she hadn't commented on his provocative statement, he certainly didn't show it. "I'll just get a few of my things," he murmured, turning on his heel and walking back out the door.

Laura let out her breath and leaned weakly against the foyer wall for a moment.

By the time Quinn returned, Laura had his bed made up with fresh sheets. He dropped his duffel bag on the floor and glanced around the obviously masculine room. "Who used to sleep in here?" he asked.

"My father." Laura, too, looked around the room, which was still just as her father had left it, from the medical books lined on a low bookshelf to the framed snapshots of Laura and her mother on the dresser.

Quinn's gaze paused on the books. "You said he was a doctor?"

"Yes. He and Amos were partners."

"I knew they were good friends, but I hadn't realized they were partners." He paused a moment, then looked back at Laura. "When did you lose your mother?"

"She died when I was eighteen."

"This was their house?"

"Yes. I grew up here. I moved out a few years after I graduated from college, but I moved back four years ago when Dad's health started going downhill."

Quinn shrugged out of his parka and draped it over a rocking chair. Laura turned away to avoid looking at the way his flannel shirt hugged his powerful torso. "I hope you're comfortable here until we get the heater in the cottage fixed. Let me know if there's anything you need."

He shook his head, slowly, hands deep in the pockets of his worn jeans. "I won't need anything." He paused, then said flatly, "It's a wonder people aren't lined up to take advantage of you."

He must have been thinking of their conversation earlier, in the kitchen that afternoon. He was so very cynical. Laura found herself almost feeling sorry for him again. "There have been those who have taken advantage—or have tried to—in the past few years," she said evenly. "But don't make the mistake of thinking I'm naive, Quinn. I'm not."

He started to say something, obviously changed his mind, and shrugged. "Whatever."

His shrug had drawn her eyes to his shoulders, which looked so wide and solid in his lightweight flannel shirt. She thought they also looked a bit hunched, then realized that he still had not warmed up from being in the bitter cold outside. How long had he been without heat, she wondered, before he'd been compelled to swallow his pride and seek warmth?

"You're still cold. Let me make you some hot chocolate."

"No, that's—"

She wouldn't allow him to complete the refusal. "I'm going to make some for myself, anyway. You may as well join me." She turned and walked out of the room, wondering if he would follow. He did.

Chapter Four

Quinn didn't want to go with Laura. He didn't even like hot chocolate. So what the hell was he doing following after her on command? His gaze settled on her hips as she walked down the hallway to the kitchen, appreciatively noting their slight sway. He was sure the tempting walk was unconscious on her part. Laura was not a woman who deliberately sent out sexy signals—or at least not to him. She'd seemed completely comfortable to stand in front of him in her nightclothes. Not that the fuzzy robe belted over a high-necked lavender flannel gown was in any way revealing. But there was still something soft and vulnerable about her dressed this way. Something Quinn found entirely too appealing. He should have stayed in her father's bedroom, he decided, even as he followed her through the swinging door into the kitchen.

Laura snapped on the kitchen light as she passed it, and Quinn's head jerked around when they were greeted by a noise from a corner of the room. It sounded like—a duck? What the hell was a large white duck doing sleeping on a scruffy rug in one corner of the kitchen? He was even more disconcerted to spot the sleek gray cat curled up alongside the duck, a cat with only a stub where his right back paw should be, who was now looking at Quinn with narrowed, sleepy eyes and a soft, questioning meow. Where the hell had these two boarders been hiding during the past week and a half?

"Are you aware that you have a duck and a three-legged cat in your kitchen?" he asked dryly.

"Doo and Sabu," Laura explained, watching Quinn's face with a grin. "They sleep inside when it's this cold. Don't worry, they're very clean. Go back to sleep, guys," she added to the animals.

"You're a strange woman, Laura Sutherland," Quinn told her, and he wasn't teasing. Damned if he would ever understand her, he thought as he watched her fill a kettle with water and set it on the stove to boil.

"I have to be, Mr. Gallagher," she replied, completely without offense. "I take in some very strange tenants." She shot him a look that included him in that category, then rummaged in the cabinet for instant cocoa.

There didn't seem to be anything to say to that comment, so Quinn dropped into a straight-backed kitchen chair and watched her until he remembered what she had called him. "You called me Quinn earlier," he commented.

"Did I?" She poured boiling water over the drink mix in two thick mugs. "Sorry."

He shook his head impatiently. "You don't have to call me Mr. Gallagher. I'd rather you call me Quinn."

"I would have thought you'd prefer sir," she mused, setting his mug on the small butcher-block table beside him and sipping her own beverage as she took a chair opposite him.

He felt his hackles rise and deliberately blocked out the irritation as he tasted the cocoa. He wouldn't allow her to make him angry, he told himself firmly. What was it about her that made his rigid control so hard to maintain?

"You were a cop before you quit to write, weren't you?" Laura asked, seemingly out of the blue.

Quinn raised an eyebrow and nodded.

"I read it somewhere when *Under Investigation* was released in the theaters," she explained, correctly reading his questioning expression. "It's true, isn't it?"

"Yeah."

"How long were you a policeman?"

He didn't like personal questions, usually didn't answer them, but he could hardly refuse now that he'd been asking her things that definitely fell under the heading of personal. That's what he got, he thought grimly, for giving in to curiosity about her. "Almost fourteen years," he finally answered.

This time her eyebrows shot up. "When did you quit?"

"Two years ago, when my first book was published."

"You're thirty-five now, but you were a cop for fourteen years. You started young, didn't you?"

"How the hell do you know how old I am?" he asked, startled. He knew *that* information hadn't been in any article.

Laura flushed. "Amos mentioned it."

"Just what else did Amos tell you about me?" he demanded, eyes narrowing. He had expected his one friend to respect his privacy, he thought angrily.

"Nothing much," she answered evasively. "But you *were* young when you started out, weren't you?" she continued, turning the subject back to his former career.

He exhaled a bit impatiently, but answered, "I guess. My older brother was a cop. When I was nineteen, I got recruited through him as a narcotics officer assigned to New York public high schools. Went in undercover as a student to track down the suppliers. I looked young for my age then."

Laura looked at him for a long time, searchingly, until he shifted uncomfortably in his chair. He knew what she was thinking. He no longer looked young for his age. Almost fourteen years of police experience had long since drained the youth from his face. He looked at his watch. Two-thirty. "Don't you have to work tomorrow?"

"Yes." But she wasn't ready to drop the subject of his past, it seemed. "Why did you quit? Did you always want to write?"

He shrugged, avoiding her curious eyes. "I quit because I felt like it. Writing was something else I was good at. A way to keep eating."

"Is your brother still a policeman?"

"My brother is dead."

The stark words fell like a rock between them. Quinn stared at Laura through narrowed eyes, silently ordering her to keep any sympathy she might feel to herself. She started to say something, eyed the expression on his face, then changed her mind. A few moments later, however, she took a deep breath and dared another question. "Is that why you quit? Because your brother was killed?"

She seemed to assume that his brother had died in the line of duty; Quinn neither confirmed nor denied that assumption. He never talked about his brother to anyone. Frowning deeply, he glared at her. "What is this, an interview?"

She bit her lip at his curt tone, and he found himself regretting the sharpness with which he'd spoken. It seemed he was always offending her, when offending her was the last thing he wanted to do. Fighting the urge to drag her out of her chair and kiss away the tooth marks she would leave on her lower lip, he made an effort to speak in a conciliatory way. "There wasn't any one event," he told her quietly. "I simply quit. Two years after my brother died," he added reluctantly.

She nodded. "I didn't mean to pry," she said, pushing away her mug as if the fragrant chocolate had lost its flavor for her. "I was only trying to get to know you better."

"It's okay," Quinn muttered, standing to dump his own barely tasted drink into the sink. "I'm just not used to personal questions." That was as close as he could get to an apology.

She seemed to accept the unspoken apology as it had been offered. "I *do* have to work tomorrow. I'm supposed to leave in four hours, as a matter of fact," she added with a slightly rueful grimace. "Guess I'd better try to get two or three hours' sleep first."

"Sorry I kept you up."

She smiled at him with just a hint of shyness. He found that shyness strangely appealing. "I got a few hours' sleep before you came to the door," she told him. "I had gotten up for a drink of water when I saw you head this way."

Quinn wondered instantly why she'd been looking out at the cottage, but he didn't ask. There were some things he'd be better off not knowing, he told himself. He waited until she'd rinsed their mugs, patted the cat and duck and turned out the kitchen light before trailing after her down the hallway to their adjacent rooms. Not knowing why, he paused to look at her at the doorway of the room where he would be sleeping—assuming, of course, that he slept at all. "Thanks for the hot chocolate," he said, the word *thanks* sounding a bit rusty from lack of use.

She nodded, her sudden shyness masked but not yet completely disguised. "You're welcome. Good night, Quinn."

It wasn't a conscious move that he made next. There was no forethought, no prior intention on his part at all. Almost before he was aware of what he was doing, he put out a hand, snagged her by the back of the neck and pulled her to him, his fingers buried in her thick golden curls. There was only time for a glimpse of large, startled brown eyes before her face was too close to see clearly. And then his mouth was on hers. She stiffened for a moment, then, to his amazement, her lips softened beneath his and she began to kiss him back.

Quinn closed his eyes and lost himself in the kiss that he hadn't consciously planned but now realized that he fully intended to have. Touching her only with his lips and the hand at the back of her head, he was still aware of every inch of her delectable body so close to his. With only a slight shift of his weight he could have her pressed against him from breast to knee, but he refrained from making that move. The kiss alone was devastating enough.

Wanting—needing—to taste more than her lips, he slid his tongue between her teeth, groaning deep in his throat when hers welcomed him. God, she tasted good. His body tightened painfully, urging him to pull her down and take her right there in the hallway. Ignoring that urge, ignoring the need for oxygen, ignoring a shrill warning signal from somewhere back in his brain that he was in danger of losing some long-protected part of himself to her, he slanted his mouth to a new angle and deepened the kiss even more. Her muffled whimper was almost his undoing. He realized that his fingers must be digging painfully into her neck, and he consciously loosened his grip as he slowly, so very slowly, pulled his mouth away from hers.

He stared at her for a long, silent moment, taking in every detail of her flushed, startled expression. Her brown eyes were wide, searching, asking him questions he couldn't answer. He made a conscious retreat, physically and emotionally—backing away from her even as he deliberately hardened his face into his carefully cultivated unreadable mask. "Good night, Laura," he said, then turned before she could answer and closed himself in the bedroom, the door shutting on anything she may have said in answer.

Without taking off his boots, he threw himself onto the old double bed, lying on his back with his arm across his eyes. He shouldn't have kissed her, he told himself angrily, his entire body throbbing. He wanted her, he ached for her—dammit, he was beginning to need her. He shouldn't have kissed her.

Bundled into her down coat, knit cap, scarf and gloves, Laura slid behind the wheel of her Subaru just under four hours after parting with Quinn in the hallway. She hadn't slept a wink. She wasn't sure she would ever sleep again.

Quinn had kissed her with more raw hunger and need than she'd even encountered. She'd never been kissed like that in her life. It had made her want to offer whatever he wanted, whatever he needed. Had made her ache with needs of her own.

He shouldn't have kissed her, she thought as she guided the small car down the highway at a faster-than-usual speed. Her lips still tingled, her mind still reeled, her body still craved. He shouldn't have kissed her.

The cottage heater would be out for at least a week. Judy, the tall, dark-haired woman who finally showed up after noon on Friday to repair it, explained to a disgruntled Quinn that it would take that long for her to obtain the part needed by the older, no-longer-in-production unit. She left with a promise that she would have the problem solved in as short a time as possible.

Quinn wondered what else could go wrong on this "working vacation." Not only had he lost his privacy by being forced to move into the main house with its idiosyncratic occupants, he was also having to deal with his unexpected and wholly unwelcome attraction to his temporary landlady, an attraction that had been haunting him all day. No matter how hard he'd tried, he couldn't get that kiss out of his mind. And he couldn't stop wanting more.

Leaning against a corner post of the front porch of Laura's house, he huddled into his parka and smoked. Knowing how Laura felt about cigarettes, he wouldn't have felt comfortable smoking inside her home. He really should move on, he told himself with a weariness that he attributed to too many sleepless nights and too many snail's-pace days. Though he'd made a satisfying amount of progress on his new book during the time he'd been here, he predicted that his sudden streak of productivity would fizzle now that he'd been forced out of the seclusion of the guest cottage.

Putting out the cigarette, he turned and headed inside, walking without hesitation to the telephone in the den.

"Amos? It's Quinn."

"Good to hear from you, boy. How are you liking Colorado?"

Quinn lounged back in the easy chair beside the telephone table and crossed his booted feet on the worn, matching ottoman. "Heat's gone out in the cottage. I've gotta move out. I'll probably be back in Florida in a day or two."

There was a pause on the other end, then Amos asked, "Isn't there room for you in Laura's house?"

Even her name made him tense. Mentally cursing his unprecedented reactions to the woman, Quinn answered with enforced nonchalance. "Yeah, I'm in the room that used to be her father's. But I'll probably head on back sometime tomorrow. You know how I feel about communal living."

"Oh, *I* know. I'm just not too sure that *you* do," Amos replied with cheerful obscurity. Before Quinn could speak again, he continued, "How's Laura? I worry about her."

A bit surprised, Quinn allowed the question to distract him from Amos's incomprehensible comment. "She's fine, I guess. Why would you worry about her?"

"Well, she's been alone ever since Graham—her father—died. I take my responsibilities as her godfather seriously enough to want to know that she's all right."

"Amos, she's hardly alone."

"I know she's not alone in the physical sense. But she's always so busy taking care of everyone else that I worry about whether she takes proper care of herself."

Quinn shifted in the chair and frowned, running his free hand through his heavy brown-and-gold hair as he cradled the receiver against his ear. "She appears to be perfectly healthy, if that's any comfort to you. I don't see anything for you to worry about."

"Glad to hear it. And she seems happy? Still flashing the most beautiful smile west of the Mississippi?" Amos asked the lighthearted questions with an almost audible grin, seemingly relieved to hear that his adored goddaughter was doing well.

"Amos, I hardly know the woman, but if the beauty of her smile is any indication of her emotional well-being, then I'd say she's quite content." Quinn's frown deepened as he spoke. Perhaps he could have phrased his answer a little differently, he thought. He certainly had no intention of telling Amos how attracted he was to Laura.

Something in Quinn's answer—or perhaps in his voice— seemed to please his friend. Amos chuckled happily before speaking more seriously. "I really think you ought to reconsider coming back to Florida just yet, Quinn. The reporters have been all but camped at the door for the past couple of weeks. They ask me a dozen times a day when you're going to be back and how they can get in touch with you. Why don't you wait until after that movie's out so that all the prerelease publicity will be over?''

"But the release date is still two weeks away."

"I'm sure Laura won't mind you staying a few weeks longer."

Quinn wasn't so sure of that, but he didn't expect her to ask him to leave. He knew her well enough by now to be aware of her unfailing graciousness and generosity. "That's not the point, Amos."

"Well, think about it, anyway. Believe me, if these reporters catch a glimpse of you, they won't give you a minute's peace. They're wanting to know if *Suicide Beat* is autobiographical. They want to make you the next cop-turned-writer hero—the next Serpico. *People* magazine called you 'the brooding, handsome young recluse wearied of a never-ending war against crime.'"

Appalled, Quinn dropped his feet to the floor and sat up straight. "Tell me you're kidding."

"'Fraid not," Amos returned with a touch of humor. "I'm reading the words straight from the article. Had a feeling you wouldn't have seen it, since such light reading is hardly your cup of tea."

"That's disgusting."

"It's Hollywood, boy. Somebody saw your photograph somewhere, decided you'd make good copy—particularly with your impressive service record and your phobia about your privacy—and now they're using you to help them sell their movie. As if that hotshot actor starring in it wouldn't draw in enough viewers by himself. Even had somebody call the other day wanting to know if you'd be interested in a screen test. Said he wanted you to play yourself in the story of your life."

That settled it. He wouldn't be going back to Florida just now. "You haven't told anyone where I am?"

"Nope."

"Don't."

"You know me better than that, Quinn."

"Yeah, I guess I do." Quinn relaxed again and patted his shirt pocket in search of a cigarette. He'd just located the pack when he remembered where he was. "Damn."

"What's the problem now?"

"Cigarette attack."

Amos laughed. "Knowing Laura's views on cigarettes, I understand. Ah, well, I've been trying to get you to quit for months. Look on it as a lesson in self-discipline."

Quinn summed up his opinion of Amos's suggestion in a few pithy words, making the older man laugh heartily before declaring that he missed having Quinn around. Oddly pleased by the words, and uncomfortable at being pleased, Quinn quickly concluded the call.

Replacing the receiver in its cradle, he turned his head to find himself being scrutinized through enormous blue eyes. "Hello, Renee."

The child smiled at the slight hint of encouragement in his voice and rushed forward. "Hi, Quinn. I have a beeber."

Quinn thought about that one. "A what?" he asked finally.

"A beeber," Renee answered patiently, leaning against his denim-covered knee. She touched her rosier-than-usual face with one chubby hand. "My head's hot."

Comprehending, Quinn placed his own hand against the damp little face. "You have a fever?" She did feel quite warm. "What's wrong?"

Renee shrugged with childish unconcern. "I sick. Read to me?"

"Renee! You mustn't disturb Mr. Gallagher." Betty twisted her hands in the doorway, her green eyes wide and distressed. They were also red-rimmed and puffy, as if she had been crying. Her mousy-brown hair was pulled back into her usual, unflattering ponytail, emphasizing the thinness and paleness of her oval face. "I'm sorry, Mr. Gallagher. She got away from me."

Quinn shook his head. "Don't apologize. What's wrong with her? She seemed fine at lunch."

"It's just a cold," Betty assured him. "Nothing serious. It makes her run a low fever on and off during the day. I just gave her some baby aspirin."

Which meant that she hadn't been crying about Renee. Quinn wondered dispassionately what was bothering the woman, what had happened since lunch to put a frightened, cornered-animal look behind the tears still brightening her eyes, but he didn't ask. He would leave that sort of thing to Laura. "Bring me your book, Renee, and I'll read to you while your mom makes dinner."

"Oh, Mr. Gallagher—"

Quinn sighed, cutting the anxious mother off in mid-protest. "I don't mind, Mrs. Pritchard. I wouldn't have offered if I did."

Renee was already crawling into his lap with a stack of Little Golden books, her flushed face beaming with pleasure. Betty hovered in the doorway for another moment, then murmured a disjointed thank you and fled to the kitchen. Quinn wondered how such a neurotically nervous and timid woman could have such a seemingly well-adjusted and gregarious child, then wondered what the hell he was doing with said child perched in his lap waiting to hear *The Poky Little Puppy*.

"Read, Quinn," Renee insisted, opening the book and pointing to the large-print words on the first page.

"'Five little puppies dug a hole—'" Quinn began obediently, his voice a bit hesitant at first. After all, he'd never read to a kid before. But then as Renee snuggled against his chest and stuck her thumb in her mouth, seemingly perfectly satisfied with his amateurish efforts, he gained confidence and forged on into the story.

Laura paused in the doorway of her den, the events of a hellish day temporarily forgotten at the sight that met her eyes. Quinn was about halfway through *Home for a Bunny*, which he was reading quite well—animal voices and all. Unfortunately, his audience was not in the least impressed. "Renee's asleep, Quinn," she said gently.

Startled by Laura's voice, Quinn blinked and looked up. "What?"

"Renee is asleep," Laura repeated, coming into the room with a smile that she knew didn't quite reach her brown eyes. Why, she asked herself in despair, did seeing Quinn with Renee always disarm her so? Surely she had more sense than to allow herself to become involved with this troubled, difficult man.

Quinn gave her one of his long, searching looks before glancing down at the child in his arms. "So she is." He closed the book and set it aside, reaching up to stroke his mustache in an almost sheepish manner. "She's sick," he said, as if his behavior required some explanation.

"She's had a cold for a couple of days. It was sweet of your to read to her."

A flash of something very near humor crossed his face so quickly she almost missed it. "It's been a hell of a long time since anyone's called me sweet," he murmured.

Her own smile was a weak attempt. She dropped onto the couch and leaned her head tiredly against its brown plaid back. "I'm sure it has. I saw Betty in the kitchen when I came in. Dinner's almost ready. I don't suppose you know where everyone else is?"

"Janet is resting upstairs and Mrs. Elliott is knitting her little fingers off in the dining room. Don't ask why she's knitting in the dining room."

"I don't have to," Laura answered, her smile becoming more natural. "She says the light's better in there. Are you always so observant about everything that goes on around you? Is that a habit left over from your former career?"

"I notice things," Quinn agreed evenly. He was watching her again, so closely that Laura had to make an effort not to squirm self-consciously. She knew what he was seeing—the ravaging after-effects of a sleepless night, a devastating kiss and a baby dying in her arms. She wished fleetingly that she had stopped to change out of her uniform and freshen her makeup before coming in search of him. She wondered for the first time why she had been compelled to seek him out almost the moment she'd arrived home, when all day long she had been determined to avoid him this evening to prevent a repeat of last night's unsettling intimacy.

"You're almost as pale as that white uniform you're wearing," Quinn observed unexpectedly. "Are you all right?"

No, she wasn't all right. For some stupid, irrational reason, she was sitting on a couch in her den wanting nothing more than to curl up in Quinn's lap as Renee had done. But she didn't want him to hold her in the same gentle, almost absentminded way he was now holding Renee. She wanted him to...

"Yes, I'm fine," she lied, staring straight into his probing gray eyes and praying that none of her thoughts showed on her face. *Diversion. Small talk.* Anything to give her time to overcome this sudden insanity. "Judy called me at work about the heater in the cottage. I'm sorry about the inconvenience."

"It wasn't your fault."

"You're welcome to stay in Dad's room for as long as you like," she continued because there was nothing else she could say. "I know it's not as convenient for you, but I'll talk to everyone again about giving you plenty of privacy to work. You can set up your computer in the study."

"I already have."

"Oh. Well, I'm sure no one will disturb it—or you."

"I made certain of that at lunch." He had told the entire gathering, quite amicably but still firmly, that his computer was set up behind the closed door of the small, comfortable study that opened off the den and he would personally break the fingers of anyone who touched it. After a moment's startled silence, everyone had laughed—even Betty. The initial discomfort with which they had greeted him at the table had evaporated after that, and it was just like the first time he'd joined them for lunch. Janet chattered, Mrs. Elliott smiled, Betty tried to blend in with the furnishings and Renee stared adoringly at Quinn. It had been a hell of a half hour.

Strangely enough, Quinn had enjoyed it.

This place was getting to him, he thought ruefully. Its inhabitants were getting to him. He looked down at the little girl sleeping against his chest, then up at the beautiful woman watching him from the couch. Something was bothering Laura. He'd sensed it the moment she'd entered the room. He knew he was part of the problem. Something had happened between them last night, and he hadn't been the only one who'd spent an entire day wondering what it had been. He saw it in her eyes every time she shot him a shuttered, wary glance. But he saw something else, too. Some deep, raw sadness that made him want to take her into his arms and kiss away the pain.

The impulse startled him. It wasn't like him. He'd been immersed in his own gloom for so long that he hadn't particularly cared about anyone else's feelings in—well, in years. Ever since Michael had died. Ever since...

Shaking his head to clear it of memories best left buried, he started to speak, but was interrupted by Betty's voice from the doorway. "Dinner's ready. Everyone else is already at the table."

Carefully depositing Renee into her mother's arms, Quinn excused himself to wash up before dinner. He noticed that Laura avoided his eyes as he passed her.

Chapter Five

The mood at dinner was rather constrained. Even Quinn, who didn't want to know these people or care about their problems, couldn't help but sense that there was tension among them. Betty looked as if she would faint if anyone said "boo," Renee was sleepy and fretful, Janet complained of a headache and Laura was still quiet and introspective.

"We're a cheery bunch tonight, aren't we?" Janet asked finally, after the main course had been consumed in near silence and peach cobbler was disappearing in the same manner. "What's wrong, Laura? Did something happen at work today?"

Quinn swallowed a bite of his dessert and reached for his iced tea, though his entire concentration was centered on the answer to the question he would have liked to have asked, himself.

Laura looked up from her untouched cobbler, moistened her lower lip and tucked a golden curl behind her ear, looking so sad and vulnerable that Quinn's fist clenched around his fork. "We lost one of the Travanti twins today," she said finally. "The boy—Anthony."

Betty's eyes widened in distress. "But I thought he was doing well," she exclaimed. "You said yesterday that he was still gaining weight and appeared healthy."

Laura nodded, her eyes shadowed by her lashes. "We thought he was going to make it. It was his sister we were worried about. But he went critical this morning and we lost him this afternoon. It's always a possibility with one born that prematurely, weighing less than three pounds at birth; but we really thought Anthony was going to be okay."

Janet placed a protective hand on her own rounded stomach. "His poor mother. Is she going to lose both the babies?"

"Not if we can help it," Laura answered flatly, her voice ringing with determination.

"Mommy, I sweepy," Renee complained, rubbing chubby fists into droopy eyes and drawing everyone's attention away from Laura. Everyone except Quinn, who couldn't look away from the sorrow on her face. He missed her beautiful smile. He wished he knew some way to bring it back to her. But he wouldn't know how to begin.

"I'll do the dishes tonight, Betty." Laura made a visible effort to shake off her depression and concentrate on the others. "You take care of Renee."

Betty made a token protest but was overruled by general consensus. Renee was carried off to bed, casting one last sweet smile back at her housemates—Quinn, in particular.

Laura wasn't exactly sure how it happened, but some ten minutes later she found herself in the kitchen with a stack of dirty dishes. And Quinn.

"Quinn, you really don't have to—"

"Rinse the dishes. I'll stack them in the dishwasher."

Laura stood for a long moment staring at his impassive face, her hand on her hip. Then she gave him an unwilling smile, shook her head and turned to the sink, murmuring, "I wonder if I will ever understand you."

"I think not," Quinn returned, his eyes meeting hers as he took a rinsed plate from her hands. He was the one to break the visual contact, turning away and busying himself with the dishwasher as if there were nothing he'd rather be doing.

"No!"

Quinn sat bolt upright in bed, sweating and swearing as he shook off the effects of another one of his bad dreams. He heard his own voice echoing in his head and hoped that he hadn't actually yelled aloud. Since the quiet household seemed undisturbed, he could only assume that his anguished shout had been a silent one.

"Damn," he muttered, pushing his sleep-tossed hair out of his eyes with one shaking hand and using the other to throw off the sheet that was his only covering. "Damn, damn, damn."

He wondered if he would ever get an uninterrupted night's sleep. He couldn't remember the last one. Shoving himself out of the bed and to his feet, he fumbled on the nightstand for his cigarettes. Digging out the plain ceramic ashtray he'd purchased the day he'd bought supplies for the cottage, he steadied his nerves with a pleasureless smoke. He thought briefly of his former resolve not to smoke in Laura's home but shoved the broken resolution to the back of his mind. He needed this cigarette.

If only he could remember the dreams when he woke up. He wanted to defeat them, to force them out of his life, but how could he control something that he couldn't even remember? He'd mentioned them to Amos once in a moment of weakness, and the doctor had suggested a few sessions with a psychologist, an idea that Quinn had rejected categorically. No way would he bear his soul to some money-hungry headshrinker, he'd proclaimed scornfully. And yet here he was, sitting in the dark and destroying his lungs because he couldn't seem to change this pattern of sleep-shattering nightmares followed by hours of wakefulness.

Amos had wondered if the dreams were related to the death of Quinn's brother, Michael. Quinn had asserted that he'd come to terms with his brother's death a long time ago, though he knew as well as Amos that he'd never quite gotten over that loss. It had been after Michael had died that Quinn had realized his own emotions were nearly dead. As deeply as Michael's death had hurt, Quinn had never cried for him. *Were* the dreams related to Michael? Stubbing out the last of the cigarette, he searched his mind for any remnant of the dream that had left him cold and weak.

Nothing.

Well, maybe something. Suddenly he could remember hearing children's laughter. He could hear it still, way back in his head, whispery echoes that made no sense to him at all. Though he'd always liked kids and occasionally stopped to talk with them on his walks on the beach in Florida, he didn't personally know any children, other than Renee. Certainly none he would dream about.

The faintest suggestion of a memory was just creeping into his mind when he was distracted by a sound from the room next to his. Laura's room. He twisted his head around, straining to hear. It came again, and this time he identified the sound. Laura was crying.

Almost as if he were tuned into her thoughts, he knew immediately why she cried. The baby who'd died that day.

She was grieving for him and his parents. Quinn clenched his fist and shook his head. Damned if he'd ever met a more softhearted woman. He wished the walls of the old house weren't so thin, so he wouldn't have to hear her pain.

He wouldn't go to her. She didn't need him—probably didn't want him. What would he say to her, anyway? He doubted that she was in the mood for sex, which was the only method he could think of at the moment to take her mind off her other problems. Actually it might take his mind off his problems, as well. Quite pleasantly, in fact.

No. He wasn't low enough to take advantage of her in her moment of vulnerability. But perhaps he should just go in and ask if she was okay. Offer some words of comfort, maybe.

He snorted. *What* words of comfort? He wouldn't know where to start. The best thing for him to do was to mind his own damned business. He threw himself on the bed, his arm over his eyes as he tried to will himself back to sleep.

Another sob, faint but still gut-wrenching, came from the other room.

"Well, hell." Quinn rolled to the edge of the bed and landed on his feet, stalking toward the door. Only at the last moment did he remember to grab his jeans and shove his legs into them.

Laura mopped at her face with one hand and pressed her other fist against her mouth, trying to muffle her sobs. She couldn't seem to stop crying. She couldn't get the Travanti baby out of her mind. For one of the few times in her busy, generally fulfilling life, she was lonely. She wanted someone to hold her.

She curled into a tight fetal position on her bed, her eyes closed against the empty darkness around her, and tried to tell herself that there wasn't anyone in particular whose arms she would like to have around her. Once she would have turned to Robbie in her pain, but that had been a long time ago. Now she was appalled to find her thoughts turning to the man in the room next to her. The man whose sad eyes had already begun to capture her heart. No. She didn't want Quinn, she told herself firmly, choking back a fresh wave of tears. She wanted someone warm. And caring. And tender. Not cold and reserved and troubled.

He came in so quietly that she didn't know he was in the room until his hand touched her shoulder. His fingers closed around her flannel-covered shoulder and she could almost believe that his touch was warm. And caring. And tender.

"Are you okay?"

Swallowing hard, she nodded, assuming that he could sense the movement even if he couldn't see her. Thank God he couldn't see her. She looked horrible when she cried. "I'm okay. I'm sorry if I disturbed you," she managed in a husky, tear-thickened voice.

He crouched beside the bed, his awkward embarrassment conveying itself to her in his voice, his touch. "You didn't disturb me," he told her, obviously lying. "Is it—are you crying about the baby who died?"

She inhaled deeply, gathering strength to dry her tears and answer evenly. "Yes."

"Why do you work in this job if you tear yourself up so over it?" Quinn sounded almost angry. His fingers tightened reflexively on her shoulder.

She wondered why he'd even bothered to come in. "I don't always," she answered defensively. "I'm usually prepared when we lose a baby, and I accept the losses by remembering all the ones we save. It's just that I wasn't prepared for Anthony's death. We've had him almost four weeks and we were so sure that he would be all right. His young parents were devastated. It hurt."

He sighed, a soft, apologetic sound in the no-longer-empty darkness. "I guess I understand. Will you be able to sleep now?"

She hesitated just a moment too long before trying to assure him that she would be fine.

He seemed to accept her words, moved as if to leave, then stopped. "Would it—would it help if I sat in here with you for a while?"

Surprised, yet pleased that he'd offered, Laura shook her head, "That's okay, Quinn. But thank you."

She was even more surprised when he sat down on the edge of the bed, spread his long legs over the covers and pulled her into his arms. "There. Now try to go to sleep."

Laura struggled to sit up. "Quinn—"

"Laura, I'm only going to hold you for a while," he explained with uncharacteristic patience. "Just until you go to sleep. Maybe it will help."

He couldn't possibly believe she would be able to sleep lying in his arms. She could think of a lot of things that were likely to happen to her in that particular position, but sleep wasn't one of them. So why was she meekly settling herself more comfortably against him?

He was bare-chested, his skin warm and smooth. He shifted her head into the hollow of his shoulder. "Try not to think about it anymore tonight," he told her gruffly, one hand stroking her back through the covers.

How could she think about anything but the feel of his skin beneath her cheek? His warm, vibrant, male-scented skin. Her hand settled tentatively on the middle of his chest, feeling every crisp, curling hair, each rise and fall of even breath, the steady, reassuring rhythm of his heart. His head moved briefly above hers. It felt almost as if he'd dropped a kiss on her hair. Ridiculous. Quinn Gallagher would hardly do anything so sweet.

She'd never sleep like this. Never be able to rest when her pulse was racing, her skin tingling, her most feminine depths slowly throbbing. In all the fantasies she'd had of lying in Quinn's arms—and only now would she admit to herself that she'd been having those fantasies since the day she'd met him—she hadn't begun to imagine how good it would really feel. She'd never be able to sleep. Never.

She relaxed slowly, starting with her toes and proceeding up to the cheek that snuggled more deeply into his shoulder.

She woke once during the night, drowsily, to find that their position had changed very little. Quinn was still lying beside her, peacefully sleeping, having climbed under the covers with her at some point. He must have gotten cold. Though she knew she shouldn't be feeling so natural, she sighed in contentment and drifted off again, shamelessly using the comfort of his arms to ward off the unhappy thoughts that would have swamped her had she been alone.

The next time she woke, the sun was shining. And she was alone.

Mack cradled the weapon in his big, callused hands. His fingers stroked the dully shining gray-blue metal, caressing it like a lover. The metal was smooth and cool beneath his blunt fingers. Smooth like ivory. Cool like a woman. He closed his eyes and pictured pink skin. Full breasts tipped in darker pink. Sleek legs. Soft . . .

"Damn," Quinn swore, clearing the computer screen with a vicious punch of a button. He was supposed to be writing a fast-moving action scene. The killers were just outside the smelly, rat-infested room where Mack was hiding, ready to burst in at any moment and splatter him all over the walls. What's more, Mack knew it. So why the hell was he fooling around with his gun?

And why was Quinn getting aroused just writing the scene?

He knew why. Because his mind was on the woman who'd spent the night in his arms, not on the story he was creating.

"Damn," he said again, shifting in his chair to ease his discomfort. It didn't help.

He tensed when he heard Laura's voice outside the closed door of the study in which he'd secluded himself. He relaxed when it was evident that she wasn't coming into the study. He hadn't even seen her that morning, though neither of them had left the house. Skipping breakfast, Quinn had told Betty he wanted to work and had closed himself in the study. No one had disturbed him. And still he'd gotten absolutely nothing written. He couldn't forget how it had felt to sleep all night with Laura in his arms.

The hell of it was that he usually didn't like to spend the night in a woman's bed. Couldn't even remember the last time he'd actually slept with a woman. On those rare occasions during the past few years when physical need had overcome his desire for solitude, he'd found himself climbing out of bed almost before his body had cooled from having sex. He made no effort to refer to it by any euphemism, for sex was all it had been.

And yet he'd lain all night at Laura's side, cradling her against his chest, throbbing with desire for her but somehow content just to hold her. And he'd gotten the best night's sleep he'd had in years. What the hell was it with this woman that even he was falling under her spell?

He muttered something vicious and explicit under his breath and attacked the keyboard again, as if he could force the keys to cooperate with his need to lose himself in the story.

* * *

"You suppose he's going to join us for lunch?" Betty asked curiously, her gaze on the closed door to the study.

Following her friend's look, Laura shrugged. "I don't know," she answered. "We'll call him when it's ready." She turned her head to frown fiercely at the lamp shade she was dusting, refusing to allow herself to dwell on thoughts of the man who'd held her through the night. She chewed her lower lip as she tucked a wayward curl behind her ear.

Unaware that Laura was trying so hard to block all thought of Quinn, Betty pressed the cap onto the bottle of glass cleaner she'd just used on the television screen and remarked, "He's an unusual man, isn't he?"

"Yes, I suppose he is." *To say the least.*

"I don't understand him very well. One minute he seems so intimidating, and the next he's reading stories to Renee."

Or letting me cry into his shoulder, Laura added silently. She smiled weakly at Betty. "He's really quite nice," she commented, inwardly wincing at the insipid description. But then, how could she be expected to describe Quinn? As Betty had said, he changed from one moment to the next. It was almost as if he tried to be cold, uncaring. Yet he continued to surprise her with glimpses of a warmer, softer side.

Laura was becoming too fascinated by Quinn, too deeply drawn to that hidden man. She was afraid she was beginning to care for him in addition to the more physical attraction she felt for him. She didn't want to be hurt, she thought apprehensively, moistening suddenly dry lips. And somehow she knew that Quinn could hurt her. Badly.

He was so very different from the man she'd loved before. Robbie had been happy and laughing, open and caring. Everyone who knew him had loved him, and Laura had been no exception. There had been no one for her since she'd lost him. And yet now she found herself falling for a man who was Robbie's opposite—withdrawn, complex, embittered, defensive. A man she didn't know well, couldn't quite understand but still couldn't seem to resist.

Reluctant to continue talking about Quinn when just the thought of him disturbed her, she changed the subject, wondering aloud if Janet was coming down with the cold that had plagued Renee. Janet had complained of another headache that morning and had been generally subdued all day. That subject reminded Betty to check on her daughter, who was playing with a favorite toy in the dining room while Mrs. Elliott, busy with her knitting as usual, kept an eye on her. Glancing once more at the closed door to the study, Laura returned to her cleaning.

Some twenty minutes later Laura hesitated in front of the door to the study. She'd almost given in to cowardice and asked Betty to summon Quinn for lunch, but Betty had just answered the telephone. Chiding herself for being silly, Laura swallowed hard, squared her shoulders and knocked. "Quinn?" she said, opening the door. "Lunch is ready."

He looked up from the computer, his expression as unreadable and unencouraging as ever. Her stomach contracted at her first sight of him since the night in his arms. He looked so very good, his beautiful hair falling over his forehead, his face cleanly shaven except for that temptingly soft mustache, the chest she'd snuggled against encased in another thin flannel shirt. He didn't smile at her as he acknowledged her words. "I'm not very hungry."

Acting on impulse, she closed the door behind her and approached the desk where he sat. "Betty said you skipped breakfast. You really should eat something."

His only response was a grunt. She had no idea what it was supposed to mean. Tempted to leave him in hungry solitude, she made herself stand firm. "About last night—"

He cut her off, speaking without looking at her. "Forget about last night."

She took a deep breath, reminding herself that he was a man who didn't deal well with emotion. "I want to thank you," she forged on in as even a voice as she could manage. "It was very kind of you to—"

He looked at her then, his mouth twisting into a rather mocking smile. "I wasn't trying to be kind."

"Oh, no?" she challenged him. "Then why did you come to me? Why did you offer to stay with me until I went to sleep?"

His hard gray gaze moved suggestively to the swell of her breasts, outlined by the green knit pullover she'd worn for cleaning, then traveled slowly down the rest of her. "Is it so surprising that I'd want to be in your bed, Laura? And you told me you aren't naive."

She was suddenly angry. How dare he reduce his impulsive kindness last night to nothing more meaningful than sex? His concern had meant a great deal to her, and she wouldn't allow him to refuse to acknowledge the genuine emotion behind his actions. He owed himself more than that, if not her. "So the only reason you came into my room was to get into my bed. Is that what you want me to believe, Quinn?"

He shrugged. "Why not? It's true."

"Sure it is. That's why you held me all night without even making a pass, right?"

"Look, I've got work to do."

She felt like stamping her foot, but resisted, knowing he would turn such a childishly futile gesture against her. "Why is it so hard for you," she asked quietly, "to admit that you have the same feelings as anyone else? That you are capable of offering kindness and sympathy and understanding and that maybe—just maybe—you need someone to do the same for you sometimes?''

"I don't *need* anyone," Quinn retorted instantly, rising in an abrupt movement to tower over her. "What I do need is to be left alone to work."

"Fine," she all but spat at him. "You might want to ask yourself, though, whether you're lying to me or to yourself." She spun on one heel, intending to slam the door behind her as she left, only to be caught by one arm and whirled none too gently around.

Quinn gave her no opportunity to resist when he pulled her into his arms. His mouth was on hers before she could sputter a protest.

If the one kiss they'd shared before had been powerful, this was doubly so, fueled as it was by anger and frustration. Laura wasted only a moment struggling against it before she surrendered to her own need to kiss him back. She opened her mouth to his insistent demand, allowing him inside. A groan rumbled low in his chest, vibrating against her breasts, and then he invaded her mouth with a hungry skill that left her weak and trembling. He held her still with one hand buried deep in the curls at the back of her head, the other at the small of her back, pressing her to him, making her fully aware of his arousal. Her own arms locked around his lean waist.

After what seemed like a very long time, Quinn ended the kiss and drew back, slowly. Breathing hard, he stared down at her, his face somewhat flushed. Making a massive effort to control her own labored breathing, she noted the signs of his agitation with a distant part of her dazed mind. At least he couldn't claim that the kiss hadn't affected him, she thought, achingly aware of the hardness of him where he still pressed against her abdomen. She watched his throat work as he swallowed and fought the urge to press her lips to the glistening hollow there.

"You going to try to pass that off as another act of kindness?" he asked her finally, his voice gravelly.

"No," she murmured, looking up at him without moving.

"Ah, hell," he muttered, releasing her to half turn away from her, one hand going to the back of his neck as he plunged the other into the pocket of his still too tight jeans. Laura continued to stare at him, waiting for him to do something. Truth was, she couldn't have moved just then if she'd wanted to.

Without lowering his hand, Quinn threw her a seething sideways glare. "I'm not one of your charity cases," he told her flatly, unexpectedly. "I don't need you messing around in my mind, trying to cure me of whatever the hell you think is wrong with me."

"I never said I thought there was anything wrong with you," she answered, one hand on her father's desk to support her still trembling legs. "I think you're a very lonely man, but it's by choice, not necessity. You deliberately shut out the people who want to be close to you. Like Amos. Like—" She stopped, looking away from him.

"Like you?"

She couldn't read his tone, so she forced herself to meet his eyes again. For all the good it did her. He'd pulled the shutters back down, closing his thoughts and feelings inside himself, closing her out. "Maybe," she whispered bravely.

His hand fell heavily to his side. "Laura, you—"

A brisk tap on the door interrupted whatever he'd intended to say. "Lunch is ready. Come eat while it's hot," Janet's voice called through the door.

Laura took a deep breath. "I'm going to eat. Why don't you come with me."

She thought for a moment that he was going to refuse, then he nodded shortly and pushed a couple of buttons on his computer. "All right. Let's go eat."

If anyone noticed that Laura was rather subdued when they sat down to lunch, no one commented. Quinn, of course, acted no differently than usual, though Laura found him looking at her rather oddly on the few occasions she allowed their gazes to meet. She could almost imagine that she saw regret in his eyes, though she told herself she must be mistaken. He'd tried to convince her that he felt nothing for her but a surface attraction, so why should she think that he wanted more?

Realizing that she'd been so wrapped up in Quinn that she'd been ignoring her other companions, Laura forced a smile and turned to Renee, teasing the child and making her laugh. She chatted with Mrs. Elliott for a moment about the progress of the afghan the older woman had been working on for weeks, then made arrangements to take Janet to her next doctor's appointment. Only then did she notice that Betty was even more quiet and frightened-looking than usual, her hand visibly trembling as she toyed with the uneaten food on her plate. Odd, she hadn't acted that way earlier, Laura thought in concern, wondering if the telephone call Betty had answered had caused her distress.

"Betty, is something wrong?" Laura asked, keeping her voice low so as not to alarm Renee.

Betty's eyes widened and she swallowed quickly, almost dropping her fork. "No. Why would you ask?" she questioned, her voice too shrill.

Laura shook her head reassuringly. "No reason. The stew is delicious, Betty."

"I'm glad you like it. Can I get you any more, Mr. Gallagher?" Betty offered, seemingly relieved that the topic had become less personal.

"No," Quinn replied, then offered belatedly, "Thanks."

Dropping his eyes to his plate, Quinn lifted a bite of the thick, rich stew to his mouth, barely tasting it as he chewed. Food wasn't what he was hungry for. His eyes turned inexorably back to the other end of the table, to Laura.

She was talking to Renee again, a tender smile curving her unpainted lips. He focused on those lips, wondering if he was the only who could tell that they were still slightly swollen from his kiss. She laughed at something Renee said and he wanted her so badly he had to swallow a moan along with another bite of stew.

The telephone rang suddenly in the other room. Quinn looked up with a frown when Betty jumped uncontrollably and knocked over her water glass. He noted that her face had gone starkly white as he stood to lift Renee out of the path of the spill.

Renee's arms went tightly around his neck. "Mommy spilled her drink," she announced unnecessarily.

"Yes, I know," he replied. "You okay, Betty?" He'd forgotten to address her by the more formal Mrs. Pritchard as he'd always done before.

"Yes, I'm—fine," the woman answered faintly, looking down at her dripping clothes. "I'll have to change."

Laura had already brought in a towel and was busy wiping up the spill as Mrs. Elliott gathered dishes out of the way. "It was just someone selling magazines," Janet reported, returning from answering the phone.

"It startled me," Betty explained, wringing her trembling hands. "So silly of me."

"Go change your clothes," Quinn instructed her quietly, seeing that she was still pale and seemed momentarily incapable of making that decision for herself. "Renee and I will go into the den for a little while."

Appearing on the verge of tears, Betty gave him a weak, grateful smile. "I'll be right back," she promised, finally moving.

"No rush." Quinn couldn't help wondering if the woman had been receiving threatening calls. She showed all the signs of it, but he was determined not to ask her, not to become involved. It was none of his business, he told himself almost angrily, carrying Renee into the den. There he helped her build a block house until Betty came in half an hour later, looking somewhat more composed, to take the child up to her room for a nap.

Knowing Laura was still busy in the kitchen with Mrs. Elliott, Quinn shut himself into the study once more to work with a fierce, stubborn concentration. He wasn't disturbed again until Janet came in much later to tell him that dinner was served.

Chapter Six

Laura slipped a tape into the VCR and tied her fuzzy robe tighter around her waist. Carrying the remote control with her, she walked over to the couch where a canned cola and a plate of Betty's homemade chocolate chip cookies waited for her. She felt almost guilty as she settled onto the couch, her bare feet curled under her, and realized how pleased she was that the entire household had turned in early on this Sunday night, leaving her a couple of hours' peace. She really did love her housemates, she thought with a weary sigh, but she was looking forward to those next two hours with only a romantic movie and a plate of cookies for company.

For one thing, the private interlude gave her a chance to sort through her feelings about Quinn.

Quinn. Just the thought of his name made her go weak, made her tremble with the memory of that ravenous kiss the day before. She closed her eyes and she could almost imagine his mouth on hers again, his body pressed so tightly to hers that their hearts had pounded against each other. A long sigh escaped her as she shivered with reluctant longing for another of those kisses. And more.

"Are you asleep?"

Laura jumped at the sound of Quinn's voice, her eyes flying open. He was standing in the doorway to the den, looking a bit uncertain, as if unsure whether she wanted to be disturbed.

They'd been avoiding each other all day. Laura had spent a restless night, imagining him on the other side of her bedroom wall, reliving the two devastating kisses they'd shared, telling herself she was a fool for being so obsessed with him. They'd shared breakfast with the rest of the household and then Quinn had worked most of the day, stopping only for another of his long walks during the afternoon. He'd spoken little at lunch or dinner—not that there was anything particularly unusual about that, she thought wryly—then had gone back into the study until she'd heard him go into her father's room as she'd changed to watch her movie. She'd assumed he, like the rest of her tenants, had turned in early.

"No, I wasn't asleep," she assured him with a smile she knew must look too bright. "I was just about to watch a movie. Come on in."

Passing several empty chairs, Quinn sat down on the couch with Laura, though he left plenty of space between them. "What are you going to watch?"

"I—uh—" She had to stop to clear her throat. He'd twisted a little so that he half faced her, and the position had drawn his shirt tightly across his solid chest. It was all she could do not to lay her head on his shoulder as she'd done Friday night, when he'd slept with her in his arms. Better not to think of that. Making herself concentrate on the conversation, she reached for a cookie to give her hands something to do. "*Ladyhawke*," she told him more steadily. "Have you seen it?"

He shook his head, his eyes seeming to linger at her throat where her robe parted to reveal a patch of skin above her scoop-necked gown. She wondered if he could see her pulse racing there.

"It's a little bizarre," she admitted, needing to say something—anything. "Two medieval lovers are put under a curse so that he's a wolf by night and she's a hawk by day and they can never be together as humans. I've seen it once before if you'd rather watch something else."

His mustache quirked with his faint smile. "No, go ahead and watch it. It sounds—interesting."

Knowing he'd probably find the movie terribly sentimental—especially in light of the stark, violent tone of the movies based on his own writings—Laura grimaced and pushed the play button on the remote control. "Want a cookie?" she offered, determinedly keeping her eyes on the screen as the opening credits began.

"Yeah, thanks." Quinn stretched his long legs out in front of him and propped his feet on the low coffee table, crossing his ankles. He'd taken off his boots and wore only thick white socks. Then he paused and moved as if to lift his feet. "Sorry, I—"

"No, go ahead," she told him quickly, reaching without thought to touch his knee. "The table's sturdy."

His leg stilled, though she felt a muscle twitch beneath her palm. She snatched her hand away, her face burning. Didn't she have enough sense to keep her hands to herself around this man? she wondered with a silent moan. She set the plate of cookies on the couch between them. Not much of a barrier, she thought with sudden wry amusement, but a barrier nonetheless.

They watched the first thirty minutes of the tape in silence. Not a comfortable silence, but one fraught with the tension of sitting within two feet of each other, each aware of the other's movements, breathing, surreptitious glances. Laura cleared her throat soundlessly and raised her lukewarm soft drink to her lips, feeling Quinn's eyes on her as she did so. "Oh, you don't have anything to drink," she blurted, putting down the can and starting to rise.

Quinn stopped her with an outstretched hand. "No, I don't need one. I'll have a sip of yours." He lifted the can to his mouth, placing his lips exactly where hers had been, his eyes never leaving hers.

Laura watched his throat work with his swallow and bit back a moan. It took a massive effort to tear her gaze from his and look back at the television. Her lips trembled with the need to feel his upon them.

She sensed when Quinn became more involved in the tale unfolding on the screen. As she'd told him, it was a love story, but there was enough rather violent adventure to hold this particular man's interest. Laura divided her attention between the movie and Quinn, noting the way he watched with such full concentration, the frown line between his brows deeply pronounced. How often, she wondered, did he do anything strictly for entertainment? She didn't think it would be often.

She was delighted when Quinn went so far as to laugh at one of Matthew Broderick's clever lines. True, it wasn't much of a laugh. More of a chuckle, actually, but it did indicate that he had a sense of humor. And . . .

"Dimples!" she exclaimed impulsively, causing Quinn to turn to stare at her.

"What?"

"You have dimples," she told him, flushing a little, "when you smile. I hadn't noticed before."

He looked a little embarrassed. "Guess I haven't smiled much since I've been here."

"No, you haven't," she agreed candidly.

He stroked his mustache with his thumb—he'd done that once before when he was feeling sheepish, she remembered—then grimaced ruefully. "I'm not a...cheerful man, Laura."

She laughed at the phrasing—and the understatement. "No, I don't suppose you are."

He seemed about to say something else, but a flurry of activity on the television screen distracted him. Throwing her one last, thoughtful look, he turned his attention back to the movie. Laura felt herself grinning as she followed suit.

Cheerful? Hardly. But fascinating—oh, yes. Definitely fascinating. And who would have believed this hard, dangerous man would have long, deeply carved dimples bracketing his mustache when he laughed? If it was the last thing she ever did, she'd see them again, she vowed, settling more comfortably against the back of the couch.

Laura told herself that she wasn't going to cry when the movie ended. She'd sobbed the first time she'd seen it, touched by the moving conclusion to the emotional story. Laura could never resist a happy ending.

This time she wouldn't cry.

Quinn watched Laura watch the movie. During the second half she lost herself in the story, her expressions mirroring her reactions to the various scenes. Watching her was more interesting to Quinn than the movie, though it really wasn't bad. He smiled a little when she winced at the violent scenes—no wonder she didn't like the movies made from his books—sobered when she went misty-eyed over the more sentimental parts. He watched her blink back tears at one particularly poignant scene in which the two cursed lovers caught just a glimpse of each other as they went through the changes that would continue to keep them apart.

Laura was an emotional woman, he mused. A romantic. His opposite, in fact.

He wondered about her love life. She didn't seem to have one, something he found quite strange in light of her deep capacity for love. She was a woman of passion; he'd found that out for himself. He still burned in the aftermath of that passion. Yet she lived in the mountains with a houseful of eccentric boarders, a cat and a duck. He wondered about the men in her life, past and present. Surely there wasn't a current lover; Quinn had known her for over a week and a half now and she hadn't even been on a date during that time. True, Quinn hadn't been out on a date in—well, he couldn't even remember how long—but he was a loner, content with his own company. Laura was different.

He wanted her. He'd wanted her when he'd known her only as a beautiful, laughing woman in a photograph; he wanted her even more now that he knew her in vibrant, tempting flesh. Everything about her fascinated him. Drew him.

Frightened him.

He frowned as the thought slammed into his mind. Of course she didn't frighten him, he repudiated immediately. What was there to be frightened of? He could sleep with her without losing himself in her. He could make love with her—say, tonight, he thought on a wave of hunger—and still walk away from her. Tomorrow? Well, maybe not tomorrow. There was no rush, was there?

She was too soft, too vulnerable. He could hurt her.

Remembering the tears she'd shed on Friday night, he swallowed hard. It tore him up to think that he could make her cry. Laura should never be unhappy.

Sighing, he turned his eyes back to the television, wishing he had a cigarette on him, knowing he wouldn't smoke it if he did. He wouldn't want to make Laura uncomfortable.

He had no business becoming involved with this woman. No business being here.

He wasn't at all surprised that Laura cried when the movie ended, even though she'd seen it before. The moment Rutger Hauer caught Michelle Pfeiffer in his arms, Quinn slanted his gaze to the woman at his side, amused to see the tears rolling down her cheeks. He could tell she was trying not to cry, and that amused him, too. Did she think he was going to mock her for her romanticism? No way. Still, he thought with a slight smile, it wouldn't hurt to tease her a bit about it.

"Dumb ending," he drawled, stretching his arms above his head.

Laura snapped her head around as if he'd insulted her. "How can you say that?" she demanded. "It was a beautiful ending!"

"Too Hollywood," he argued, straight-faced. "It would have been much more effective if they'd never broken the curse, were destined to live out the remainder of their lives together yet separate. Or if they'd died trying to break the curse."

Swiping almost angrily at the tears still glistening on her cheeks, Laura scowled and punched the rewind button on the remote control. "I should have expected that from someone whose movies are evaluated according to body count. You should write so well."

That made him chuckle. "I was only teasing," he admitted finally. "The ending was okay."

She eyed him sternly. "It was better than okay."

"You're right," he agreed meekly. "It was better than okay."

"You really liked it?"

He grinned. "The way you're defending it, you'd think *you* wrote it. Anyway, I don't write the screenplays for the films made from my books. Hell, I've never even seen the one that came out last year. Probably won't see this next one, either."

She blinked at him in surprise. "But why?"

He shrugged. "Don't care for the publicity. If I went to one of the screenings, the reporters would be all over me, wanting to know how I liked it, whether the film was true to the book, all that garbage."

"But Quinn, how do you know whether they're doing justice to your stories? What if you hated what they did to them?"

"My agent keeps an eye on them for me," he answered unconcernedly. He could tell she wanted to follow up on that particular conversation. He didn't. To distract her, he reached out to flick away one lingering teardrop. "You're the most soft-hearted woman I've ever met. Do you always cry so easily?"

"Only over sad things," she answered with a self-mocking smile. "And happy things," she added, her smile deepening.

His hand lingered on her cheek, his thumb touching the corner of her mouth. Her smile faded.

He had to kiss her again. His eyes locked with hers, he lowered his head. Slowly. Still watching her, he brushed his mouth over hers, almost groaning at the sharp pleasure of it. Had any woman's mouth ever tasted so sweet? He didn't think so.

Laura made a deep sound in her throat, a little murmur of arousal that was his undoing. Slanting his mouth more firmly over hers, he tugged her nearer, his arms going around her as he invaded the moist depths of her mouth, reclaiming territory he'd mapped before. He closed his eyes as her arms went around him, her hands flattening against his back to hold him closer. Something foreign pressed against his leg; he shoved it aside, not even noticing when the cookie plate fell to the floor. All he cared about was that there was nothing between them now, nothing to stop him from pulling her closer.

Her robe was soft under his hands, but he longed for the more satisfying softness of her skin. He slipped a hand inside the fold of the garment, his palm cupping one firm, perfect breast through her nightgown. He moaned against her mouth at the feel of the hardened, pointed nipple pressing against him, seeming to beg for more of his touch. He wanted to take her into his mouth, to taste all of her.

"I want you," he muttered, his thumb circling that tempting crest.

She drew in a sharp, ragged breath. "I—" She swallowed, her clouded eyes meeting his. "I—"

Her head lowered. "I think we'd better stop," she said finally, pulling out of his arms. "Good night, Quinn." And she stood and all but bolted from the room, leaving him staring after her, his entire body quivering with taut need.

"Hell," he growled, slapping his hand against the couch. He hadn't intended to attack her like that. She wasn't ready, hadn't known him long enough to want him the way he wanted her—even though she responded with such warm passion when he took her into his arms. Aching with frustration, he snapped off the television set and then the lights, deciding he may as well go to bed, although he was quite sure he wouldn't sleep.

And tomorrow maybe he'd think about returning to Florida, he decided grimly. There was no way he'd be able to stay under the same roof with Laura without wanting her, making every effort to have her. He hadn't liked the panic he'd seen in her eyes just before she'd walked—no, run—away from him.

Telling himself that he was going to bed and would keep away from her the next day, he still found himself standing outside her bedroom rather than the one he was supposed to be sleeping in.

Go to bed, Gallagher, he ordered himself, staring at the closed door as if he could see Laura through it. *Leave her alone.*

I can't. Exhaling sharply, he reached out and turned the knob.

Laura was standing by the bed, her robe unbelted, hanging loose to expose the white gown beneath. Her gloriously curly, wheat-colored hair fell almost to her shoulders, tempting him to plunge his hands into it. Her brown eyes were huge as they locked with his, her soft lips trembling. Quinn pulled in a breath that slashed like a razor all the way to his lungs. His voice was raw when he spoke. "I want you," he told her again. "But I'll go if you tell me to."

He watched without moving as the emotions chased themselves across her face. She wanted him, thank God, but she was fighting it. Fighting both of them. He could tell the exact moment when she lost the battle.

With a sigh of surrender, she allowed the robe to slip off her shoulders. "Don't go," she said in little more than a whisper.

He locked the door behind him.

Laura watched him approaching her, his hand already going to the top button of his shirt. She was afraid, she noted almost objectively, but she wanted him. She'd never wanted anyone else like this.

He wouldn't be a gentle lover. She toyed with the ribbon at the waist of her nightgown, wondering if she should tell him that it had been years since she'd made love. No. She'd just have to trust him.

Quinn caught her restless hand and lifted it to his mouth, his mustache brushing sensually against her skin. "Don't be nervous," he murmured, his eyes still locked with hers. "I won't hurt you."

Perhaps those piercing eyes of his really could see straight into her soul. It was almost as if he'd read her thoughts. "I know."

He wouldn't hurt her physically. Emotionally—well, that remained to be seen.

Quinn placed her hand on his chest, just above his heart. Then he cupped her face in his hands, his fingers sliding into the curls behind her ears. "You're so beautiful," he muttered, and she knew such compliments didn't come easily to him. "So damned beautiful."

They were going to make love. And it would be like nothing she'd ever experienced before. Somehow she knew her life would be irrevocably changed. "I'm not—I'm not protected," she whispered, as close as she could come to telling him that this wasn't something she did casually.

"I'll take care of it," he promised. At her questioning look, he grimaced a bit ruefully and admitted, "I picked up protection when I bought supplies in town. I knew the day I met you that this would happen, eventually."

She wasn't sure how she should feel about that confession. Should she be angry that he'd taken it so much for granted that she'd be unable to resist him? Should she be touched that he'd thought of her needs even as he'd anticipated his own?

And then he lowered his head to kiss her and she was lost. The hunger, the only partially concealed vulnerability in that kiss, went straight to her heart. If she hadn't known before that she was falling in love with this moody, hurting man, she knew now. He needed her more than anyone ever had, and Laura could never resist such need. Nor could she ignore her own need for him.

She lifted her hands to his shoulders, pressing closer to him. Her head tilted to allow him deeper access to her mouth. Quinn lifted her against him, his hands warm through the fabric covering her. He kissed her until her pulse roared in her ears, until she was quite sure she was going to faint. And then he lifted his head, allowed her a quick breath, and kissed her again.

When that second long kiss ended she found herself on the bed, flat on her back as Quinn lay over her, his mouth moving against her throat. His hands swept her body, not gently—she'd known he wouldn't be gentle—but so wondrously arousing. He'd unbuttoned his shirt and only one thin layer of cotton separated them. She could feel his skin hot against hers as if they were naked. She burned in his heat.

He lowered his head to her breasts, burying his face in the scented valley between them, then opening his mouth to kiss her through the nightgown. Pushing her breasts together with his hands, he nuzzled and tugged, dampening the fabric covering the highly sensitized tips. Laura gasped and writhed beneath him, wanting the nightgown to be gone, wanting his clothing to be gone, needing to take him into her.

His hand slipped between her thighs, pushing up beneath the gown. Laura arched against his palm. "Quinn!"

"Shh." He kissed her roughly. "The damn walls are too thin."

She bit her lip to hold back another wild moan as his fingertips slipped beneath the elastic leg of her panties. Quinn teased her mouth open with his, soothing her savaged lower lip before plunging his tongue deep inside her mouth even as one bold finger slid into her body. He swallowed her startled cry of pleasure.

With only his hand and his mouth he caressed her, harder and faster, until she was blazing almost out of control. She stiffened in protest when she felt herself nearing release, but he refused to slow down. "Quinn, wait, I—"

The words were lost in a burst of ecstasy as he pressed more insistently. She shuddered beneath him, her fingernails digging into his shoulders through the unbuttoned shirt.

He held her as she recovered, his hands soothing her in long, firm strokes. She could barely see him in the deeply shadowed room. "I wanted you to be with me," she whispered.

"We're not finished yet," he vowed, reaching for the hem of her gown.

It took only a matter of seconds for him to divest them both of their clothing. Laura sighed her contentment as she felt him against her, skin to skin, for the first time. He was warm and hard and powerfully built, his chest and legs sensually roughened with coarse, curling hairs. She snuggled against him, loving the strength in the arms that held her.

His every muscle taut with his own denied need, Quinn allowed her little time to savor. Instead he began to love her again, using his hands and mouth to restoke her desire.

No longer content to lie still for his attentions, Laura pushed against him, loosening his hold so that she was able to touch him as she'd longed to touch him. She pushed her hands through his heavy hair, finding it even thicker and silkier than she'd imagined it. She kissed the hollow of his throat that always fascinated her when he swallowed. She nuzzled into the shoulder that had given her such comfort before. Seeking out the hard flat nipples hidden in the hair on his chest, she used her lips and teeth to pleasure them, delighted with the moan he couldn't quite hold back. Her hands explored lower, finding him hot and pulsing and so very ready for her. He bit off a groan.

Laura leaned over him, her hands in his hair, her breasts flattened against his heaving chest. "This time," she told him in a husky, very feminine murmur, "I'll have you with me."

She felt the fine tremor in his hands when he reached up to cup her face. "This time," he answered in a near growl, "I couldn't hold back if I wanted to." And he brought her mouth down to his even as she lowered herself onto him.

Quinn fought to hold on to his control as Laura slowly, so tortuously slowly, took him inside her. She rotated her hips and he gripped her thighs, trying to hold her still. "Wait, I—"

She laughed huskily, the smoky sound going straight to his loins. "Seems like I was the one saying that before," she whispered, even as she arched against him.

That laugh, combined with her sensuous movements, took him over the edge. Gripped by a frenzied madness that had everything to do with the powerful, unprecedented emotions evoked by the woman in his arms, he twisted until he had her beneath him again. Driven by that madness, he thrust into her, over and over, his mouth slanting greedily over hers. Only dimly aware of the moment when she stiffened and gasped her fulfillment, he gave in to the demands of his own raging need, shuddering with the explosive force of his release.

He'd never lost control like that, never with any woman, Quinn thought when his mind cleared enough to allow something close to coherence. Even as he tried to convince himself that it had been nothing more than extraordinarily good sex, he knew he was lying.

His first impulse was to leave her bed, leave her home, get as far away from her as possible. His second was to hold her. He wasn't consciously aware of choosing the latter, but his arms tightened around her as he rolled to his side, cradling her against his shoulder.

"Quinn?" she whispered, stirring against him.

"Go to sleep, Laura," he ordered on a deep sigh. Utterly drained, he closed his eyes and followed his own advice.

Laura lay awake for a long time, staring into the darkness, certain she'd just made a drastic mistake and equally certain she'd continue to make the same mistake for as long as Quinn would allow her to do so. Though he didn't want it, he'd stolen her heart. She would never be able to deny him the love he so desperately craved, so stubbornly rejected. She resigned herself to loving him for as long as she lived, even as she tried to prepare herself for the pain that love would inevitably bring her.

She'd loved and lost before. She'd suffered grievously, but she'd survived. Somehow, she would survive again. But this time, it would be different. Robbie hadn't left her voluntarily. Quinn would. And her feelings for Robbie had been different—gentle, tame, innocent. There was nothing gentle, nothing tame, nothing innocent about these feelings for Quinn. She'd never known the kind of raw, wild passion she'd just experienced in his arms.

Yet there was tenderness in her feelings for him. She ached to comfort him, to take away his pain, teach him to love. She knew the chances were slim that he'd ever let her get that close to him.

Turning her cheek into his shoulder, she closed her eyes and tried to store the memory of how right it felt to be held by him. There would come a time when she'd need that memory.

Chapter Seven

Quinn wasn't sure what woke him. It wasn't the dream, he knew that. He lay staring up at the darkened ceiling, acutely aware of the woman curled up against him. He didn't turn his head to look at her, but then he didn't have to. He could clearly envision her as he'd seen her earlier—arching beneath him, leaning over him to smile in sensual challenge, saying his name in a tight, exciting whisper that twisted his insides.

Laura.

Oh, God, what had he done?

She'd been so giving, so unreserved in their lovemaking. She hadn't had to tell him that her previous experience hadn't been extensive—or that it had been a while since she'd been with a man. Somehow he'd known.

She wouldn't have gone to bed with him if she hadn't convinced herself that she was beginning to care for him. He couldn't imagine what she might find to care for in a man like him. He frowned deeply. Did she feel sorry for him for some reason? Did her soft heart recognize another misfit, another stray with no place to call home? Everything within him rejected the idea of her pity, though he couldn't have said what it was he really wanted from her.

She stirred against him and his arm tightened reflexively, snuggling her closer. Snuggling. Hell, when was the last time he'd snuggled?

He had just about decided to get the hell into his own bed when the sound that had awakened him came again. A cry of pain from somewhere above his head. Moments later it was followed by a sobbing scream.

Quinn was on his feet and into his jeans before the scream had died away. Aware that Laura had jumped from the bed to follow him, he threw himself out the door and bolted for the stairs, long years of police experience urging him into action.

The door to Janet's room was open. Mrs. Elliott and Betty hovered over the young woman who sobbed loudly as she curled on the bed, clutching her swollen stomach. "What's wrong?" Quinn demanded.

"Janet? Are you all right?" Laura asked, right on Quinn's heels as he approached the bed.

Mrs. Elliott answered. "We were just about to come for you, Laura. Janet is in labor. Her water just broke."

"It's too soon," Janet sobbed. "It's not—aaagh." Her words slid into a keening moan as her young body was rocked by another fierce contraction.

"Mommy?" Renee's voice called from another room.

"Betty, go take care of Renee," Laura instructed quietly, sitting on the edge of the bed to take Janet's hand in hers. "We'll take care of things here."

"I'll get the car warmed up," Quinn offered, moving toward the door.

"Quinn, wait," Laura called after him, stopping him in his tracks. He turned to her in question. Janet was already gasping in pain as another contraction ripped through her—too soon, he realized in dismay. His eyes met Laura's.

"I don't think there's time to get her to the hospital. And I don't want to deliver a premature baby in a car," she told him quietly. "Mrs. Elliott, call an ambulance, please. And then gather the things we'll need for the baby."

The retired nurse nodded and left the room, her thick quilted robe swishing around her slippered feet.

"No!" Janet moaned, gripping Laura's hands. "Laura, it's too soon."

Laura stroked the damp brow and spoke soothingly. "Shh, sweetheart, it'll be okay. We're going to take care of you, all right?"

Quinn drew a deep breath. "I'll wash up." When Laura looked at him in surprise, he startled her with a flashing grin. "It won't be the first baby I've helped deliver," he told her.

He thought he saw a bit of the tension leave her face as she returned his smile. "That's good to hear," she answered. "It's always so handy to have an ex-cop around."

"Isn't it, though?" he murmured, dragging his gaze from hers.

When he returned to the bedroom only minutes later, Janet was lying on her back, a sheet draped over her. Laura bathed the young woman's flushed, tear-streaked face with a damp cloth while Mrs. Elliott stood to one side, stacking clean towels on a chair she'd pulled close to the bed. "I'll go down and wait for the ambulance," the older woman whispered to Quinn, patting his arm as she passed him. "Laura told me you've had experience with this sort of thing. Frankly, I'm getting too old for all this excitement."

Quinn gave her a faint smile. "I think I am, too."

She chuckled and shook her head as she left the room.

Close to panic, Janet wasn't giving Laura much assistance in preparation for the impending delivery. She refused to let go of Laura's hands, saying over and over that it was too soon and that she was frightened.

"Janet," Quinn said firmly, sitting beside her and pulling her hands gently away from Laura's. "Laura's a lot more experienced with this than I am. Let her go wash up and you can hold my hands, okay?"

He was aware of the gratitude—as well as the surprise—in the look Laura gave him before she quickly left the room. And then he gave his full attention to Janet, who had started crying again. "Come on, Janet. This isn't the way you want to greet your kid, is it?"

"I don't want to lose my baby," Janet whispered tearfully. "I'm afraid."

"I know," he assured her, tightening his hands on her small, clammy ones. "But you're going to do just fine. You're lucky that you're surrounded by people who know what they're doing, you know. Laura takes care of premature babies every day, Mrs. Elliott was a nurse, and I even delivered a baby once, myself. Single-handedly."

Janet took a hiccuping breath and looked at him doubtfully. "You did?"

"Sure. Hold on, now, grip my hands," he instructed as she bowed upward on another contraction. "Breathe deeply, Janet. Deep. That's right. Good."

As the contraction ended, he glanced back at Laura, who had returned and was kneeling on the bed between Janet's raised knees. "How's she doing?"

She looked worried when she met his eyes, but her voice was calm for Janet's benefit. "She's almost fully dilated. The baby has dropped into the birth canal. It won't be long. How long have you been in labor, Janet?"

"I don't know. I wasn't feeling too good all day, but I woke up about an hour ago feeling sick. I thought it was just false labor or something until my water broke and then...the pains...started—oh, God."

"Breathe, Janet. Deeply." Quinn leaned over her to look straight into her eyes, keeping his voice low and firm. Her fingernails were digging into his hands, but he thought she looked a bit calmer, less panicky as she relaxed with the end of that wave of pain. "Want to hear about the baby I delivered?"

"Yes," she gasped immediately. "Tell me about it."

"I was working narcotics in New York. I was about twenty-four, twenty-five, at the time—had never even seen a baby born. Picked up this woman for dealing—that's right, Janet, breathe. Again. Good. Anyway, the woman—I forget her first name but I remember her last name was Smith—was hugely pregnant and aggressive as hell. Resisted arrest."

"I need to push!"

"Can she push, Laura?"

"Yes, until I tell her to stop."

"Take a deep breath and hold it, Janet. Now push. Two. Three. Four. Five. Okay, breathe. You okay?"

"Tell me—tell me about the woman—"

"She grabbed her stomach and screamed that she was having a baby. I didn't believe her, thought she was trying to get out of the arrest. My partner had just taken off after her old man, who'd bolted when we broke in on them, and I was there in this dingy little room alone with her. You're doing fine, Janet. Atta' girl."

"Was she—in labor?"

"Oh, yeah. I kinda figured that out when her water broke and she started screaming even louder. I was going to run out for help but she threw herself at me, begging me to save her. I realized then that she was little more than a kid herself and scared spitless. So was I."

"I—I find that—hard to believe."

"Believe it."

"And you delivered the baby?"

"Yeah. It came fast, like yours is doing. She must've been in labor for some time before we got there. Backup arrived just about the time the baby slipped out into my hands. It was a boy."

"Quinn, tell her not to push this time."

"Okay, Janet, you heard Laura. Don't push."

"I have to! I can't—"

"Grip my hands. Harder. And breathe. Fast. Faster. Good."

"Okay, she can push now."

"Come on, Janet, let's get this over with."

"Was—that woman's baby—okay?"

"Sure was. As they were carrying her out, she told me she was going to name him after me."

"She—did?"

"Yeah. Said she was going to call him Pig Smith."

Janet gave a startled, breathless laugh, then leaned into one last powerful contraction.

Quinn jerked his head around as Laura let out a gusty breath. "It's a boy," she announced exultantly.

His eyes on the tiny, blood-streaked body, Quinn waited tensely for some sign that the infant was alive. He blew out a sigh when the baby squirmed and cried, a weak, tentative sound, but a cry, nevertheless. "You hear that, Janet? It's a boy."

Janet was crying again, still clinging to Quinn's hands. "Is he okay? He's so tiny."

"He'll be fine," Laura answered, wrapping the baby in the waiting towels. "He's really not as small as I'd expected. Close to six pounds, I'd guess. Quinn—"

Understanding, he reached for the baby so that Laura could finish what she had to do for the mother. She smiled tremulously at him as she passed the fragile bundle to him, their hands meeting for a moment. Resisting the futile urge to take her in his arms and hug some color back into her tension-strained face, Quinn turned back to Janet, placing her son in her arms and then helping her hold him as she suffered through the pains of afterbirth.

Laura was tempted to throw her arms around the ambulance team when they arrived with the equipment necessary to ensure that Janet and her son would be given proper care until they were safely hospitalized. Janet made her promise that she'd follow the ambulance to the hospital, just to make sure everything went smoothly. Quinn immediately offered to drive.

Throwing on just enough clothing to be presentable, Laura buttoned herself into her quilted coat and ran out to the car. Quinn was already behind the wheel, the heater going as he waited for her. He'd pulled on a shirt and a pair of boots and had buttoned his parka all the way up. The night air was bitterly cold and the first few flakes of snow were beginning to fall.

"You okay?" Quinn asked as he put the car into gear and pressed the accelerator.

Laura leaned back wearily against the seat and lifted a hand to her head, running her fingers through her tangled hair. She wasn't particularly surprised to note that her hands were trembling in delayed reaction. "I'm fine. Lord, what a night."

"Yeah." He drove in silence for a moment, then asked, "You really think they're going to be okay?"

"I think so. The baby seemed healthy enough, though small. I wish I'd known earlier that Janet was in labor. Maybe if I'd checked on her before I—went to bed." Remembering suddenly that she hadn't gone to bed alone, she looked quickly down at the hands she'd clasped tightly in her lap, feeling her face warm with a blush. There hadn't been time before to think about what had happened in her bed, but now it was hard to think of anything else.

"Now don't start blaming yourself," Quinn chided without looking at her. "You couldn't have known she was going into premature labor. You just went with her to the doctor last week and he didn't indicate this could happen, did he?"

"No, none of us were prepared."

"Think it had something to do with her physical neglect during her first couple of months?"

"I don't know. Maybe." Impulsively she turned to rest a hand on his arm. "Quinn, thank you. You were wonderful with her."

He looked embarrassed by her praise, his habitual frown deepening as he stared out at the road ahead. "You did all the work."

"I couldn't have done anything if you hadn't calmed her down. She was coming awfully close to outright panic."

"Yeah, well, she was scared, but she did okay when she had to."

"Thanks to you."

He scowled deeper and grunted an indecipherable response.

Laura removed her hand from his arm—reluctantly—and laced her fingers together again. "Was the story you told her true?"

"Yeah."

"Your job must have been very exciting. Do you use some of your own experiences in your books?"

"Yeah."

She sighed in exasperation. "Is it so hard for you to make conversation?"

He threw her a quick, emotionless glance. "I'm tired. I'm not in the mood to make conversation. If you want noise, turn on the radio."

Blinking back a swift, unexpected rush of tears, she turned her head and stared blindly out the passenger window. His kindness to Janet and the unspoken rapport between him and Laura during the crisis had almost lulled her into forgetting how rapidly his moods could change, how easily he could hurt her. She suspected that he'd turned on her deliberately this time, because he was uncomfortable that she'd gotten too close to that softer side he so persistently guarded. His barriers had weakened when they'd made love, and again when they'd worked together to deliver Janet's baby, but now they were firmly in place again.

What had happened to him, she wondered bleakly, to cause him to feel the need to keep everyone else at such a distance? What had made him so afraid of making himself vulnerable to anyone? And how could she overcome an obstacle she couldn't understand?

Each time he allowed her a glimpse of the caring, compassionate man she sensed inside him, it hurt more when he closed her back out. And each time she found it harder to resist loving him.

She was, undoubtedly, a fool. Because she knew even as she smarted from his latest unprovoked attack that she wouldn't stop trying to reach him.

Quinn tightened his hands on the steering wheel until his knuckles were white, his eyes trained unblinkingly on the ambulance visible through the lightly falling snow ahead of them. He'd hurt her, he thought angrily, all his senses trained on the unnaturally quiet woman huddled in the passenger seat. Dammit, he hadn't meant to hurt her.

He had to leave her alone, before he hurt her even more.

It was dawn by the time Janet and her baby were settled into the hospital and pronounced in good condition, considering what they'd both been through. Bone-tired, Laura sighed in relief when the doctor assured her that both mother and son would be fine.

"The snow's starting to come down harder," Quinn told her, returning from a restless walk, the faint smell of cigarette smoke clinging to him. Laura sensed that he hated hospitals and was ready to get out of this one. She wondered what kind of bad memories hospitals evoked for him.

"Let's just tell Janet we're going," she suggested.

He nodded. "Okay, but we'd better make it quick. I don't want to get stranded halfway ho—halfway to your place."

Home. He couldn't even say the word, Laura thought, turning her face around so that he couldn't see the weary tears that had welled up again. Blaming her emotionalism on stress and exhaustion, she led the way to the room Janet had been assigned.

Janet was almost asleep. Laura leaned over her and brushed a limp strand of red hair out of the young mother's pale face. "We're leaving now, Janet. I'll be back as soon as I can, okay? You and the baby are both going to be fine."

"Thanks to you and Quinn," Janet murmured faintly, making an effort to smile. "I owe you. Both of you."

"Get some rest now," Laura told her, dropping a kiss on Janet's cheek.

"Quinn?"

At the soft call, Quinn stepped closer to the bed. "Yeah, Janet?"

"Thanks, okay?"

"Sure."

Janet managed a pale semblance of her usual broad grin. "I'm naming him after you and Laura, but I won't be calling him Pig. His name is Laurence Quinn. I'll call him Larry. You like it?"

"Yeah. I like it a hell of a lot better than Pig."

Janet chuckled and closed her eyes. "See ya."

Watching with what felt like a golf ball-sized lump in her throat, Laura saw Quinn's hand lift as if to touch Janet's cheek. And then his fingers clenched and he dropped the hand back to his side, his expression unreadable again. "See ya, Janet."

Laura thought of that physical withdrawal during the near-silent ride home. Was it so very hard for Quinn to reach out to anyone? Why? And what had their lovemaking meant to him? Nothing more than sexual gratification? Her heart twisted with that unpleasant thought.

She wanted to talk to him so badly—about his feelings for her, his reactions to the baby's delivery, his past...anything. She wanted to lay her head on his shoulder and rest—at the very least to reach out and touch his hand. How terribly ironic, and how very sad, that she'd made love with him yet didn't feel free to do any of those things.

Dropping her head back against the seat, she closed her eyes. It was easier not to think at all than to try to work out her jumbled emotions just then. She sighed and let sleep claim her.

It had been a long time since he'd seen snow like this. Quinn turned off the car and sat for a moment staring out at the foglike whiteness surrounding them, already covering every outside surface. Then he drew in a deep breath and turned to look at Laura.

She was sleeping, her head lying back against the seat, face turned toward him. She looked so beautiful, so damned fragile, that he hurt. He rubbed his chest slowly, annoyed and rather bewildered to realize that he actually did hurt.

She was getting to him. She was the most giving, unselfish woman he'd ever known, and for some reason he couldn't begin to understand, she had offered him so much already, seemed willing to offer more. Yet he couldn't accept her generosity because he had nothing to offer in return. Absolutely nothing. Anything he may once have had to give to a relationship had died somewhere on the back streets of New York and Miami. Had died with Michael, and later with....

He frowned as a bit of ugly memory shuddered through his mind then vanished as if deliberately obliterated. Shaking his head like a man emerging from a dream—a nightmare?—he inhaled sharply and climbed out of the car. He shivered when he was immediately covered with snow. Damn, it was cold. Rather a shock to a system that had spent the past three years in sunny Florida.

Laura stirred when he scooped her into his arms. Her eyes opened, squinting as wet, stinging snowflakes blew into her face. "Quinn?"

"Yeah?"

"What are you doing?"

"Carrying you inside."

She shivered and nestled deeper into his shoulder. "I can walk," she mumbled without much enthusiasm.

He was already inside the front door. "Yeah, I know."

The house was quiet, the other occupants still catching up from the sleep that had been disturbed earlier. Quinn's long strides made short work of the hallway to Laura's bedroom. He set her on her feet by the bed, helping her to catch her balance as he impassively began to remove her jacket and then reached for the hem of her heavy sweater. She stood quietly as he undressed her, forcing himself to concentrate on the task rather than the creamy, slender body being revealed to him. Her nightgown lay over the foot of the bed; he snatched it up and tugged it over her head.

"I really am capable of dressing myself," she complained, pushing her hair out of her eyes as she gazed at him with heavy-lidded eyes.

"Yeah," he said again, because he couldn't think of anything else to say.

The bed covers were still tangled from earlier; Quinn scowled at his body reacted to the sensual memories those tumbled sheets evoked. Smoothing out the major wrinkles, he urged Laura into the bed with one hand, then pulled the sheet and comforter to her chin with the other.

He'd just started to walk away when she caught his hand. "Where are you going?"

He looked around at her, then had to quickly look away. She was entirely too tempting lying sleepily against the pillows, her golden-wheat curls tumbled heedlessly around her face, her mouth soft and unpainted. "To get some sleep."

"You can do that here." When he started to speak, her hand tightened around his. "It's too lonely in there," she said softly, almost pleadingly.

If only you knew, he thought bleakly. He looked at her again, intending to refuse, and their eyes met. He sighed. "Move over."

She chuckled quietly as he stripped out of his clothes. "You're always saying that," she told him even as she followed his curt order.

He didn't answer, but slid into the bed beside her. He wasn't sure which of them made the move that brought her into his arms. He suspected that he'd been the one.

Holding her tightly, he buried his face in her hair for a moment, his entire body tight with emotions he refused to examine, then forced himself to loosen his grip before he hurt her. Tucking her against his shoulder in a position that was becoming dangerously familiar, he let out a long, tight breath and closed his eyes.

Laura's hand was lying over his heart when he fell asleep, was still there when he woke four hours later. It was surprisingly difficult for him to move it so he could get up.

He headed straight for the shower—and didn't complain when the water ran cold for the first few minutes.

Chapter Eight

It's a good thing you're off work this week. Look at that snow," Betty commented, her eyes on the kitchen window as she washed up after breakfast.

Laura sipped her freshly poured coffee, her gaze following Betty's. The snow was still coming down outside, adding to the inches already covering the ground. The radio report had predicted that it would continue for the rest of the day and on into the next. Like Betty, Laura was glad the snowstorm had waited until the first day of her vacation to hit. Otherwise, she'd have found herself sleeping over at the hospital.

"I called the hospital a few minutes ago," Betty went on, seemingly unaware that Laura had been exceptionally quiet since she'd gotten up a few minutes earlier, the last of the household to arise. "Janet is doing just fine. She told me the baby is beautiful and healthy."

"We'll have to get the bassinet set up in her room," Laura responded absently. "I thought we had a bit more time to get ready for a baby in the house."

"It's so nice of you to let her stay here until she gets on her feet."

Laura shook her head. "I like her. And it'll be fun having a baby around. I'm sure we'll all spoil him terribly."

"At least she won't lack for baby-sitters while she's attending classes."

"I wish you'd reconsider letting me raise your pay, Betty. You shouldn't have to take on baby-sitting in addition to your other chores without being compensated for the extra work."

Betty's voice was uncharacteristically firm when she answered. "You pay me too much as it is, particularly since room and board is included. Besides, I love babies. And Renee will adore it."

"Mmm." Laura smiled a bit skeptically. "She'll adore it until she realizes she's sharing Mommy's attention."

Betty laughed. "Well, I never said there wouldn't be adjustments to make."

After pouring herself another cup of coffee, Betty slipped into the chair opposite Laura at the small kitchen table. "Mr. Gallagher working again this morning?"

Laura swallowed too quickly, forcing a cough. Damn. Just the mention of his name...

"Yes, I suppose he is. I haven't seen him this morning," she answered as casually as possible. He'd gone when she'd awakened, just like the last time. He'd resumed his usual pattern—advance and retreat.

She wondered what it would be like to wake up with him.

"Laura," Betty began hesitantly, "would you like to talk about it? I mean, you certainly have listened to my problems often enough. I'd like to return the favor if it would help."

Laura looked up in surprise. "Talk about what?" she asked, genuinely confused. She hadn't thought anyone in the household knew that there was anything unusual going on between herself and Quinn.

It seemed that she'd underestimated Betty. "It's pretty obvious that you're falling for him," Betty told her, almost apologetically. "And that he's a hard man to get close to. I'm afraid you're going to be hurt. I just don't think I could bear to see you hurt. You give so much to others, and you ask so little for yourself."

Moved, Laura reached across the table to touch her friend's hand. "Thank you for being concerned, Betty, but I'm fine. Really. You're right, of course," she felt compelled to add, wanting to respond to Betty's genuine solicitude with honesty. "I do care for him. And he isn't a man who'll allow people to care for him. He's been very badly hurt, I think, though he hasn't talked to me about it. Maybe he never will."

"But you're going to keep caring for him, anyway."

"I can't help it," Laura admitted, staring soberly down at the coffee cup she cradled in both hands. "It's too late to try to stop."

"Too late?"

Laura was almost relieved when Renee chose that moment to burst into the kitchen. "Mommy, mommy! Quinn drawed me a picture, see? It's me!"

"This is wonderful," Betty said in surprise, studying the slightly crumpled sheet of paper her daughter had thrust into her hands. She glanced at Laura. "Look at this."

Laura accepted the paper with curiosity. Sure enough, the drawing was of Renee. She'd been sketched in pencil, a chubby little figure in a snowsuit, one long braid dangling out of her hood. She stood in the center of a deserted playground, implied by quick strokes of the pencil in the background. Laura noted the slide, the swings, the merry-go-round. Her eyes narrowed on something else in one corner, a dark scrawl that may have started out as an object but had ended as no more than a blot. Something about that scribbled area bothered her; she couldn't have said what it was. The rest of the sketch was lightly done, almost whimsical, but there was something dark, something almost savage about that corner of the page.

"You wike it, Aunt 'aura?"

Dragging her gaze from the sketch, Laura looked up at Renee. "Yes, Renee, I like it."

"Renee, you haven't been disturbing Mr. Gallagher while he's trying to work, have you?" Betty asked reprovingly.

Renee's blue eyes rounded innocently. "Him said it was okay," she insisted. "Him said come in when I knocked onna door."

"Oh, Renee—"

"Him wouldn't wet me pway with the ca'puter, but him drawed me a picture."

"You *have* been disturbing him. Renee, when Mr. Gallagher is busy..."

"Mr. Gallagher will say so," Quinn's voice finished from the doorway. He entered with the quiet power that was so much a part of him, Laura observed, hoping her expression wasn't as transparent as it felt when his eyes briefly met hers. "Good morning, Laura."

"Good morning, Quinn," she managed.

"Recovered from all the excitement yet?"

If only she could read something in his face—tenderness, warmth, anything. "I'm not sure," she answered slowly.

He accepted that with only a quirk of an eyebrow before turning to Betty. "Don't scold Renee, Betty. She did knock before she came into the study. If I'd been involved in something critical I would have told her to come back later. Any coffee left?''

"Yes, I'll—"

He made a short, flat movement with his hand, indicating that she was to remain seated. "I'll get it."

"Renee just showed us the picture you drew for her, Quinn," Laura told him. "I didn't realize you were an artist as well as a writer."

He shrugged and rubbed his mustache with his thumb before pouring his coffee. "I'm not. Knowing how to sketch just came in handy sometimes when I was a cop."

"Did you ever have any art training?"

"No. I've got to get back to work now. See you at lunch." Without looking at Laura, Quinn left the kitchen, ruffling Renee's hair and making her giggle as he passed.

Laura looked helplessly at Betty when Quinn was gone. "I must be out of my mind."

Betty somehow managed to look amused and sympathetic all at the same time. "I'm hardly qualified to give advice on men, Laura. My own choice was drastically wrong. But I do think Quinn Gallagher's a good man, deep inside. I've watched him with Renee. And Janet told me how good he was to her last night."

"Yes, he is a good man. But he's so withdrawn. I don't know if he'll ever let anyone inside those barriers he's put up."

"If anyone can get in, you can," Betty answered optimistically. "You'll just have to get to know him as best you can, find out why he thinks those barriers are necessary."

"You know, you're right," Laura agreed thoughtfully. "I do need to learn more about him." She thought of the purchase she'd made a couple of days after Quinn had moved into the guest cottage. Perhaps she knew where to find one clue to Quinn's past.

After breakfast, Laura stepped out on the screened back porch to feed her pets, spending a pleasant ten minutes tickling Sabu's ears and stroking Doo's feathers. Sabu had belonged to her father. The cat, a stray, had been hit by a car, resulting in the amputated leg. Graham had brought the cat home to recover, and Sabu had become a permanent occupant. She honestly didn't know where the duck had come from. Sabu had brought the plump white bird out of the woods one day and Doo had been with them ever since. Some people might think it odd that the cat had chosen to make a pet of the bird rather than a dinner. Laura accepted it quite easily.

She spent the next two hours reading *Suicide Beat*. Quinn's book alternately appalled and fascinated her. He wrote very well, though he wasted no words on description or unnecessary dialogue. The book was mostly action, stark, violent action, punctuated by brief, grim snatches of the characters' thoughts. It broke her heart that Quinn seemed to slip so easily inside the criminal mind. There were unexpected flashes of humor in the tale, but even that was a sardonic, detached mockery of the people involved—those on both sides of good and evil. At times the differences between the two sides became very hard to distinguish. She knew he'd portrayed it that way on purpose.

She'd forced herself almost halfway through the book when Betty called her to lunch. More than once she'd found herself blinking back tears, not for anyone within the book but for the angry, cynical, lonely man who'd written it.

Quinn wasn't sure how to read the looks Laura gave him during lunch. Her expression was solemn, thoughtful, as if something were bothering her. He wondered if it had anything to do with that sketch he'd drawn for Renee.

He wished he hadn't drawn it. It had been an impulse, really, something to amuse her and to distract her from wanting to experiment with his computer. He'd picked up the pencil and a sheet of paper and the drawing of Renee in the playground had been the result. He wasn't too crazy about playgrounds, ever since an ugly incident a few years ago that had almost gotten him killed. One didn't exactly look back on the scene of that close a call with fond nostalgia, he thought ironically.

Regardless of the reason he'd chosen to draw that particular setting, he'd been restless ever since, unable to concentrate on his work, pacing up and down the study. Maybe it was all that damned snow outside. The way it was piling up, still coming down, he knew there was no question of getting off this mountain for the next few days. But he needed to get out for a while, even if he had to slog through snow to do it.

It was either go for a long walk or carry Laura into her bedroom and throw himself on her. It had been all he could do to leave her bed this morning without waking her. He'd looked at her lying there, sleeping so peacefully, and he'd ached to repeat the incredible lovemaking of the night before. He tried to tell himself that it couldn't possibly have been as good as he remembered, that it could never be quite that good again. He told himself that he shouldn't try to find out. He wasn't being fair to her.

And then she smiled at him from the other end of the dining table and his entire body hardened in response. Hell.

"Think I'll go for a walk," he said when everyone had finished eating. "It's been a long time since I walked in snow."

Mrs. Elliott looked up and started to say something, but Laura spoke first. "Do you mind if I go with you?"

Having her go with him was rather defeating the purpose of putting her out of his mind. But at least they'd be outside, nowhere near her bedroom. "Suit yourself."

"Quinn, dear, just a moment. I have something for you," Mrs. Elliott said in her fluttery voice, already moving toward the stairway.

Quinn looked after her with a frown. *Quinn, dear?* When the hell had he become Quinn, dear?

Laura met his eyes and barely stifled a giggle, obviously reading his astonishment on his face. His mouth twitched in response. "What does she have for me?"

Laura shrugged, though he could tell by looking at her that she had at least an idea.

Mrs. Elliott bustled back into the room. Smiling sweetly at him, she held up a large, thick, royal blue sweater. "I noticed that you only have those flannel shirts—I suppose you don't need heavy sweaters in Florida—so I knitted this for you. I just finished it this morning. Perhaps you'd like to wear it on your walk. Do you have a hat and gloves?"

Quinn looked at the beautifully worked garment, then at the blue-haired little lady waiting for some show of approval from him. "Yes, I—uh,—that's very nice of you. Thank you."

His awkward thanks seemed to satisfy her completely. She patted his arm. "You're welcome, dear. Enjoy your walk. I'll go help Betty now." She left him still staring down at the sweater. No one had ever knitted a sweater for him before.

He looked up at Laura who was watching him with soft, almost tender eyes. Feeling compelled to say something, he cleared his throat. "That was—uh—"

"Nice of her," she finished for him, smiling as she repeated the words he'd used to Mrs. Elliott.

"Yeah." He shoved his free hand into his pocket. "If you're going with me, you'd better get your coat."

"Yes, sir," she replied cockily, sketching a quick salute at him before hurrying off to her room. Quinn followed more slowly, deciding he might as well change into the sweater. He didn't want to hurt the old lady's feelings, after all.

Laura tugged an off-white wool sweater—another of Mrs. Elliott's creations—over her head, then ran her fingers through her curls to smooth them, not easy with the static electricity the sweater had generated. She hurriedly grabbed her red knit hat, scarf and gloves, stamped her feet into knee-high boots and then reached for her favorite slate-blue coat. She knew better than to expect Quinn to wait for her if she dawdled.

She wondered if he'd have the sweater on. She'd been almost unbearably moved by the little scene. Quinn had obviously been touched by the gesture, though he hadn't known how to show it. Hadn't wanted to show it. It was so hard for him to demonstrate his feelings. Which, of course, made her think of the way he'd made love to her. It was the only time she'd known him to completely lose control of his obsessive detachment. She wanted to believe that she'd reached him in a way no other woman had. Such beliefs were dangerous, because they made her hope.

He was wearing the sweater. It fit perfectly, emphasizing his wide shoulders, powerful chest and trim waist. The rich blue looked wonderful on him, deepening the color of his gray eyes, glowing against his dark tan. His hair had tumbled onto his forehead again and she longed to brush it back. She wondered what he'd do if she gave in to the impulse to do so. Would he smile for her or would he jerk away from her touch? She wasn't brave enough to find out; she didn't think she could bear it if he pulled away from her.

Without a word, he buttoned up his parka and tugged on a pair of heavy black gloves. Already bundled into her own things, Laura finished winding her muffler around her neck. "I brought you one of Dad's hats," she told him, offering a thick knit cap. "I haven't seen you wearing a hat since you've been here, so I wasn't sure you had one."

"I don't like wearing hats," he cut in flatly.

"Quinn, it's really cold out there," she argued. "It's silly to go out without something on your head."

He made an impatient gesture, his mouth hardening. "Look, I'm a grown man, okay? I don't need everyone in this household trying to mother me."

It hurt, but she refused to lower her outstretched hand. "I'm not your mother, Quinn. I'm a nurse. And a grown man should have enough sense to protect himself from the elements."

His eyes blazed hotly, but his voice was icily cold. "Fine. I'll wear the damned hat."

Not exactly an auspicious beginning to their walk, Laura thought with a sigh, following as he stamped out the back door. But at least he was wearing the hat.

Between the five-inch-deep snow and Quinn's long, angry strides, she had a hard time keeping up with him. Finally deciding she wasn't going to break her neck trying, she slowed down and allowed him to get ahead of her. Gloved hands deep in the pockets of her down-filled coat, she gazed moodily around her as she walked, unusually impervious to the beauty of the winter wonderland surrounding her. All her thoughts were centered on Quinn.

Watching him ahead of her, she thought he looked as though he wanted to run or break something or beat someone up. Though her knowledge of him was frustratingly slim, she thought she knew why he was turning savage. He was feeling threatened. She compared him to a wild animal, finding himself trapped in a situation he didn't know how to handle, striking out at anyone who came too close. She still didn't know enough about his past to understand him fully, but she was beginning to realize that Quinn was motivated by a compulsion to hold himself aloof from his fellow humans. It didn't take a psychologist to realize that he was afraid of being hurt again. How many times, she wondered, had he been wounded before he'd felt it necessary to go to such extremes to protect himself?

And couldn't he see that it wasn't working? He wasn't the type who could live in total isolation. If he were, he wouldn't rent a room from Amos when he could have a place of his own. She was sure he'd have some good excuse if confronted about that choice, but the fact was that he was lonely. Nothing more.

For that matter, he could be staying in a hotel somewhere right now. Even when he'd chosen to get away for a while, he'd ended up staying with others. Oh, sure, Amos had sent him here and he'd originally planned to stay in the guest cottage. But he was still here.

If only she could get him to talk to her, to accept his own need for someone. How she wished he would realize that he needed her. She had so much to give him, if only he would accept it. And somehow she knew he had a great deal to offer in return, if only he would allow himself.

They'd been walking for perhaps ten minutes when Quinn's shoulders relaxed and his strides shortened. Finally he turned, his face impassive as he waited for her to catch up. He'd chosen to stop beneath a huge, dense cedar, its white-coated branches providing a makeshift awning from the steadily falling snow. He leaned back against the thick, rough trunk, one leg bent to prop his boot against the tree, his hands in his pockets. Their eyes met and Laura could see the apology he didn't know how to make.

"Your nose is red," he told her.

She smiled. "Your cheeks are red," she countered, standing close to him.

"It's cold. Want to go back?"

She shook her head. "I've lived here all my life, remember? I'm used to the cold. How about you? Can you take it?"

"I grew up in New York. I can take it."

"What was your family like, Quinn?"

He shrugged. "Average. My dad was a plumber, my mom a schoolteacher. They married in their late twenties, had my brother a year later, then thought they couldn't have any more kids until I came along almost ten years after that. My mom died when I was in high school."

"Is your father still living?"

A muscle moved sightly in his jaw. She saw it only because she was watching him so closely. "Yeah. He remarried and moved to Phoenix years ago. We aren't close."

"I'm sorry."

He shrugged again.

"I lost my mother early, too. It hurts, doesn't it?"

He reached inside his parka and pulled out a pack of cigarettes, a noncommittal grunt his only response to her tentative question.

She persisted. "Tell me about your brother. What was his name?"

He pulled off one glove to light a cigarette, cupping his gloved hand around the flame from his disposable lighter. Drawing deeply, he shoved the lighter back into his pocket, lowered the cigarette with his bare hand and blew the smoke away from her. "Michael," he growled, just when she'd decided he wasn't going to answer her question. "My brother's name was Michael."

"Were you close?"

"Yeah."

"You were so much younger; you must have admired him a great deal."

"He was a good man. A good cop."

"Is that why you went into police work? Because you wanted to be like him?"

His eyes narrowed at her through a thin stream of smoke. "We talked about this before. I told you how I ended up being a cop."

"But did you really want to be a police officer, or did you want to write even then? Did you go into a career you really didn't want just to please your brother?"

"What the hell are you trying to do?" he asked in sudden temper. "Why are you asking all these questions?"

She faced him bravely, her chin lifted. "I'm simply trying to understand you, Quinn. Is that so hard to believe after what's happened between us?"

"Nothing special has happened between us," he retorted immediately, though he didn't quite meet her eyes as he said it. He lifted the cigarette to his lips again—hiding behind it, she told herself in exasperation.

"The hell it hasn't," she answered succinctly, drawing on his own mannerisms to hide the hurt. Before he could say anything else, she changed the subject. "I read the first half of *Suicide Beat* this morning. When I finish it, I'm going to read *Under Investigation* and your latest one, *Crimson Justice*. I bought them last week."

She'd succeeded in startling him, anyway. And he didn't look at all pleased by her announcement. "Why are you reading those? They're hardly your type of books."

"I'm reading them because you wrote them."

"Don't read them for my sake. Stick to your fairy tales. They suit you better."

"The policeman who was killed in the second chapter of *Suicide Beat*—he was so nice, so idealistic. Was he based on Michael? Is that the way Michael died?"

"Don't you read the fine print at the beginning of all fictional novels?" he growled. "It says something about the characters not being based on anyone, living or dead. Fiction is just that—fiction."

"You told me yourself that you draw on your own experiences to write your books. You must also use the people you knew as the basis for your characters," Laura pushed on relentlessly, determined to draw some kind of response out of him. She wondered if this was the time to tell him about Robbie's death. Perhaps in sharing their grief and their anger, Quinn would open up to her more. "Were you thinking of Michael when you wrote about the man you called Neal? Is the angry, bitter protagonist a projection of yourself?"

He threw the cigarette on the ground and smashed it savagely beneath the heel of his boot. "Psychology 101, right? Probably required by all nurses in training. Well, forget it, Laura. I'm not one of your patients."

"Dammit, Quinn, talk to me! Tell me about Michael, tell me about the other people you loved and lost. Tell me why you won't let anyone—why you don't want me to get close to you."

He opened his mouth to retort, then sighed and closed his eyes for a moment before looking at her again. When he did speak, his voice was low, calm, unemotional. "Let it go, Laura. Don't start trying to look into my head, my past. You'd do better to forget about last night altogether. When the roads are clear, I'll get out of here, head back to Florida."

"I can't just forget about last night, Quinn," she answered quietly. "And I can't stop trying to reach you. Don't you know that I—"

"No!" He caught her shoulders in his hands, one gloved, the other still bare. His eyes bored into hers. "I know what happened between us isn't something you take lightly, Laura. I know you don't give yourself indiscriminately. This...attraction between us caught both of us by surprise. But don't start telling yourself that it's anything more than physical. It's not."

"Maybe not for you," she whispered, her hands lifting to rest on his chest. "It is for me."

"Laura, you're too soft. Too giving. Someday you're going to be badly hurt. I don't want to be the one to hurt you."

"You wouldn't have to hurt me, Quinn."

His fingers tightened. "Don't you see that I have nothing to offer you? Nothing! You can't love a dead man, Laura."

She almost recoiled at his words. She'd thought he was talking about Robbie—but the look on his face made her realize he referred to himself. "Quinn, I don't know how to break this to you, but you're very much alive."

"Not inside. Not where it counts," he answered grimly. "That's what I've been trying to tell you. I can't offer you anything because there's nothing left to give."

"Oh, Quinn." She was unable to prevent herself from lifting a hand to his hard, set jaw, stroking him with unsteady, wool-covered fingers. "For such an intelligent man, that's about the most idiotic thing I've ever heard. Of course you have something to give—you have everything to give! It's not me you're protecting. It's yourself."

He jerked his head back, breaking the contact between them, releasing her shoulders as he did so. "Don't delude yourself, Laura."

"I'm not the one living a self-delusion, Quinn. You are."

He swore. "No wonder you prefer fairy tales. You can't see the difference between fantasy and reality."

She didn't blink, nor hesitate to throw the accusation right back at him. "No wonder you write such bleak, unhappy stories. You've blinded yourself to the good things in life."

He turned away from her. "I'm going back to the house."

"I'm not giving up, Quinn," she threw after him recklessly. "I'm not going to stop trying to make you see that you're wrong about yourself."

He kept walking.

"I love you," she told him, her voice so soft she hardly heard it herself. She didn't know if he'd heard or not, didn't even care. He wouldn't have believed her, anyway. Not yet. Maybe not ever.

Chapter Nine

Laura wasn't surprised that Quinn barricaded himself in the study again after their walk. He was hiding from her, of course; she wondered if he was having any success at hiding from himself. She finished *Suicide Beat*, finding the ending as uncomfortable as she'd expected it to be. She didn't really learn anything more about Quinn than she'd already figured out for herself, but some of the events in the book were so brutally depicted that she thought they must have come from his own experiences. She tried to imagine how she would react to such ugliness. It wasn't easy, but she guessed that she, like Quinn, would have to find a way to stay totally detached from the things she saw, the things she had to do.

She thought of Sam Jennings, a psychologist at the hospital who was a casual friend. She'd even been out with him a couple of times, though she'd never felt more than liking and admiration for him. Sam had told her that he'd once led a therapy group for police officers in Denver, where he'd worked before moving to Greeley. Maybe he could help her understand Quinn better. She'd make a point of talking to him on Monday, when she returned to work. Not that Quinn would appreciate her doing research on him behind his back, she thought with a grimace, but she'd warned him that she wasn't going to give up. If he'd been so determined to keep her from becoming involved with him, he should never have entered her bedroom.

"He reminds me a bit of my husband, Oliver," Mrs. Elliott mused, startling Laura out of her own thoughts.

Laura was sitting in a rocking chair in the den, Renee dozing in her lap on the pretext of watching television after dinner. Mrs. Elliott sat knitting on the couch, while Betty curled into an armchair with a book—one of Laura's romance novels. As far as Laura knew, Quinn was still in the study. "Who reminds you of Oliver, Mrs. Elliott?" she asked, glancing at the television program she'd been ignoring and wondering if the woman was referring to one of the actors.

"Quinn," Mrs. Elliott clarified, smiling at her as she changed the color of yarn on her needles. "You remember Oliver, of course, Laura. Doesn't Quinn remind you of him?"

A bit dubiously Laura thought of Mr. Elliott, a World War II veteran who'd lost both legs to an enemy mine and had spent the remainder of his years in a wheelchair. Like Quinn, he'd been rather quiet, but he'd been a gentle, sweet-natured man who'd absolutely adored his wife. The feeling had obviously been mutual. "Well—"

Mrs. Elliott laughed softly. "Of course you don't see the resemblance. Oliver was so much older when you knew him. I was thinking of when he was young and he'd just come home from the war. Oh, my, he was so angry, so bitter. You see, we were married only a few days before he shipped out and he was ashamed to come home with no legs. He tried to drive me away from him, but I simply wouldn't allow it. I loved him. And eventually I was able to convince him that he was every bit as much a man when he returned to me as he was when he left."

Fascinated, Laura studied the older woman's reminiscent expression. She'd had no idea that Mrs. Elliott had such a romantic past. She should have known better, she thought with compunction. Everyone had an interesting past if only others would take the time to listen; it was the main reason she'd always enjoyed the company of older people. "How did you convince him?"

The faintest of pink blushes touched Mrs. Elliott's pale, lined cheeks. "Oh, I was quite forward. I kept after him until he couldn't reject me any longer. Once he realized that I just wouldn't give up, he did a complete about-face. He used to tell me all the time that he'd given me my chance to run and once I'd passed up the opportunity I no longer had any choice. I was his, and he had no intention of letting me get away." Her smile trembled a bit, then steadied. "I never wanted to get away, of course. We had a wonderful life together. We were married for forty-five years."

Aware of a hollow feeling in the pit of her stomach, Laura murmured a response. Would she have a chance to convince Quinn that they could be happy together, whatever shortcomings he believed himself to possess? She rested her cheek on Renee's silky head, snuggling the drowsy toddler deeper into her arms. Would she ever hold a child of her own?

With one of her always surprising moments of uncanny perception, Mrs. Elliott smiled gently at Laura. "It won't be easy, dear, but it will be worth it. He's a good man."

Laura flushed. Were her feelings for Quinn so obvious already? Uncertain what to say, she opened her mouth then closed it when Renee stirred and murmured, "I sweepy, Mommy."

Betty set her book down. "All right, darling. Tell everyone good night."

Renee gave Laura a hug and a kiss, then crawled down from her lap to toddle over to the couch where she lifted her chubby face for Mrs. Elliott's kiss. "Night, Mrs. Ewwiott."

"Good night, sweetie."

Betty held out her hand to her daughter. Renee looked around the room with a frown. "Where's Quinn?"

"He's working in the study. You can see him in the morning."

"Kiss him night."

"No, darling, we can't disturb him. Come on, now."

Renee's lower lips trembled and her blue eyes filled with tears. "Wanna kiss Quinn night," she insisted. "Him wants a kiss."

Laura wasn't so sure about that, but she couldn't resist the child's plea. She glanced at Betty, who was beginning to look harried, and sighed. "I'll take her in."

Betty chewed her lip. "Are you sure?"

Suddenly amused, Laura nodded. "Yeah. I don't think he'll bite." Not in front of Renee, anyway, she thought with an urge to giggle. One would think that they were, indeed, sharing their home with the wild animal Laura had compared Quinn to earlier. "Come on, Renee."

Dimpling her satisfaction, Renee caught Laura's hand and bounced at her side to the study. Laura knocked once, then opened the door. "Quinn? Renee wanted to tell you goodnight."

Quinn looked up from the computer with a lifted eyebrow, just in time to catch Renee as she eagerly launched herself at him. "You gonna bite, Quinn?" she asked, grinning at him.

One corner of his mustache lifted with a smile. He shot Laura a quick, amused glance then looked back down at the little girl in his arms. "I might," he told her in a mock growl. "I was just thinking about having a snack." Pulling her closer, he made a snapping motion with his teeth.

Renee giggled. "I not a snack! I a girl!"

"So you are," he replied in feigned surprise, causing her to laugh even harder.

"Kiss?" she invited him, lifting her face expectantly.

He tousled her hair, then touched his mouth to her cheek, making her giggle again and inform him that his mustache tickled. "Night, Quinn."

"Good night, Renee." He released the child, who immediately headed for the door.

Laura had watched the scene with bittersweet emotions, telling herself that it was quite unreasonable to envy a three-year-old. But how she'd have loved to be so comfortable with Quinn, not to have to worry about everything she said to him. To be able to throw her arms around him and cheerfully demand a kiss. She turned to follow Renee out of the room.

"Laura."

Turning back in response to his voice, she found him standing right behind her. He'd moved so quietly she hadn't heard him approach. "Yes?"

He reached behind her to close the door. "I don't bite," he told her.

Uncertain how to respond, she clasped her hands loosely in front of her, studying him through her lashes. "I know."

With a hand under her chin, he lifted her face, forcing her to look at him directly. "Laura, I—" He stopped, then exhaled sharply. "Ah, hell."

And then his mouth was on hers, hot and demanding, and she forgot about everything else. Her arms went around his neck even as his encircled her waist, pulling her closer. His tongue stabbed erotically into her mouth, making her long for another kind of penetration. She moaned and tilted her head back to deepen the kiss, responding with all the turbulent, convoluted emotions swirling within her.

Quinn leaned into her, pressing her back against the door, his hands moving possessively over her slender curves. He lifted his head to stare down at her with glittering eyes, then kissed her again, less forcefully this time, more seductively, asking for a response rather than demanding one. She couldn't resist him when he was difficult and autocratic, she'd never be able to deny him when he was gentle and persuasive.

She buried her fingers in his thick, soft hair, her eyes tightly closed as she savored the moment, knowing it could end at any time. His mouth slanted to a new angle and she followed his lead, her pulse throbbing heavily, her breasts swelling in unconscious appeal for his touch. Quinn's hand slipped to the small of her back, his fingers spreading over the top of her hip to hold her to him. He was boldly aroused, his thighs rock-hard against hers, his hips moving just enough to make her shiver with desire. "Quinn," she gasped when he released her mouth again.

"I wasn't going to do that," he muttered, his face buried in her hair.

"I'm not sorry you did," she answered, holding him closer.

His fingers clenched in the curls at the back of her head, tugging just hard enough to lift her face to his. "I want you." His voice was low, intense, his eyes narrowed. "But I don't want to hurt you."

"Why don't you let me worry about me?" she suggested in little more than a whisper. "I want you, too."

His mouth lowered toward hers, then stopped. With a muffled curse he released her and turned away. "You'd better go back to your friends."

"Quinn." She reached out for him, but he evaded her hand. She let it drop, knowing he'd managed to close her out again. This time. At least she knew for certain now that he was fighting himself much harder than he was fighting her. And she had no intention of making it easier for him. "Good night, Quinn," she told him softly. "If you get lonely later, my door will be unlocked."

He didn't answer, but his shoulders went rigid. Satisfied, she turned and left the room, closing the door quietly behind her. And then she leaned against the wall outside the study, taking several long, deep breaths to calm herself before rejoining Mrs. Elliott and Betty in the den.

"Not here, dammit! Not here!" Quinn heard the anguish in his own cry even as he clawed his way to consciousness. It had been too much to hope that he'd managed to keep quiet in the throes of the nightmare this time; he felt the soft hand stroking his damp forehead just before he forced his eyes open.

"Quinn, it's all right. You were having a nightmare. It's over," Laura's voice crooned at his ear.

Chagrined, he turned his head to find her kneeling by the bed, her concerned expression just visible in the shadows. He took a deep breath to calm his rapid pulse, clearing his voice before he spoke. "Go back to bed, Laura."

She moved, but only to sit on the edge of the bed, her hand still cool against the side of his face. "It must have been a terrible dream. Would it help to talk about it?"

He shook his head. "No."

"Sometimes it does," she persisted. "If you could just tell me about it—"

"I can't," he muttered, embarrassed that she'd caught him in the middle of one of the dreams. "I can't remember it."

"You don't remember any of it?" she asked in obvious surprise, dropping her hand.

He shook his head again. "I never do. I've tried, believe me."

"You have these dreams—these nightmares often?"

He sighed. "Sometimes. Sorry I disturbed you."

"You were saying 'not here.' And when I came in, I thought I heard you mutter something about a playground. Does that mean anything to you?"

He frowned. "A playground?"

"Well, I thought that was what you said, but it was hard to tell. Since you'd drawn that picture for Renee earlier, I thought—"

He moved restlessly against the pillow, cutting off her words. "I don't know. I can't remember the dream."

"Did something bad happen to you in a playground once? There was something in the picture you drew—a dark spot in one corner that you'd scratched out. Do you remember what it was?"

Quinn pushed his hand through his hair and raised himself on one elbow. "I was just scribbling. Don't start looking for deep psychological meaning in a simple sketch, Laura."

"I'm only trying to help, Quinn. I know how awful it is to be plagued by nightmares. I had that problem myself a few years ago. Fortunately I had my father to talk them out with me. Eventually they stopped."

He hated the idea of Laura waking up in the night, haunted by the cold horror that he'd come to associate with his dreams. He wanted to ask about her nightmares, but couldn't. Still, he sensed that she genuinely wanted to help him.

If only she could.

"I tried to talk to Amos about the dreams once," he admitted, "but I can't talk about something I can't even remember."

"*Did* something ever happen to you on a playground, Quinn? Could it be that the drawing you did for Renee triggered the dream tonight?"

Tempted to snap at her to leave it alone, he made himself consider her question, instead. "I was involved in a shoot-out on a playground once. It would have been about three years ago, just before I transferred from New York to Miami. The playground incident was rather routine, really. The only thing I can remember about it was that I took a bullet in the shoulder."

"That sounds terrifying enough," she commented with an odd catch in her voice. "Could that be what you were reliving in your dream?"

He shrugged, brow furrowed in confusion. "I doubt it. It wasn't the first time I was hit, not even the most serious wound I received in the line of duty. I was working in Miami only a few weeks later."

"How long after that did you decide to quit?"

"Almost a year, I guess. I just woke up one day deciding I was tired of the same old routine, needed to move on to something else. I'd been working on a novel to wind down when I was off duty, so I decided to finish it and see what would happen if I submitted it to a publisher. I told you once before, there wasn't any single, traumatic incident that led to my quitting the force. To be honest, I simply burned out. It's not all that uncommon after fourteen years in vice work." He found his thoughts wandering as he finished.

The effects of the nightmare were rapidly wearing off and he was becoming intensely aware that Laura was sitting on the side of his bed in the middle of the night, that she had on a soft, light-colored nightgown and he was wearing nothing but a sheet and a thin blanket.

"Quinn—" she hesitated, then braved on "—tell me how your brother, Michael, died."

That caught his drifting attention. "Why?"

Laura bit her lip at the unencouragingly bitten out question. She'd lost him, she thought regretfully. In the aftermath of the nightmare that had drenched him with sweat and made him cry out in a voice that had torn her heart, he'd let his guard down enough to talk to her, really talk to her, if only for a few moments. But her question about Michael had been too much, too precipitous. Because she couldn't stand having him withdraw from her so abruptly after the fleeting intimacy they'd shared, she reached out and framed his face in her hands, recklessly, willing to risk his rejection. "Quinn, please. Don't shut me out again. You don't have to talk about Michael if you don't want to."

"Dammit, Laura." His tone was exasperated, but his free hand lifted to cover one of hers. "Don't you know you're playing with fire?"

"I'm not playing, Quinn," she whispered, her thumb stroking the corner of his mustache.

"You're going to get burned, anyway."

"So you keep telling me." She leaned closer and pressed her lips to his, quickly, just because she wanted to. Because she thought she'd die if she didn't. He hadn't pushed her away, she thought, tentatively deepening the kiss. He'd stiffened, but he hadn't pushed her away. "Don't send me away," she murmured against his lips.

"I should," he answered, but he couldn't hide his reluctance to do so.

"No. You shouldn't." She rubbed her lips back and forth against his firm, warm ones, loving the way his mustache tickled her skin. She slipped one hand down to his chest, her fingers spreading through the rough hair. His muscles rippled beneath her palm, proving that he wasn't immune to her touch.

"I hope you know what you're doing."

Her hand glided lower, stopping just above the covering that had slipped below his waist. "I know what I'm doing." She kissed him again, her tongue darting between his lips to briefly touch his.

Quinn cleared his throat. "Yeah. I guess you do." And he brought her mouth firmly down on his, lowering himself back against the pillow so that she lay sprawled across his chest.

She could have laughed with relief, but his skillful hands soon had her gasping with pleasure, instead. He swept her nightgown over her head, though the sheet still lay across his lower half. She felt his arousal, heavy and demanding, through the thin fabric as she rubbed her breasts against his bare chest, her lips thrusting lightly into his. The little laugh that escaped her when he groaned was breathless, husky, sounding wicked even to her.

She lowered her head to nibble at his neck, then wriggled lower to nuzzle against his hardening nipples. He groaned again when she circled one with just the tip of her tongue. "Honey, you do know what you're doing," he muttered, holding her head to push himself into her mouth.

It was the first time he'd called her by anything but her name. She gloried in the simple endearment, and in the way his breathing became more and more ragged as she caressed him with her hands and her lips. The strongly defined muscles of his flat stomach contracted beneath her mouth as she moved downward, stopping to press a kiss here, to taste the skin there. Her hand preceded her mouth, sliding beneath the sheet to stroke him, moving lower to cup him. Quinn gasped and arched into her palm, impatiently sweeping the sheet away to join the blanket he'd already pushed aside. Their legs tangled and Laura closed her eyes in pleasure at the sensation. Flesh to flesh, heart to heart.

He pulled her mouth back to his, ravaging it in a sudden rush of passion, holding her so tightly she could hardly breathe. She returned the embrace with matching fervor, her hands coming up to hold him. "I love your hair," she whispered when he allowed her to surface for oxygen. She threaded her fingers into the silky brown and gold strands, pressing a kiss to his forehead.

His own fists were clenched in her tangled curls. "I like your hair," he admitted rather awkwardly, reminding her that compliments didn't come easily to her lover. "Sometimes it looks almost alive, the way it curls and bounces around your head."

She laughed softly. "Sometimes it *feels* alive when I'm trying to make it behave. I have to pin it back at work, but it keeps escaping. I've thought of cutting it, but—"

"No." The denial was immediate and succinct. "Don't cut it."

Whatever she may have said next was lost in a gasp when he rolled suddenly to pin her beneath him, his lips taking hers again even as his hand moved downward, finding her hot and wet and ready for him. His fingertips stroked her until she was arching beneath him, begging incoherently for him to stop tormenting her and complete the embrace. His thumb revolved against her and she cried out, the sound muffled by his quick mouth.

And then he thrust deep, deep inside her and she clung to him helplessly as he carried her with relentless speed to the ultimate peak of sensation, urging her into a climax so powerful, so shattering that she wasn't sure she'd emerge whole. Moments later he shuddered in her arms, moaning his own satisfaction. Her name left his lips in a broken whisper, the sound bringing hot tears to fill her eyes and trickle down her flushed cheeks.

He caught the tears with his lips, but didn't speak of them as he shifted to cradle her head on his shoulder. She wondered if she'd ever again be able to sleep comfortably in any other position.

Quinn slept soundly through the remainder of the night— so soundly that Laura finally had the chance to discover how it felt to wake up with him.

It felt right. So very right to open her eyes and find him on the pillow beside her, his features relaxed in sleep. Only now did he look his age, or younger, his unguarded repose removing years from his face. She realized that it was his practice of deliberately concealing his emotions that made him look older when he was awake.

Once again he'd made love to her as if he couldn't get enough of her, held her as if he hadn't wanted to let her go. Once again she'd allowed herself to hope.

He stirred on the pillow and she held her breath. Would he reject her again when he opened his eyes to find her still with him? She didn't expect him to greet her with open arms and a smile, but it would tear her apart this time if he snapped at her in resentment that he'd allowed her too close again.

His dark lashes lifted, unveiling gray eyes that showed none of the bleariness one could expect of someone just waking. Finding her looking at him, he frowned a bit, then reached out and pulled her to him with a hand hooked behind her head. "Good morning," he said, just before he kissed her.

She wanted to throw herself on him, to shower him with kisses of gratitude for not ruining her morning. She contented herself with returning his kiss and his greeting. "Good morning, Quinn."

"Is it still snowing?"

"I don't know. I haven't looked out. Does it matter?"

He shrugged. "Guess not."

"Are you hungry? I'm sure breakfast will be ready in a few minutes."

"Yeah. I'm hungry." He drew her mouth down to his again, and his kiss was ravenous.

She laughed delightedly when he drew back to eye her meaningfully. "That wasn't the kind of hunger I was talking about, but I suppose I could take care of that, too."

He smiled faintly. "That's tempting, but I guess we'd better get up before someone comes looking for you. I'd hate to shock Mrs. Elliott."

"I'm not sure we *would* shock Mrs. Elliott," Laura murmured, but she reached for her nightgown and slipped reluctantly from the bed. "You can have the first shower."

He raised his eyes slowly from her breasts to her face. "Thanks."

"You're welcome." A bit self-consciously she pulled on the gown and walked toward the door.

His voice stopped her just as he reached for the doorknob. "Laura?"

She smiled over her shoulder. "Yes?"

"Nothing's changed, you know."

She could feel her smile dim, but she only nodded and stepped out of the room.

Quinn was wrong, of course, she told herself as she entered her own empty bedroom. Everything was changing, had already changed. He just wasn't aware of it yet.

Chapter Ten

The snow had stopped falling, but not before depositing several more inches on the ground. Quinn stared moodily out the window in the study. It would be several days yet before he'd be able to leave. The hell of it was that he really didn't want to leave, anyway. Knowing he would hurt her, knowing he had nothing to offer her, knowing there was no future in staying with her now, he still wasn't ready to leave Laura.

He'd never known anyone like her. She just gave and kept on giving, asking so little in return. When was the last time he'd met anyone who gave without demanding? Amos, maybe; the old doctor was a generous man who seemed to enjoy doing for others. But Laura outshone even Amos.

He couldn't help wondering why she cared for him. It was all wrong, of course. Laura was a woman who deserved flowers and romance, tenderness and compliments. He was a man who could offer none of that. So it was wrong for him to keep taking what she offered. But, oh, how sweetly she offered.

He closed his eyes, blocking out the snowy vista outside the window, remembering the way she'd given herself to him the night before. Such compassion after his nightmare, such passion when they made love. How could any man resist that?

Exhaling sharply, he turned back to his computer. The book was getting close to being finished. In wry amusement, Quinn reflected that it seemed to be headed toward a comfortable ending this time. Not what Laura would consider a happy ending, perhaps, but one she'd like better than the conclusion of his other books. She'd even slipped into his work, he thought, his amusement fading abruptly. Damn.

"It's a good thing we did our shopping last weekend for Thanksgiving dinner," Betty commented during lunch. "We won't be getting into town for a couple of days."

Quinn had almost forgotten about Thanksgiving, though he'd known that was the reason Laura was taking this week for vacation time. Today was Tuesday, so Thanksgiving was only two days away. He wondered what this household did to celebrate that particular holiday, but didn't ask. Thanksgiving for him was just another day; he wasn't particularly thrilled about dwelling on blessings—or the lack of them.

"The weatherman predicted a warming spell on the radio this morning," Laura said, buttering a roll. "Maybe the snow will be gone soon." Then her hand stilled and she looked quickly up at Quinn, her eyes distressed. He assumed she'd just remembered that he'd told her he was leaving as soon as the roads cleared. He offered no smile of reassurance because his plans hadn't changed. After a moment, she finished buttering the roll and carried on with the luncheon conversation, though Quinn sensed that her cheerfulness had become a bit forced. He wondered if anyone else noticed.

After lunch Quinn decided to stop by his room for a cigarette, which he planned to smoke on the back porch. He'd sort of made friends with the cat and the duck during the past few days as he'd compromised with his conscience and his occasional nicotine cravings by smoking on the porch rather than in Laura's home.

Unusually restless that morning, Renee had left the table before the others were finished with lunch, supposedly to play with her building blocks. Quinn found the child in the hallway outside the doors to his room and Laura's, surrounded by papers and photographs that had obviously come out of an ornately carved wooden box lying open in front of her.

"Whatcha got there, Renee?" he asked, knowing the toddler had gotten into something she shouldn't have.

"It's Aunt 'aura's," she replied warily. Funny thing about kids, Quinn thought with an urge to grin; they always knew what would get them into trouble, but sometimes they judged a particular adventure to be worth the consequences.

"I don't think Aunt Laura would appreciate your being in her stuff, do you, kid?" He knelt down to retrieve the papers before something was destroyed. He made no effort to examine the things he gathered, but he paused when he discovered a ring—an engagement ring that looked just about Laura's size, its round, impressively sized diamond flashing brilliantly in his hand. He stared at it for a moment, then dropped it into the box as if it had burned him.

"Who this, Quinn?" Renee inquired innocently, holding out a framed photograph of a handsome young man with black hair and smiling dark eyes. There was something written in the lower corner of the photograph—"For Laura, my future bride. I love you. Robbie."

"Quinn, have you seen—oh, there you are, Renee," Laura said from behind him. "Oh, sweetheart, have you been into my room again? You know you're not supposed to go in there without asking permission."

Renee's lower lips trembled pitifully. "I sorry, Aunt 'aura."

Laura grimaced ruefully at Quinn. "She knows very well that I can't resist that look." She sighed dramatically. "All right, Renee, I'm not going to scold you this time, but please don't do it again. Okay?"

"Okay. I go pway with my dolls now." Renee prudently made her escape before Laura changed her mind about the scolding.

Laura chuckled and shook her head as she knelt to recover her scattered possessions. "I know, I spoil her terribly. But I just can't bring myself to fuss at her when she—" Her voice died away as she noticed the photograph still in Quinn's hand.

He handed it to her and reached beside him for a bankbook, which had fallen open, facedown. Closing it, he added it to the neat stack in the wooden box. "I didn't realize you'd been married," he said offhandedly, almost surprised that his voice sounded so casual when he was consumed by a sudden inexplicable urge to smash the face of the handsome, smiling man in the photograph.

"I haven't been," she replied quietly, adding the last of the scattered papers to the large box and closing the lid. "I was engaged five years ago, but my fiancé—died."

"I'm sorry," he said awkwardly, uncomfortable with the realization that he'd wanted to hit a dead man. He still felt like hitting something. The wall looked inviting, but he restrained himself.

Laura stood as he did, the box clutched in front of her. "It seems like a long time ago now."

"What was he like?" Quinn heard himself asking, though he really didn't want to know. Couldn't imagine why he'd asked.

Her face grew tender with memory and Quinn's urge to smash his fist through the wall grew stronger. "He was a doctor, had just finished his residency. He was kind and thoughtful, always available to listen or lend a hand. Many people were surprised to find out that he also had a terrible temper, though it was slow to ignite."

She'd loved him. She made the man's temper sound like a damned virtue. Quinn muttered something about having to get back to work, then escaped before he had to say anything else.

Laura carried the box back into her room, placing it on the low table where Renee had found it. On an impulse, she opened the lid and pulled out the photograph of Robbie. She looked at it for a long time before pressing her lips to the glass front and then replacing it in the box. She'd loved Robbie with the sweetness of first love; now her heart was given entirely to another man. Another man who might never learn to accept the gift.

She wondered if she'd only imagined that Quinn had been jealous when he'd asked about the photograph. He wouldn't be feeling possessive of her if he didn't feel something for her, would he?

She sighed and reached for another of his books, knowing that only Quinn could answer her question.

Quinn stared for a long time at a blank computer screen, his thoughts dark and tangled. He didn't know why he'd asked Laura that question, and he didn't understand his feelings. He knew only that he wanted her, that he craved her smiles, her touch, the way she looked at him with such caring in her deep brown eyes. That he hated the idea of another man having his hands on her, having her look at him that way.

She'd lost people she loved, just as Quinn had. And yet she still cared, still opened her heart and accepted others inside, still made herself vulnerable to losing again. While he, on the other hand, had made a religion out of not caring for anyone. Where did she find the strength, and when had he lost it? And was there any chance of his ever learning to care again, enough to satisfy a woman whose capacity was seemingly unlimited?

If anyone could teach him, Laura could. He just wasn't sure he had the courage to allow her to try.

Betty received another phone call the next afternoon. Quinn happened to enter the kitchen just as she slammed down the extension, her hands shaking, her face parchment white. She started when she turned to find him watching her. "Oh—I—uh—did you need something?"

"I was just on my way out for a smoke," he answered, hesitating in the doorway. Reluctant to get involved in her problems, he still couldn't help asking, "Is something wrong, Betty?"

"No. I was just—" She stopped, wringing her thin hands in front of her. "It was just—a telephone call that was upsetting."

"Want to talk about it?"

She shook her head. "No. Thank you, anyway, Mr. Gallagher." She was the only one in the household who hadn't begun to call him Quinn.

"Well—" What the hell was he supposed to say, anyway? "If you need anything, let me know."

She thanked him again, seemingly as embarrassed as he was. He walked out to the porch, closing the kitchen door behind him. He'd already lit a cigarette by the time he noticed Laura. Wearing her slate-blue coat, she was sitting in a wrought-iron patio chair in one corner, Sabu in her lap. She smiled at him. "I wondered when you were going to realize you weren't alone."

He blew smoke out his nose. As always, the sight of her smile had gone straight to his gut. He hadn't touched her since yesterday morning, had forced himself to go to his own room and stay there the night before. She'd made no effort to change his mind, only bidding him good night with that tender-sweet smile that told him she knew he was running from her, running from his own need for her. "What are you doing out here?"

"Cabin fever," she returned lightly, stroking Sabu's back until he purred in pleasure. Quinn could certainly identify with the cat. He'd be tempted to purr, too, if Laura were stroking him.

"Oh." He raised the cigarette to his lips, then paused. "Uh—you mind?"

"Don't be silly, Quinn. You've been so thoughtful to come out to the porch. I'm not going to ban your bad habit here, too."

He chuckled at her teasing tone and drew on the cigarette. "I suppose I should quit."

"I'm sure you've cut back drastically as it is."

He nodded. "Yeah. It's not quite as convenient to come out to the porch."

"Colder, too. You should wear your coat when you're out here. Screening doesn't exactly keep the cold out."

He shrugged. "This sweater's warm enough."

"I think Mrs. Elliott has started on another one for you. She's decided you're going to wear that one out."

He frowned. "This is only the second time I've worn it."

"Quinn, you've only had it three days."

"Oh. Yeah. Well, it's comfortable."

"How's the book coming along? Is it almost finished?"

"Yeah. Couple more chapters and I can get it in the mail." He'd checked in with his agent the day before; she'd been impressed at the speed with which he was working. She, too, had been a bit concerned about the slump Quinn had fallen into during the past few months in Florida.

"Couldn't this one have a happy ending?" Laura asked with exaggerated wistfulness. "I just finished *Crimson Justice*. Did you *have* to kill the good guy at the end?"

He almost smiled, remembering his thoughts in the study the day before. Yes, Laura would definitely like the end of the new book better. "Just who *was* the good guy?"

She sighed in exasperation. "Now don't start that. I know you were trying to point out that the cop wasn't a whole lot better than the crime boss in some ways, but he was still a police officer. In my opinion, he was the good guy."

"Some might say that was a rather naive opinion."

Her eyes narrowed indignantly. "Some might say that you work just a bit too hard at being the cynic."

"Whatever." He liked it when she got mad. It brought bright color to her cheeks, added sparkling bits of gold to her brown eyes. Made her seem just a bit more touchable, less saintly. More like the woman who'd made him moan in bed.

She glared at him a moment longer, then looked back down at Sabu. "The playground scene in the book was quite effective. The way you described it made it seem almost haunted—no one there but the cop and the bad guy, the swings moving in the breeze, whispery echoes of children's laughter underlying the sound of guns. Is that the way you remember the playground where you were shot?"

He grunted. He still didn't like the idea of Laura reading his books. He'd tried to tell himself that they were too grim for someone with her rosy outlook on life, but now he wondered if he'd been reluctant for her to uncover pieces of himself, of his past, between those covers. He changed the subject. "Have you talked to Betty lately?"

"I talk to Betty all the time. Did you have a specific topic in mind?"

"She seemed upset just now when I came through the kitchen. She said something about a phone call that had disturbed her. I thought you might want to check on her."

Laura looked troubled. "I will. I have been worried about her lately. She's so jumpy—well, more so than usual. She hasn't talked to me about it and I hate to pry, but I am concerned."

"You think she could be receiving threatening phone calls? Maybe from her husband?"

"It's possible. She's jumped every time the phone rang lately."

"If it is, she needs to have a restraining order put on him. Then she can have him thrown in jail if he continues to bother her."

Tilting her head in thought, Laura nodded slowly. "I'll see if I can get her to talk about it. If that's really happening, I'll make sure it stops."

"You'd better stay out of it. Domestic problems like that can be dangerous to outsiders. Let the police take care of it."

"I can't just stand back and do nothing. If Betty's in trouble, I have to try to help her."

Quinn ground out his cigarette in the small ceramic bowl he'd unearthed for an ashtray a few days before. "When are you going to admit that you can't take care of everyone's problems, Laura?"

"I can't help caring, Quinn," she answered softly.

"You care too much," he returned, his hands in the pockets of his jeans as he frowned at her. "You're going to get hurt."

She returned the frown, hers undeniably confused. "Why do you keep saying that, Quinn? Why are you so sure that I'm going to be hurt—by you, by others?"

"Because people who care too much *get* hurt," he answered in sudden savagery, the old, dull pain twisting in his chest. "Sometimes they even get killed."

"Like Michael?"

He started to turn away, then inhaled and nodded. "Yeah. Like Michael."

"Was Michael the one who cared too much?"

"Yeah," he answered again, his voice completely unemotional—as *he* was, he assured himself. "He was like you—a sucker for any stray, animal or human. He was always helping little old ladies across streets, putting money in charity buckets, standing up for the rights of the weak and helpless. He cared too much about everyone—his family, his wife, strangers. It tore him up when Mom died, almost destroyed him when his wife left him, and in the end he was killed by strangers."

"His wife left him?"

"Yeah. The bitch accused him of being too dedicated to the job. Started playing around on him, then finally ran off with some bum. Michael always thought that woman hung the moon; it almost broke his heart when she took off."

"How did he die?"

Quinn had told himself he'd learned to live with it, that he could talk about it now without feeling as if someone were slashing away at his insides with dull knives. It seemed he'd been wrong. "The story's not all that uncommon," he said finally. "He was off duty, driving home to his place in Queens. He saw a car broken down on the side of the road, a woman standing beside it, and he stopped to lend a hand. The woman who'd flagged him down pulled a gun, two guys who'd been hiding behind her car jumped Michael for his wallet. When they saw that he was a cop, they shot him and left him for dead. He lived just long enough to tell what had happened to him; he died in surgery a couple of hours later.''

He steeled himself for Laura's outpouring of sympathy, but all she said was, "I'm sorry, Quinn.''

"Yeah, well, Michael cared about people and he died. If he'd passed that car without stopping, he'd still be alive.''

"He thought he was helping someone. I think you'd have done the same thing.''

He'd asked himself at least a hundred times if he would have stopped; he'd wished at least a thousand times that it had been him. Michael hadn't deserved to die that way.

"So you've decided that it's best not to care for anyone at all," Laura commented when Quinn was silent.

"I haven't decided anything," he said with annoyance. "I just burned out, Laura. On police work. On life. I was never as caring as Michael, anyway. Somewhere along the line, I lost even that.''

She set her cat down on the porch and stood, moving to stand in front of him, her gaze locked in challenge with his. "So now you don't care for anyone, right?''

"I—''

"Not Amos?''

"Amos is a friend," Quinn admitted. "Probably the only friend I have. But I'm not tied to him. I don't feel any real compulsion to return to Florida because of him.''

"I see. And Renee? You don't care for her, either?''

He glared at her, his hands pushing deeper into his pockets. "She's a little girl. A cute kid. Sure, I like her.''

"And me?" she dared at last. "What am I to you, a convenient lay?"

"Dammit, Laura!"

"Do you care for me at all, Quinn?"

His hands came out of his pockets to grip her shoulders. "You know damned well that I do."

"How much?" she demanded, still holding his eyes with hers, daring him to lie to her.

"Too much," he muttered. And he kissed her, grinding her mouth savagely under his.

She knew she'd pushed him too far, but she couldn't seem to stop pressing, digging for emotional responses from him. She wasn't disappointed with the response she'd gotten this time. Even as she lifted her arms around his neck and tilted her head back to facilitate his rough kiss, she told herself she should be pleased that at least he'd admitted he cared for her. She closed her eyes and lost herself in his kiss, pushing aside the plaguing doubts and savoring the feel of his arms around her, his mouth on hers.

His eyes were stormy when he drew back to look at her. "What do you want from me, Laura?"

Laura pulled her lower lip between her teeth, knowing that Quinn had neatly turned the confrontation around until she was the one backed into a corner. Any answer she made to that question—any honest answer—would be the wrong one as far as he was concerned. And the more honest she was with him, the more he'd withdraw. Still, she wouldn't lie to him. "All I'm asking is for you to give us a chance."

He half turned away from her, his hands deep in the pockets of his jeans. "I don't think we have a chance. You want things that I can't give."

"I've never asked for more than you're capable of giving. I think you underestimate your own capacities. Please, Quinn, couldn't we try?"

Still without looking at her, he phrased his words carefully. "If I agree to... whatever it is you're asking, what would expect from me?"

"I only want you to talk to me, Quinn. About your past, if you want to, or about the present; it doesn't matter. Just don't keep shutting me out. And stop protecting me from myself."

His mouth twisted into a humorless smile. "Maybe I'm trying to protect you from me."

"I'm not afraid of you. I couldn't be."

"Maybe you should be."

She looked at the way he was standing: his hands deep in his pockets, his face averted, his shoulders hunched a bit, probably from the cold on the unheated porch but adding to the overall appearance of isolation. He looked vulnerable at that moment, more so than she'd ever seen him before. She wanted to take him in her arms and hold him as she would Renee; to bring laughter and joy back into his life; to heal the raw wounds still hurting him so terribly. Tenderness swept through her along with a love so deep that she knew she'd never get over it. She hadn't chosen an easy man to love, but she'd chosen one who needed that love desperately. Without stopping to think about her actions, she took the steps that brought her to him, reached up and framed his face in her hands. "Maybe you're the one who should be afraid of me," she told him almost whimsically, knowing how much she was asking of him. How much more she would ask.

"Maybe I am," he answered in little more than a husky whisper.

"Don't be." She went up on her tiptoes to kiss him. Her mouth had barely touched his before he swept her into his arms.

When the long, earth-shaking kiss ended, Quinn held her away from him. "You'd better get inside before I throw you over my shoulder and haul you into your bedroom," he warned her hoarsely.

Tempted to allow him to do just that, she managed to get a grip on her raging desires and nod. "All right. I'll go talk to Betty. You really should go in, too, Quinn. It's so cold out here."

He eyed her grimly. "It's this or a cold shower. I'll be in soon."

It was only after Laura had entered the house and gone off in search of Betty that she remembered Quinn hadn't really agreed to give them a chance to see where their tenuous relationship was headed. She tried to take heart by reminding herself that he hadn't refused, either. Only then did it occur to her that she still hadn't told him about Robbie's death.

Quinn spent another long, restless night in his room, using every ounce of willpower he possessed to keep himself from going to Laura. He couldn't think when he was in bed with her—hell, he thought, he couldn't think when he was in the same room with her. And he needed to think. About the request Laura had made of him. And about what it was he wanted from her in return.

By Thursday morning the only conclusion he'd come to was that he still wanted her. Badly. She had only to smile at him and say good morning and he was achingly aroused, disgusted with himself for having lost all control of his physical responses.

He was reminded of the date when he entered the den and found the rest of the household watching Thanksgiving Day parades on the television. "You used to live in New York, didn't you, Quinn?" Mrs. Elliott asked, looking up from the red and black sweater she was knitting.

"Yeah," he answered, even as he noted that the sweater looked just about his size. It was a nice pattern, but he wondered what he was going to do with all these sweaters when he got back to Florida.

"Did you ever see the Macy's parade while you were there?"

He hadn't thought of it in years, but, as a matter of fact, he and Michael had made an annual event of the parade back when they were young. They'd find a good viewing spot and wait there for hours, regardless of the weather, Michael keeping a close eye on his younger brother in the pressing crowds. "Yeah, I saw it several times," he replied around a knot in his throat. Then he surprised himself, and apparently Laura since she looked startled, by adding, "My brother used to take me when I was a kid."

He hadn't talked about Michael so much since he'd lost him.

"Did you see Snoopy?" Renee demanded, lying on the floor on her stomach and pointing to the enormous beagle balloon currently floating across the television screen.

"Snoopy wasn't in the parade back then," Quinn answered.

Laura patted the couch beside her, sending him a singularly intimate smile. "Why don't you watch it with us?" she invited him.

If he refused, she'd think he was running from the memories again. She'd be right. Determined to prove—whether to her or to himself, he wasn't sure—that he wasn't an emotional coward, he nodded. "Okay. For a few minutes."

He left several inches between them when he sat down, but then he reached out and laced his fingers through the hand she'd used to pat the couch. Her grasp was warm in his, her smile becoming a bit tremulous. He turned his gaze reluctantly toward the screen.

"Quinn, don't take your hat off, it's too cold. You don't want to get sick again, do you?"

"Aww, Mike, I hate wearing hats."

"Look, I promised Mom I'd make you keep it on, okay?"

Sigh. *"Okay, Mike, I'll keep it on."*

"I'm out of peanuts, Mike. Can I have some more?"

"You ate all those already?"

"I'm hungry!"

"You're always hungry. Here, you can have the rest of mine."

"Don't you want em, Mike?"

"It's okay, kid. You can have em."

"Hey, Quinn. Here he comes! Can you see him?"

"No, I can't! Where is he?"

"Here, kid, climb up on my shoulders. Now can you see?"

"All right! It's Santa! Hi, Santa! Hey, Mike, he waved at me. Didja see him?"

"Yeah, I saw him. He waved right at you, Quinn."

"Quinn?" Laura's voice was soft as it intruded on his distant thoughts. Almost thirty years distant.

He turned his head with a frown, only vaguely aware that Betty and Mrs. Elliott had left the room to work in the kitchen. Renee had lost interest with the parade some time before; she had gone to play with the dollhouse set up in one corner of the dining room. "Yeah?"

"Are you okay?"

He swallowed hard. "I miss him, Laura. I miss him so damned much."

And then her soft arms were around him and his face was buried in her hair. He didn't—he couldn't—cry, but he was aware that Laura shed a few tears for him.

Oddly enough, it helped.

Chapter Eleven

Perhaps it was a day for memories. Maybe because it was the first real Thanksgiving dinner Quinn had had in years. As he put away two helpings of turkey and dressing, as well as the many side dishes Betty, Laura and Mrs. Elliott had prepared, and a generous slice of pumpkin pie, he found himself thinking of the holiday dinners his mother had made so many years ago. His mother had always gone all out for holidays. He could see her clearly in his mind, urging Michael and him to have another helping of corn, another slice of pie. Quinn had never gotten along very well with his father, a disgruntled man who spent too much time drinking and chasing women, too little time with his wife and sons. But Quinn had loved his mom and his brother. Their holidays had been happy ones until his mother had died of cancer when Quinn was fifteen.

Was that when it had begun? he wondered. Had that been the first time he'd realized how much loving could hurt?

He looked at the other end of the table, where Laura was chatting to Mrs. Elliott about the call she'd just made to Janet in the hospital. A woman like Laura should be surrounded by her own loving family on holidays—a husband to cherish her, children to adore her. He scowled as he reluctantly pictured the man to whom she'd been engaged, Robbie. Had he lived, Laura would probably have already started on the family Quinn imagined for her. Instead, she was sharing her Thanksgiving dinner with an odd assortment of life-scarred strays, and nothing in her brilliant smile indicated that she'd rather have it any other way.

Betty and Mrs. Elliott insisted on doing the lunch dishes despite the offers of help they received from both Quinn and Laura. Wryly noting the smiles the older woman turned toward Laura and him, Quinn realized that Mrs. Elliott was matchmaking. Seemed like everyone was pushing him into Laura's arms. And at that moment he wasn't particularly inclined to fight them.

For once he was strangely reluctant to close himself into the study, telling himself he deserved a few hours away from work and Thanksgiving was as good an excuse as any. He didn't quite know how it happened, but he found himself involved in a game of Candy Land with Renee and Laura. They played on the floor in the den, the television playing unnoticed behind them, Renee sitting so close to Quinn that she was practically in his lap. He found the game rather boring; Renee loved it.

"I win again," Renee pointed out gleefully, sliding her little gingerbread man playing piece into Home Sweet Home.

"I keep getting stuck at the Cherry Pitfall," Quinn grumbled, glaring at the board.

Laura patted his hand. "It's only a game, Quinn."

Quinn gave her a look that told her exactly what he thought of the game, making her laugh. Her laughter faded when his eyes fixed steadily on her unpainted, smiling mouth. He wondered if his sudden desire was so obvious to her.

"Look, Quinn," Renee said suddenly, distracting them as she pointed to the television on which an old *Star Trek* rerun was playing on a cable channel. "Him wooks wike you."

Startled, Quinn looked from the unsmiling Vulcan to the grinning child. "I do not have pointed ears," he said with mock sternness, ignoring Laura's peal of laughter.

"Him wooks wike this." Renee formed her chubby little face into a stern scowl, her rosy mouth pointed downward.

Quinn couldn't hold back a chuckle. Was that really the way he appeared to Renee—to everyone? "Little girls shouldn't frown."

Though her blue eyes twinkled mischievously at him, Renee held the exaggerated expression.

"Okay," Quinn told her with a deep sigh. "You leave me no choice but to find that smile." Before she had time to react, he tumbled her to the carpet and tickled her, making her dissolve into helpless giggles.

Laura's breath caught in her throat as she watched Quinn playing with Renee. He was smiling one of his rare, full smiles, his dimples deeply carved, and his hair had fallen onto his forehead in the manner she loved so much. Her chest ached with love for him even as her body throbbed dully with the desire he'd ignited with only a look just moments before.

Betty broke up the play by appearing in the doorway to claim Renee for her nap. Renee went very reluctantly, and only after Quinn had promised to read a story to her later if she'd be good. When they were alone, Quinn looked up to find Laura's eyes on him. He went still, his own eyes darkening. "Don't look at me like that."

She didn't have to ask how she was looking at him; she knew her heart was in her eyes just then. Knew and didn't really care. "I can't help it."

He groaned and snagged her by the back of the neck, pulling her to him for a quick, rough kiss. "I'm not going to allow you to fantasize me into someone I'm not," he told her when he released her.

Giving in to the temptation to brush that heavy forelock back into place, she then slipped her fingers down to his cheek. "You're the one who doesn't know the real Quinn Gallagher. The one who has tried to turn him into something he's not—cold, unfeeling, humorless. You're none of those things."

"Laura—"

She cut him off with a swift, gentle kiss. "You think about it. I've got a few things to do."

She made herself walk away from him then, knowing he needed some time alone. Nor did she offer to accompany him when he went out for a walk later. She was being very careful not to push him, though she couldn't resist those occasional reminders that she knew him much better than he thought.

Laura wasn't there when he woke that night, drenched with sweat, the nightmare slipping from his mind the moment his eyes flew open. Breathing hard, he pounded his fist against the mattress. Dammit, why couldn't he remember? he thought in anguish. Why couldn't he remember so he could fight it?

He knew he wasn't going back to sleep anytime soon. Painfully aware that Laura was only a thin wall away from him, he climbed out of bed and pulled on his jeans, deciding he'd go into the kitchen. Maybe a turkey sandwich would help. He looked at Laura's closed bedroom door for a long time before forcing himself to turn and head for the kitchen. He refused to take any more from Laura until he knew how much he was prepared to give in return.

The kitchen was already occupied, he discovered when he pushed open the door and walked in. Betty sat at the table, clad in an unflattering plaid robe over a high-necked gown, her face in her hands as she sobbed quietly. Submerged in her own misery, she hadn't heard Quinn come in. He was tempted to turn around and leave, but he knew even as the thought crossed his mind that he wouldn't give in to it. "I think it's time you told someone what's going on, Betty."

Betty jumped, her sobs turning into a gasp. "Oh, I—I hope I didn't disturb you."

Quinn pulled out another chair at the small table, swung it around and straddled it, crossing his bare arms across the top of it. "What's wrong?"

"Nothing, I—"

"You've been receiving threatening phone calls, haven't you? Your husband?"

Her face couldn't have gone any whiter, but her eyes rounded. "How did you know?" she whispered fearfully.

"The signs were fairly obvious," he answered, trying to keep his own voice gentle. "Why don't you tell me about it, Betty? Maybe I can help."

The distraught woman mopped at her face with the back of one trembling hand. "I don't think anyone can help. The only thing I know to do is to take Renee and leave."

"Where would you go?"

"I don't know. Somewhere. Anywhere."

"Betty, you can't let him do this to you. You can't let him do it to Renee. What kind of life would she have on the road?"

"I—" She turned her head away, her breath catching in a sob. "I'm afraid. He said he'd take her from me."

Fighting down a sudden surge of fury against the unknown man, Quinn forced himself to continue to speak quietly. "So it *is* your ex-husband?"

"He's not my ex, not quite. I've filed for a divorce, but it's not final yet. I married him when I was just seventeen. He was different then. Then he lost his job, and then another, and I had a miscarriage and the medical expenses piled up, and he—he started to drink. When he's had too much, he gets mean, violent. It was as if he blamed all our problems on me."

"He physically abused you?"

"Yes," she murmured, her voice holding shame.

Quinn didn't try to convince her that it hadn't been her fault, that she hadn't deserved the beatings, though he knew battered wives had to learn to believe those things. He'd leave counseling to professionals. "Did he ever hit Renee?"

Betty shook her head. "No. He ignored her most of the time when she was a baby. But during the past year he'd started yelling at her over everything she did. I was afraid he would hit her, and that's what finally gave me the courage to leave him. Laura took me in, thank heaven, or I don't know what I would have done. But now Gene has found me. He started calling two weeks ago, telling me that he was going to punish me for leaving him, that he was going to take Renee and go someplace where no one could find him."

She started to cry again. "He doesn't even want her. He only wants to use her to punish me."

"He's not going to get her, Betty."

"I don't know what to do, Quinn." It was the first time she'd called him by his first name.

"Call the police. Then file a petition for a restraining order against him."

"He said if I call the police he'll—he'll kill me."

Quinn looked at her steadily. "He'll have to go by me to get to you. I'll talk to the cops with you tomorrow, okay? I used to be one, I know the language."

"I—no, not tomorrow."

"Betty," Quinn began impatiently.

She nodded. "I know. It has to be done. Just give me until Monday, okay? I have to work up the courage," she admitted with a self-deprecating little smile.

He nodded. "Okay. We'll go Monday." And he knew as he spoke that he'd just committed himself to another few days in Colorado, that he almost seemed to be looking for excuses to stay.

"Quinn, thank you."

"No problem. You'd better get some sleep. Renee's an early riser, isn't she?"

Betty managed a weak smile through her tears. "Yes, she is. Good night, Mr.—good night, Quinn."

"Good night, Betty."

His time in Colorado wasn't exactly turning out as he'd planned, Quinn reflected ironically when Betty had left the room. He'd intended to stay in the guest cottage, alone. Aloof from the people who lived in this household. Instead, he'd ended up assisting with the delivery of a baby, had an elderly woman busily knitting sweaters for him, had found himself adopted by a three-year-old and had now volunteered to help that child's mother battle her abusive husband. Not to mention his involvement with Laura, the most unexpected development of all.

He shook his head and rose, the turkey sandwich no longer sounding appetizing. He really should have stayed in Florida, he thought almost angrily, striding down the hallway toward his bedroom. He'd have been surrounded by reporters, but at least he wouldn't have found himself involved in their problems. Damn.

He'd almost made it into his room when Laura's door opened. She stopped, startled, when she saw him standing there, her hands going to the tie of her robe. "Oh. Hi."

"What are you doing up?"

She shrugged. "I couldn't sleep. I thought I'd try a glass of milk."

"The kitchen's a popular place tonight."

She didn't seem to know what to say to that, but stood still, looking at him with so much longing that his stomach tightened. He'd warned her once not to look at him that way. "Laura," he groaned, his hands clenching at his sides.

"I guess I'd better go have that milk."

He caught her arm as she moved past him. "You don't want milk."

Her eyes met his. "No," she murmured. "I don't really want milk."

Quinn lowered his head, his mouth thoroughly possessing hers. Laura moaned softly and slipped her arms around his neck.

Until he'd carried Laura in from the car the night Janet's baby had been born, he'd never in his life carried a woman to bed. But then, he'd never felt like this about any other woman. Moving swiftly, impatiently, he bent and slid an arm beneath her knees, swinging her up against his chest in one bold, graceful move. And then he strode into his bedroom, barely pausing to kick the door shut behind him before tumbling with her to the bed.

Laura laughed softly as his hands went insistently to the tie of her robe. "God, that sound drives me crazy," he muttered, kissing her to taste the husky, sultry sound. No other woman had ever driven him this close to the edge with nothing more than a low laugh.

She wriggled out of her robe and shoved it over the side of the bed, then helped him remove her gown. He ran his hands over her soft curves, wondering if he'd ever get enough of touching her. He swallowed a groan when Laura's hands fumbled with the button of the waist of his jeans. It took him only moments to strip out of his only garment.

"Oh, Quinn," she sighed when his legs tangled with hers. "You feel so good."

He wrapped his arms around her and slid his hands downward, filling them with soft, rounded derriere. He brought her up against him, though he held off from that final joining. His restraint was slipping quickly, but he fought to hold on, wanting to give her as much pleasure as he could before seeking his own satisfaction. If he could give her nothing else, perhaps he could give her that.

When he was sure that he had himself firmly under control, he pressed her against the pillows and began a slow, thorough exploration of her warm, restless body. His lips slid down her throat to linger at the pulsing hollow, where he tasted the slightly salty sheen of perspiration. Moving down to her swollen breasts, he used his hands, his lips, his tongue and the edge of his teeth until she was aching mindlessly, begging him to stop, begging him not to stop. His laugh sounded more like a groan as he planted kisses from her breasts to her navel, then rubbed his face across the tiny swell of her stomach, deliberately allowing his mustache to tickle her. Her muscles contracted beneath his mouth, her hands tightening in his hair.

"Quinn. Oh, Quinn, *please*!" Her hoarse plea almost ended it; he paused for several deep, steadying breaths before lowering his head to her inner thighs.

She stiffened a bit when his mouth moved inward; Quinn gentled her with soft strokes and murmured reassurances. When he sensed that her momentary shyness had passed, he continued until her breaths were coming in broken sobs, her body trembling beneath him. Only then did he allow himself to settle between her raised knees. He kissed her lingeringly, then entered her with one long, smooth thrust. Laura cried out against his mouth and arched to take him even deeper.

It took all the strength he had to hold back his own release until he was sure that Laura had found hers. He groaned his approval when she convulsed around him, her fingernails digging into his buttocks, her legs locked fiercely around his hips. Drawing out her pleasure as long as possible, he waited until her grip on him eased. Only then did he close his eyes and lose himself in his own satisfaction. Laura held him as he shuddered with an explosion of pleasure made almost violent by the sternly enforced delay, her voice crooning in his ear.

A long time later he lay awake, cradling her in his arms as she slept, and he stared at the ceiling, wondering if she'd really told him she loved him or if he'd only imagined it.

The blanket-swaddled bundle in Laura's arms squirmed as she carried it across the front porch. A diaper bag dangled against her hip, its straps slung over her forearm. "I don't think he likes all these blankets," she commented as her bundle wriggled more vigorously.

Walking slowly, her hand on Mrs. Elliott's arm, Janet smiled broadly. "Larry likes to be free to move around."

The front door flew open just before Laura reached it. "Let me see that baby," Betty demanded, a bright smile of welcome lighting her face.

Laura stepped around her. "Let's get him inside first." She walked into the den and started to unwind the blankets, finally revealing a tiny, disgruntled face. She laughed. "He certainly knows what he likes and doesn't like early enough."

She barely managed to clear the baby of the blankets before Betty took him. Renee bounced at their feet, demanding to see "'arry."

Janet grimaced good-naturedly. "I forgot she couldn't say her Ls."

"She'll learn," Laura answered, setting the full diaper bag down beside the couch. She turned to hug Janet. "It's nice to have you home."

Janet returned the hug with touching fervor. "It's nice to be home, Laura."

How easily they used that word, Quinn thought, standing unnoticed in the doorway as he watched the household welcome its newest resident. Home. It was a measure of Laura's warmth and easy acceptance that the others were made to feel so welcome in her home, never once feeling as if they were imposing on her generosity. She had quite a talent for making each one feel like a valuable member of the unit, whatever the limitations that had made them misfits elsewhere. He knew how the others felt; she'd done the same with him. Made him feel wanted, even needed. So why was he standing here now feeling like an outsider?

His gaze lingered on Laura, surrounded by her chattering friends, and he realized with some dismay that part of his problem was plain jealousy. He wanted her alone. He didn't want to share her.

Had it already come to that?

Just as he was about to turn and leave the room, Janet looked up and spotted him. "Hi, Quinn! Come meet my son." She said the last two words proudly.

Caught, Quinn gave in and entered the room. "I've already met him, remember?"

"So come meet him again." Janet carefully took the baby from Betty and turned toward Quinn. "Isn't he beautiful?"

Quinn looked down at the tiny, round face topped by wispy copper hair. "Yeah, Janet. He's beautiful," he lied diplomatically. He half smiled as a tiny hand wrapped around his tentatively proffered finger. "Got quite a grip for such a little guy," he commented.

He looked down in response to a vigorous tugging at the leg of his jeans. "What's the matter, Renee?"

Pouting, the child lifted her arms. "Up."

Quinn obediently picked her up as Janet sat down with the baby and the others stifled laughter.

"Well, I like that," Betty muttered in mock indignation. "She didn't mind when I looked at the baby, but she's jealous of Quinn."

"Face it, Betty, your daughter has her first crush," Laura answered with a smile.

Quinn frowned at her, making her smile broaden, then turned his attention back to Renee. "Don't you like the baby, Renee?"

"Him can't even pway wif me," she complained.

"Not yet," he agreed, "but he'll be crawling around before you know it and then you'll be able to play with him. He'll need someone to show him around, you know. Teach him how to play."

Renee thoughtfully eyed the infant sleeping in his mother's lap. "I teach him?"

"Sure, you could teach him."

She slanted him a sly look from beneath her long eye-lashes. "You help me? You could pway wif us."

Quinn hesitated, wondering how to tell her that he wouldn't be around when Larry was old enough to play. He looked at Laura, but she avoided his eyes. Betty came to his rescue, reminding Renee that it was nap time. When she'd carried the reluctant toddler off to bed, Quinn pushed his hands into his pockets. "Want to join me for a walk, Laura?" he heard himself asking impulsively.

Laura looked at him then, her expression startled. He didn't need that reminder that it was the first time he'd actually requested her company. Expecting her to accept immediately, he frowned when she seemed to take time to consider his offer. It had never occurred to him that she might turn him down. It seemed that he'd begun to take her a bit for granted, he mused, mystified by his own actions. He had changed since he'd arrived here, and he couldn't even understand himself lately. At least in Florida he'd been in control of himself.

"Yes, I think I'd like a walk," she said at last, reaching for the outerwear she hadn't yet taken to her room.

Quinn hadn't realized he'd tensed until he felt his muscles relax at her words. "I'll get my coat," he muttered, turning on one heel.

They'd just stepped out on the front porch when a battered, red four-wheel-drive truck stopped in front of the house, and Judy, the tall brunette who'd looked at the broken cottage heater the week before, jumped out lightly. "Got the part we needed, Laura. I'm here to fix your heater."

"Great. Just go on in, the cottage is unlocked. Need any help?"

The other woman laughed. "From you? Listen, I've seen you with a wrench in your hands, remember?" She looked

Quinn over, then gave Laura a wink of approval. "You go on with what you were doing. I'll have the heater working in an hour or so."

"Thanks, Judy." Laura looked up at Quinn, her face carefully expressionless. "Ready?"

He nodded and stepped off the porch. In the warmer temperatures of the past couple of days, the snow had started to melt a bit, leaving patches of mud here and there. Quinn stepped around those patches as he led the way along the path of sorts that led into the woods surrounding Laura's house. A squirrel darted across the path and bolted up a tree; a cardinal provided a splash of scarlet on a low, bare branch ahead of them. Quinn noted those details even as he wondered why Laura was being so quiet. For the first time it was Quinn trying to think of something to say, some way to initiate a conversation. "Have you known Judy long?" he asked after a while.

She nodded. "We grew up together. Her dad used to be the repairman; Judy took over his business when he retired."

"Oh." So much for that topic. Quinn cleared his throat, groped for a cigarette, then changed his mind. His hand dropped. "I finished the book this morning."

"Did you? Are you satisfied with it?"

He nodded. "Yeah, it's okay. I think you'll like this one better than the others—if you read it."

"I'll read it."

He picked at a pinecone. "Do you go back to work on Monday?"

"Yes."

"I promised Betty I'd go with her to the police station Monday afternoon. She's going to have a restraining order filed against her husband."

Laura slanted a glance at him but kept walking. "That's very nice of you. It will be easier for her to have someone with her."

"Yeah, well, she doesn't deserve to have to live in fear. And the bastard needs to know he can't threaten her and get away with it."

"I hope it works."

"Yeah." Dammit, what was wrong with her? It was like pulling teeth to get her to say anything this afternoon. That wasn't like her. He stopped walking and dropped his hand on her shoulders. "Laura, is something wrong?"

"Why do you ask?" she questioned in return.

"You're being so quiet. Is something bothering you?"

She buried her hands in the pockets of her coat and looked down without answering.

Concerned, Quinn caught her chin in his hand and brought her face back up to his. "Tell me," he insisted.

She pulled out of his loose grasp. Taking a few steps away, she stopped and rested her hand on the trunk of a tree, her face in profile to him. "You're leaving, aren't you?"

Taken by surprise by her words, he frowned. "What?"

"You're planning to leave. You've finished your book, which is why you came here, isn't it? That's why you couldn't answer Renee's question about playing with her and Larry. You knew you were leaving soon and you didn't know what to tell her."

He groped for words. "Laura, I never intended to move in permanently. You knew I was only here on vacation."

"I knew," she almost whispered, her gloved fingers tightening on the tree trunk. "When are you leaving?"

"I don't know."

She plucked absently at a piece of bark. "Are you going to move back into the guest cottage?"

He was rather surprised to realize that the thought hadn't even occurred to him. "Do you want me to?"

"No," she answered without hesitation, looking at him over her shoulder.

Taking a step closer, he wrapped his arms around her waist and pulled her back against him. "It might be easier for you if I did."

She took a deep breath and shook her head against his shoulder. "No." The smile she gave him then was part coy, part shy. "It's too far to walk in the middle of the night."

Groaning, he turned her in his arms and rested his forehead against hers. "I've never known anyone who could actually make me feel humble. Until I met you."

"And I've never known anyone who could make me feel the way you do," she replied, slipping her arms around his neck. "Please kiss me, Quinn."

His mouth was on hers almost before she'd finished the sentence. He didn't want to talk any longer about the time when he'd leave; the subject was too painful to deal with at present. For both of them.

Chapter Twelve

Phone call for you, Laura."

Laura set down the chart she'd been holding and looked up at the nurse who'd summoned her. "Thanks, Patricia." Casting one last glance at the tiny patient she'd been monitoring, she nodded to another R.N. to take her place, then headed for the nurses' station. Patting an escaping curl back into her loosening chignon, she lifted the phone to her ear with the other hand. "Laura Sutherland."

"Laura, it's Quinn. Is this a bad time to call?"

Surprised, Laura clutched the receiver tighter. "Quinn? Is something wrong?"

"No, nothing's wrong. I'll be in town later to go with Betty to the police station and I thought maybe I'd have her drop me off at the hospital afterward and you and I could go out for something to eat. If you want to, of course," he finished a bit awkwardly.

He was calling to ask her for a date. Absurdly touched, Laura smiled. "I'd love to, Quinn," she assured him. "I'm off duty at three, but I'd like to change first—I keep extra clothes in my locker. Do you want to meet me in the canteen at three-thirty? It will be too early for dinner, but we could do a bit of sightseeing first, if you'd like. I know you haven't seen much of the area while you've been here."

"Sure, that's fine. I'll see you around three-thirty, then."

"New guy, Laura?" Patricia, the blonde who'd summoned Laura to the telephone, inquired when Laura stood staring down at the receiver she'd just replaced in its cradle.

Laura blinked and looked up. "What did you say, Patricia?"

The younger woman laughed. "I asked if you've got a new guy. The smile you're wearing could definitely be described as besotted."

Laura felt herself flushing. "Well, he is pretty special," she admitted.

"Hmm. Do I hear wedding bells?" Patricia teased with the ease of a co-worker of three full years.

"Hardly," Laura answered with a sigh, some of her pleasure in Quinn's unexpected invitation fading. "He has a real phobia about commitment."

Patricia laughed again. "Don't they all? Hang in there, kid; if anyone can change his mind, you can."

"I wish I had your confidence," Laura murmured, straightening the top of her uniform. "Guess I'd better get back to work."

"Aren't you going to tell me any more about this man?" Patricia wailed.

Laura grinned over her shoulder as she headed toward the nursery. "Nope."

"Oh, c'mon, Laura, I tell you all about *my* guys!"

Laura only laughed and kept walking, though her smile didn't last long. Actually, she would have loved to tell her friend all about Quinn; but talking about him now would only make it harder to deal with Patricia's sympathy when Quinn left. And he *would* leave. It had finally occurred to her on Friday, just before the walk she'd taken with him. No matter how badly she wanted to hold him, she wouldn't be able to unless he wanted to stay. And until he accepted that the preconceptions he'd been living by for the past few years were nothing more than self-perpetuating inaccuracies, he'd never feel free to commit himself to her. She'd tried to show him that he had so much more to offer than he realized; now it was up to him to face the truth.

She hadn't meant to confront him on their walk Friday about his plans to leave, but when he'd demanded to know what was bothering her, she'd told him honestly. He'd held her, but he hadn't promised to stay. Nor had she wanted him to make promises he wasn't sure he could keep.

He'd made love to her on each of the three nights since that walk, slipping into her room after the rest of the household was asleep. Each time he'd taken her to heights of pleasure that surpassed everything that had come before. Just when she thought she'd discovered the ultimate of sensation, the peak of sensuality, he'd made love to her again to show her that there was, indeed, even more.

Why couldn't he understand that a man so giving, so caring in bed, was capable of just as much giving, just as much caring during the day?

"Laura! She smiled at me! She really smiled at me!"

Pushing her personal problems to the back of her mind, Laura smiled brightly at the animated brunette standing beside one of the warming cribs. "That's wonderful, Mrs. Travanti! Maybe she knows she'll be going home with you in just another few weeks."

The other woman smiled mistily down at the tiny baby who'd survived against the odds. "That's what the doctor told me. She's really going to make it, isn't she?"

"Yes, Mrs. Travanti. Angela is really going to make it."

Though her eyes reflected the sadness that remained from the loss of her other baby, Mrs. Travanti continued to smile. "It only goes to prove that miracles do still happen, doesn't it?"

Laura looked from mother to baby, her heart swelling. "Yes," she murmured. "Miracles do still happen."

Laura kept only one change of clothing at the hospital, so it didn't take her long to get ready for her date with Quinn. Slipping into the long-sleeved, wrinkle-resistant shirtwaist dress, she adjusted the full skirt and tightened the belt around her slender waist. She'd exchanged her white panty hose for beige, and she pushed her feet into taupe pumps. She'd already brushed out her hair and freshened her makeup. Checking her appearance in a mirror, she was satisfied with the results. The bright green dress made a nice change from her pristine white uniform or the jeans and sweaters she usually wore at home.

It was only twenty minutes after three when she entered the hospital canteen. Quinn wasn't there yet, but she was greeted almost the moment she entered by a man's voice calling her name. "Hi, Sam." She crossed the room to the small table occupied by Sam Jennings, the staff psychologist she'd known for some time.

"Join me?" he offered hopefully, indicating his own freshly filled cup of coffee.

"Thanks, I will. Be right back," she agreed, deciding she'd have time for a quick soda before Quinn arrived. Pulling a dollar bill from her wallet, she dropped her coat and purse into one of the four chairs at the table and walked to the snack bar.

She joined Sam a few minutes later with her diet soft drink, shaking her head at him when he started to rise as she approached. "Don't get up." She slid into the chair opposite him. "How've you been, Sam?"

"Busy. You look very pretty today, Laura."

"Why, thank you. You don't look bad yourself," she teased, eyeing his neat gray suit and sedately striped silk tie. "Big plans?"

"I'm speaking at a civic meeting later on," he replied, brushing a hand over his neatly combed, silver-streaked dark hair. An attractive man in his late thirties, Sam was tanned and blue-eyed, the subject of quite a few fantasies among the nursing staff. Laura was very fond of him but had never thought of him as anything more than a friend, which was exactly the way he seemed to feel about her.

"Oh? What's your topic?" she asked with unfeigned interest.

"They've requested the basic stress management lecture," her friend answered with a self-deprecating shrug. "Dull stuff."

She cocked her head in exaggerated skepticism. "Dull? From you? No way."

"Thanks. You must have plans for this evening, as well."

"As a matter of fact, I do," she replied, sobering a bit as she thought of Quinn. "I have a date."

"Someone I know?" Sam asked curiously, cradling his coffee cup between his hands as he watched her with the uncanny perceptiveness that was part of his profession. Laura had often imagined that he was a mind reader as well as a successful counselor.

"No, you don't know him. But I've wanted to talk to you about him."

Studying her expression, Sam rested his elbow on the table top and propped his chin on his fist. "This is serious, isn't it?"

She nodded, not surprised that he'd read her so well. "Yes. For me, anyway."

"And for him?"

She sighed and stared into her soft drink. Instead of answering him directly, she toyed with her straw and asked a question. "Didn't you once tell me that you used to counsel police officers who were getting close to job burnout?"

"That's right. I worked with the Denver Police Department for a time."

"Quinn—the man I'm seeing—is a former vice cop from New York and Miami. He quit about two years ago and now he writes. Maybe you've read something he's written. Quinn Gallagher."

Sam's eyebrow shot up. "I've read *everything* he's written. His work is fascinating."

"Then you probably know as much about him as I do," Laura mused rather glumly. "Knowing you, you've already analyzed him from his work."

Sam chuckled. "I wouldn't say that, exactly, but I do feel that I have some insight into his personality from his books."

"He's not happy, Sam. He calls himself an emotional dead man—his own words." Laura felt rather guilty talking about Quinn so frankly, but she was desperate. She wasn't sure she could bear losing him.

"He's probably repressing his emotions," Sam offered. "Vice is a tough field, Laura. Relationships are almost impossible to sustain because the officers stay undercover for months at a time, unable to carry on normal personal lives, unable to trust anyone. They become cynical, disillusioned. After more contact with the criminal element than with normal society, they begin to wonder if everyone is like that, if there are any decent people left. Narcotics, in particular, has a high rate of burnout. The officers have to learn to bring their frustrations and emotions out into the open, to deal with their bitterness and anger, or they simply overload. Some learn to live with that life, some transfer to other areas of police work, some even convert to the other side. Others—like your Quinn—quit."

"He quit," Laura agreed, "but he hasn't left it behind. He has terrible nightmares that he can't even remember when he wakes up. They're tearing him apart."

"That's probably because there's something he hasn't dealt with, something he's still repressing. If it's deeply traumatic, he'll have to face it eventually. It'll keep eating at him until he does."

Which was exactly the conclusion she'd already reached on her own. Laura sighed again and pushed her barely touched soda away. "I don't know how to help him, Sam. He won't let me close enough."

"Would he let me try?"

She shook her head. "I doubt it. He's so damned guarded, so isolated. Just when I think I'm getting closer to him, he pulls back." She looked up. "Oh, Sam, he's so special. There's a side of him that's warm and giving and caring and thoughtful. And then there's that other side, wary and bitter and hurting and angry. That's the side that takes over when he feels threatened or vulnerable."

"We're all multifaceted, Laura. We all have our defense mechanisms. Quinn's are stronger because he's needed them to be, for some reason. All I can suggest is that you be patient, keep offering to listen if he needs to talk, share your feelings and emotions with him in the hope that it will encourage him to share his. And urge him to get counseling, if you can. He needs to know that it's not a weakness to seek help."

She spread her hands on the table in a gesture of surrender. "I have to keep trying for as long as he'll let me. I'm in love with him."

"Then he's a lucky man." Sam covered her hands with his. "You just keep in mind that there's always a shoulder available to you if you need it."

She linked her fingers with his. "You're a good friend, you know that? Thanks, Sam."

"Sure, anytime. Hey, did I tell you what that stupid dog of mine did last night?"

Laura grinned, knowing Sam would have a hilarious anecdote about his not-very-bright Great Dane, and recognizing the ploy as a means of helping her put her worries aside for a few minutes. "Okay, Sam, tell me what Tiny did last night."

Quinn climbed out of the car then leaned back into the open door. "You'll be okay driving home?"

Her eyes still a bit red-rimmed from the upsetting ordeal of filing a police report against her estranged husband, Betty forced a weak smile and nodded. "Of course I will. You and Laura have a nice time, okay? It'll be good for both of you to get out of the house."

"Okay. See you later."

"Quinn. Thank you," Betty said quietly.

He nodded and straightened, closing the door firmly behind him. Glancing at his watch as Betty drove away, he noted that it was almost three-forty. He brushed his hair away from his forehead with one hand and headed for the door of the hospital.

He had no trouble finding the canteen. Nor did he have any problem spotting Laura. She was the beautiful woman in the green dress holding hands with and smiling at some guy in a tailored suit and a silk tie.

Quinn couldn't remember the last time he'd been subject to sheer, red-eyed rage. His impulse to put his fist through a wall when he'd seen the photograph of Laura's fiancé had been nothing compared to the urges swirling inside him at seeing her with this man. He watched with narrowed eyes as she laughed at something the jerk said then started talking animatedly to him, using one hand to gesture while the other remained clasped with his. She looked completely relaxed, unguarded, seeming to find a great deal of pleasure in the conversation. When had she ever looked at Quinn that way?

She hadn't, of course. She'd always been prepared for him to turn on her, to push her away. And she'd been totally justified in her caution, he realized grimly. He'd snarled at her, he'd cut her short, he'd ignored her when he could. He'd bet the guy in the suit would never treat her so shabbily. That other guy probably treated her with the kindness and respect she deserved. Damn.

As if suddenly sensing his presence, Laura turned her head and looked straight at him, her eyes widening when she saw him standing there. Her face lit with a smile and Quinn felt as if someone had kicked him in the chest. How could she possibly look so happy to see him? As if she'd completely forgotten the other man's existence she stood and held out a hand to Quinn, inviting him to join her. Never in his life had a woman looked at him in quite that way. He didn't deserve to have Laura feel that way about him, but he was selfishly glad she did. He stepped forward.

Catching his left hand in her right one, Laura greeted him almost breathlessly. "Hi, Quinn. How did things go with Betty?"

"Okay. How was your first day back from vacation?"

"Fine. The little Travanti girl is doing much better. She's gaining weight and the doctors say she'll be able to go home in a few weeks. Isn't that wonderful?"

He couldn't remember who the little Travanti girl was just then, but since Laura was so obviously delighted with the news she was giving him he smiled and nodded. "Yeah, that's great."

"Oh, Quinn, I want to introduce you to a friend of mine." Still holding his hand, Laura turned her head toward the man in the gray suit, who'd stood and was watching them closely. Too closely, in Quinn's opinion. "Sam Jennings, this is Quinn Gallagher. Quinn, Sam's a psychologist here at the hospital. He's read all your books."

"Nice to meet you, Quinn," Sam said, extending a hand and smiling pleasantly. "I'm quite an admirer of yours. I just finished *Crimson Justice*. It was really fascinating."

Quinn had never been comfortable meeting people who'd read his books; he didn't write for the attention or to gain fans. He was even less comfortable now, knowing Jennings was a shrink—and that Laura had been holding hands with him. He shook the other man's hand briefly, then pulled his own back. "Thanks."

"Sam is particularly interested in your books because he used to counsel police officers in Denver," Laura added, seeming to choose her words carefully.

Quinn shot her a narrow-eyed look. "Is that right? Are you ready to go, Laura?"

She nodded and gathered up her purse and coat. "Yes, I'm ready. See you later, Sam."

"Sure. Maybe we can get together for lunch later this week."

"I'd like that."

Quinn's hand tightened on hers and he turned, almost pulling her along with him as he walked rapidly out of the canteen. "Where's your car?"

"This way," she answered, turning down a hallway. "Quinn, is something wrong?"

He released her hand and shoved his in the pockets of his parka. "Why?"

"You look angry," she commented carefully as she slipped into her coat.

He *was* angry. He was furious, as a matter of fact. And he was doing a lousy job of hiding it. Coming to a stop, he glared down at her. "Do you make a practice of accepting a date with one man as you're leaving to go out with another one? We consider that rude where I come from."

Laura's eyes went wide in astonishment. "I didn't accept a date with Sam! I simply agreed to have lunch with him one day. Quinn, he's a friend. Nothing more. And besides," she went on, her own voice warming with annoyance, "I can't believe *you* would have the nerve to lecture *me* on manners!"

That stung, even though he knew she was justified in her accusation. Muttering a curse beneath his breath, Quinn started walking again, his eyes on the exit door ahead of them. "You sit around holding hands with all your male friends?" he heard himself asking.

"Sometimes," she replied coolly, pushing through the door before he could reach it and heading without pause for her Subaru. "When I feel like it."

"Fine."

"Fine." She stopped at the front of her car and threw her head back to glare at him. "Are you going to let this jealous snit of yours ruin our evening? Because if you are, we may as well just go home."

Stunned, Quinn felt his jaw sag. He tightened it. "I am *not* jealous," he ground out between clenched teeth.

"No?" she challenged. "Then just what *is* your problem, Quinn?"

What was his problem? What did she *think* was his problem? He was—he was—

"All right, dammit, I'm jealous," he growled, now as furious at himself as he was with her. "There. Are you happy?"

Laura continued to glare at him for a moment and then she bit her lip in a futile attempt to control a sudden smile. Her brown eyes went soft with humor.

Quinn stiffened as he noted the signs of her amusement, then his own mouth twitched into a rueful smile. "Well, hell," he breathed gustily. Ignoring the people in the parking lot around them, he reached out and snagged her by the back of the head, pulling her to him for a kiss that was part apology, part possession. "You make me crazy, Laura Sutherland," he muttered against her lips.

Her hands at his waist, Laura smiled beneath his mouth. "You think you don't do the same to me? Think again, Quinn Gallagher."

He lifted his head. "So we're both crazy. Where does that leave us?"

Her smile tremulous, she lifted a hand to touch his cheek in the gesture that never failed to get to him. "That is entirely up to you."

Not knowing how to respond to that, he stepped back. "You want to drive?"

"No, you drive," she replied, handing him her keys. "I'll navigate."

He unlocked the passenger door for her. "That ought to be interesting."

Laura chuckled and slid into the seat. Shutting the door behind her, Quinn tossed the keys into the air, caught them with a downward slash of his hand, and strode around the front of the car to the driver's seat.

"Other than your name and your temper, how much of you is Irish?" Laura asked whimsically several hours later as they dined on prime rib and fluffy baked potatoes at a cozy table in an intimate corner of an Old West-style restaurant she'd thought he would enjoy.

Quinn glanced up from the dinner he was attacking with relish. "I don't have a temper."

She only looked at him.

He grinned. "Okay, so I've got a bit of a temper."

She kept looking.

His grin widened. "All right, I admit it. I have a temper. A real Irish temper. Now are you satisfied?"

She laughed, loving the relaxed mood they'd fallen into during the past three hours. Deliberately putting their quarrel at the hospital behind them, they'd made an effort to enjoy their time together since, and they'd done so. Quinn had exerted himself to be charming—and she was amazed at how charming he could be when he tried. "You still haven't answered my question."

"How much of me is Irish? All of me," he replied casually. "My father's second generation, my mother was born in Kerry County and moved to New York when she was about ten. She kept her brogue until she died. I used to love to hear the stories she'd tell before bedtime."

"Have you ever been to Ireland?"

He shook his head. "Maybe I'll go sometime. Mom always wanted me to."

"Don't you ever talk to your father? Wouldn't you like to see him sometime?"

Quinn shrugged. "He never had much use for me when I was a kid. I doubt that he's got any more use for me now."

Laura shook her head. "I just think you should try to stay in touch with him. I'm afraid you'll be sorry you didn't after he's gone."

"I'll give him a call sometime." Quinn turned his attention back to his plate. "This prime rib is the best I've ever had."

She smiled. "This is Colorado, remember? We know how to cook beef."

"I've never been this far west before."

"Really?" She looked at him across the table, lean and tanned, his hair finger-brushed off his forehead, his mustache thick and silky. Though he'd worn a white shirt and navy slacks that evening, he looked much more natural in the plaid flannel shirts and jeans she'd always seen him in before. "For an Easterner, you fit in quite well. I can imagine you as a cowboy."

"Can you?" he murmured, smiling. "I'd probably bust my butt. I haven't spent much time on horseback. I used to be a big fan of Westerns though. Books, movies, TV shows. Roy Rogers was my idol when I was a kid."

"You'd enjoy the Independence Stampede, then."

"What's that?"

"It's a week-long celebration in late June and early July here in Greeley. We have a lot going on during that week— night shows with big-name entertainment, rodeos, barbecues, carnivals. They advertise the world's largest July Fourth rodeo, and the whole thing wraps up with a huge parade and spectacular fireworks. It's a lot of fun."

"Sounds impressive."

"Why don't you check it out this year?" she suggested daringly.

His eyes were suddenly shuttered as they met hers. "That's still seven months away. I don't usually plan that far ahead."

No, he wouldn't plan that far ahead. Even that would be a commitment of sorts, just the sort of thing Quinn so carefully avoided. Laura stifled a sigh and drained her wineglass.

"What do you want to do after dinner?" Quinn asked unexpectedly. "Is there anything to do in Greeley on a Monday evening?"

He seemed reluctant for the evening to end, Laura thought. She knew the feeling. "We could go to a movie," she offered, "or dancing."

"I'm not much of a dancer. What movies are playing?"

"I'm not sure. We can pick up a newspaper when we leave here and check."

"Okay. Unless you want to go on home?"

It was the first time he'd called it home. Laura thought wistfully of how nice the word sounded from him. "No, I'm in no hurry," she assured him.

He nodded and finished his dinner without further conversation.

Sitting in the passenger seat of her car as Quinn watched from behind the wheel, Laura turned the pages of the newspaper to the entertainment section, where she scanned the listings of films currently playing in the area. Her attention caught by one particular title, she glanced at Quinn. "What about this one?"

He looked over her arm at the newspaper. "Which?"

"*Under Investigation*. They're showing it again at the mall."

Quinn groaned. "That's been out for months. What else is playing?"

"I'd like to see it, Quinn. Aren't you even curious about it?"

"Laura, you'd hate it. You didn't even like the violent scenes in that movie we watched on your VCR."

"I know. But I still want to see it. Quinn, it's based on *your* book."

He exhaled sharply. "I'm aware of that. I've got the money sitting in a bank to prove it."

"The critics liked it."

He summed up his opinion of critics' opinions with a few well-chosen words.

Laura laughed. "We can see something else if you'd rather. I can always watch this one another time."

He shook his head. "If you're determined to watch it, you may as well see it with me." He started the car. "How do we get there?"

They stood in line with clowning teenagers at the ticket window. Quinn looped an arm casually around Laura's waist, and she felt as giddy as the young girls giggling at their boyfriends. In the lobby he bought her a box of buttered popcorn and a soft drink. "Can't watch a movie without popcorn," he assured her gravely. "Let's just hope this film doesn't kill your appetite."

She didn't exactly like the movie. She watched most of it cringing and peering through her fingers.

"For a nurse, you sure are squeamish about blood," Quinn murmured at one point.

Since Janet's favorite part had just ended—the scene where the avenging cop obliterated the face of the man who'd framed him—Laura shuddered and leaned closer to Quinn. "It's not the blood, it's the violence," she whispered in reply. "And how do they make it look so real?"

He draped his arm around her shoulders. "Hollywood magic. Sorry you came?"

Sorry? When she was sitting this close to him in a darkened theater, his arm around her, his breath warm on her cheek? She'd gladly sit through one of those slasher movies if she could stay in just this position. Not that she'd be content for long just to sit by him. "No, Quinn. I'm not sorry."

With his free hand, he stroked her cheek, then turned her face toward his. "Neither am I," he told her. And then he kissed her and she lost all interest in the action on the screen.

Chapter Thirteen

Betty, Mrs. Elliott and Janet were in the den when Laura and Quinn came home, Janet rocking Larry as she fed him his bottle. "Hi," she greeted them. "Did you have a good time?"

"Yes, we did. How's Larry?" Laura asked with a smile, slipping out of her coat and leaning over the back of the rocker to coo at the baby.

"He's wonderful, of course. What else?"

Laura walked around to the couch, where she placed a hand on Betty's shoulder. "You okay, Betty?"

Betty nodded. "Yes, I will be if the police can stop Gene from making those calls. Renee wanted me to tell you and Quinn good-night for her."

"I finished your new sweater, Quinn. I put it on the bed in your room," Mrs. Elliott announced, looking up from the afghan she'd been knitting between sweaters. "I hope you like it."

"Thanks, Mrs. Elliott. I'm sure I'll like it just fine."

Laura looked around with a frown when Quinn spoke. She'd noticed a change in him since they'd entered the house. During their date he'd been more at ease than she'd ever seen him; now he seemed tense, restless. She didn't know what had happened to make him react that way.

Betty closed the book she'd been reading. "I think I'll turn in."

Mrs. Elliott put away her knitting. "So will I. I am rather tired."

"I think someone else is ready for bed," Janet commented, smiling down at the baby dozing in her arms. She stood gracefully with him. "Good night, everyone."

"Good night, Janet."

Carrying her coat over her arm, Laura turned toward her own bedroom with a quick glance at Quinn. Would he join her tonight? Or would he stay away as a result of whatever was bothering him now?

After the wonderful evening they'd shared, she couldn't bear the thought of sleeping without him that night.

Quinn didn't leave her in suspense long. Without even pausing at his own door, he followed her into her bedroom and closed the door behind him. The lock clicked beneath his fingers and then he turned to look at her. Laura caught her breath at the hunger written on his face. Responding to that visible desire with the full extent of her own need, she held out her arms.

Supporting himself on one elbow, Quinn rested his head in his hand and gazed down at the woman lying on the bed beside him. Her eyes were heavy-lidded, her mouth still swollen from the hard kisses they'd exchanged during their lovemaking. The floral comforter covered her to the tops of her breasts, leaving her shoulders and throat bare. He stroked her throat with his free hand, feeling her tremble beneath his touch. Even after the passion that had burned between them, the desire they shared still simmered just beneath the surface, ready to be restoked.

His fingers tangled in her hair and he leaned over to drop a light kiss on her lips before resuming his position looking down at her. This was the way he liked it, he mused; just himself and Laura. He'd enjoyed having her alone all afternoon and evening, had regretted having to bring her home where he had to share her with so many others. He didn't even like the thought of her leaving for work in the morning, where her day would be filled with other people. People like Sam Jennings. Would she think of Quinn when she was having lunch with that other man?

He was rapidly becoming obsessed with Laura, he realized, beginning to scowl.

Noting his frown, Laura tilted her head on the pillow in inquiry. "Quinn, is something bothering you?"

"How do you make room in your life for all the people you have in it? How can you keep giving to others and still have anything left for yourself?"

"Now what brought that on?" she asked, puzzled by his questions.

"It seems like something or someone's always demanding your time. When you're not actually working at your job, you're worrying about the critical babies. Around here you're constantly with Mrs. Elliott or Betty or Renee or Janet or the baby." He paused, then shrugged ruefully. "Earlier you accused me of being jealous. I guess you were right in more ways than one. I don't like sharing you."

He could almost have believed the expression that crossed her face then was hope. "I'm not sure what you're trying to say, Quinn."

He twirled a strand of her hair around his finger and avoided her eyes. "I want you to go back to Florida with me, Laura," he heard himself saying then. He didn't know when he'd come to that decision, but now he knew it was what he wanted. "We can get a place on the beach—God knows I make enough money for the both of us these days."

She went totally still. "You want me to—go with you to Florida?" she repeated carefully.

"Yeah. We're good together, Laura. You know it. You've said you care for me, though I honestly can't imagine why. And I care for you. Very much." That was as close as he could come to expressing his feelings for her; even that was difficult for him to say.

"Quinn, of course I care for you," she told him softly, her hand lifting to his cheek. "I love you."

His eyes closed as his throat tightened. He'd suspected Laura felt that way, but hearing her say the words staggered him. He hadn't realized the words would mean so much to him. He couldn't even remember the last time he'd heard them. "God, Laura."

"Surely you're not surprised."

"I guess not." He cupped her face in his hands. "I won't be an easy man to live with, Laura. I can't give you all the words you need to hear. But I want you with me. I'll try to make you happy."

"Quinn, are you asking me to marry you?"

He tensed. "I didn't say anything about marriage. We don't need that."

She closed her eyes for a moment before opening them again to look up at him. "I can't go to Florida with you, Quinn. But you can stay here. Please stay."

"I don't want to stay here," he answered bluntly.

"Then I'm sorry. The answer is no."

He tried to ignore the pain that slashed through him at her words. He couldn't ignore the anger. "You're saying no because I'm not interested in getting married?"

"No," she murmured, "that's not the reason. Not solely, anyway."

"Then why, dammit?" he demanded. "You just said that you—that you—"

"I love you," she answered for him, her mouth twisting into a smile that held no humor. "You can't even say the word, can you, Quinn?"

"Is that the reason you're turning me down? Words?" he asked scornfully. "Honey, I could give you words, but they wouldn't be worth a damn if I said them only because you wanted to hear them."

"You think I don't know that?" She jerked away from his hand and sat up, clutching the sheet and comforter to her breasts. "Quinn, you're asking me to give up my job and my home, abandon the people who depend on me and go with you to Florida just because you happen to want me. For now. You haven't made any promises of how long it would last because you don't make plans for the future. I don't know what made you decide to ask—whether it was the jealousy you say you're feeling or just the aftermath of good sex—but neither of those is enough reason for me to give up the life I've worked so hard to build for myself and follow you to Florida on a whim like some . . . some groupie."

Quinn swore furiously and rolled to reach for his pants. "Okay, fine. If that's all you think I'm offering, then forget it."

"I can't believe this," she muttered, standing to wrap herself in her robe. She snapped on her bedside lamp and glared at him. "You're acting as if I've actually insulted you."

He snatched his shirt off the floor and shoved his arms into it. "Now why the hell should I feel insulted? You're the first woman I've ever cared about, the only woman I've ever asked to live with me, and you turn me down without even giving it any thought and then accuse me of only wanting some bimbo groupie."

"Quinn, you're taking it all wrong. I *am* flattered that you asked me to—"

"I had no intention of flattering you," he cut in coldly. "And I don't need the polite little thank-you-for-doing-me-the-honor speech."

"You're angry."

"Bingo." He grabbed his shoes and socks and headed for the door.

"Quinn—"

"Hey, no problem, okay? You're the one who kept urging me to take a chance on us, right? Well, fine. I did. And I got it thrown right back in my teeth. Nice advice, Laura." He slammed her bedroom door behind him as he left, paying no regard to the thin walls of the older home. It had barely closed before he opened it again for one last word. "And by the way," he told her, his eyes stormy gray as he looked at her, "if all I wanted was a groupie, I'd have given one of those goddamned interviews to *People* magazine."

And the door slammed again, followed almost immediately by the crash of the door to the next room.

Laura stood where she was for a full two minutes before her own temper kicked in. Without thinking, she jerked open her door and then Quinn's. He was standing by the bed, lighting a cigarette—his usual method of venting his emotions, she seethed. "So you think you took a chance, do you? You very generously offered to allow me to give up everything I own and live with you in Florida until you get tired of me and ask me to leave. How did you find the courage to take all that risk, Quinn?'' she asked sarcastically, making no effort to keep her voice down.

He blew out smoke in a savage exhale. "So what do you expect me to do? Live with you here? Keep sneaking into your room after all your housemates go to bed so we don't ruin your saintly reputation?''

"I never asked you to sneak into my room. I'm not ashamed of our relationship, Quinn. And what's so bad about living here? You haven't seemed all that unhappy here.''

"I'm just not the kind to live in a commune.''

"Oh, you like being alone, do you?''

He cast her an angry, impatient look. "That's right. I do.''

"Of course. And that's why you live with Amos in Florida when you can afford any place you want, right?''

"I live with Amos because it's convenient. I met him in a bar a couple of times and he offered to rent me a room, with his housekeeper providing meals and cleaning. That's easier than trying to keep up a place of my own. Leaves me free to pick up and leave whenever I feel like it. I don't rent from Amos simply to share his company.''

"I knew you'd have an excuse," she muttered, impatiently pushing her tangled curls away from her face.

"It's not an excuse, it's fact!''

"Fact as you see it. I've never seen anyone so determined to lie to himself as you are, Quinn Gallagher. Nor anyone so very good at it. You honestly believe all the garbage you've spouted at me, don't you?''

"I've never lied to you. And I don't lie to myself.''

The word she used wasn't one she used often, but it pretty well summed up her opinion of his statements. "I suppose you still claim to have no emotions?'' she asked mockingly.

He flushed a bit. "Right now I'm damned mad, if that counts," he answered flatly.

"It counts for something," she agreed. "Now why don't you tell me how you feel about me?"

"I told you, dammit!"

"You said you care for me. Well, you've told me that before and it didn't change a thing. Tell me what you *really* feel, Quinn."

He drew on the cigarette and glowered at her without answering.

"No, you won't, will you? Because admitting you love someone means you make yourself vulnerable, and the great Quinn Gallagher has decided he's not going to be like everyone else. You think you're above the risks and problems that most people accept everyday because they realize it's all just a part of being alive."

He half turned away from her, his body defensively tight. "You don't know what you're talking about."

"Don't I?"

"No, you don't. What do you know about real life? You live in some kind of ivory tower here, playing Lady Bountiful to the homeless, taking care of sick babies during the day. You've lost people to illness, but you don't know anything about the darker side of life. Well, lady, I've seen it. I've lived it. And I've lost to it."

Laura took a deep breath, angrier at that moment than she could ever remember being. Ever. "So I've never seen the darker side of life. You're so arrogant! How do you think Robbie died, Quinn?"

He threw her a quick, guarded look. "I don't know."

"No, of course you don't know. You never asked, did you? You didn't want to get that involved in my life because you were so busy licking your own wounds. Well, I didn't lose Robbie to some unfortunate illness, Quinn. I lost him to a madman with a gun, just the way you lost your brother. Only you didn't have to watch Michael die. You didn't have to hold him in your arms and watch the blood pour out of him onto you and know there was absolutely nothing you could do to save him."

"Oh, God."

Ignoring his choked words, Laura spun away from him, her eyes closing as she relived a time she'd managed to put behind her. "Robbie worked in a public health clinic in Greeley. He didn't enter medicine to make money, but to help people, and he thought his talents would be best put to use for those who couldn't afford to pay for adequate medical care. He was a good doctor; my father said he'd be one of the best. I was supposed to meet Robbie at the clinic one evening after he closed up so the two of us could go out to dinner. When I got there the front door was open and I knew something was wrong."

"Laura—"

Continuing to ignore him, still not opening her eyes, she went on in a flat, emotionless voice. "I found him in the back room. The medical cabinets had been ransacked and Robbie had been shot once in the chest and once in the head. I called the police and an ambulance and then sat and held him in my arms as he died. I'd missed the junkie who shot him by no more than a few minutes; if I'd arrived just a little earlier, I'd have probably died with him."

She opened her eyes then and turned to look at Quinn, noting his pallor with an odd detachment. "I know what it's like to have nightmares, Quinn. I know what it's like to be haunted by images you can't forget, plagued by what-might-have-beens. But I learned to put it behind me because I let people help me. I *asked* for help. I talked for hours to my father and my friends, and I saw a psychologist for a time. I surrounded myself with people I love and people who love me because I needed that love, because my life would have been empty without it. Do you think I *wanted* to fall in love again, particularly with a man I knew would hurt me? Don't you know that I was scared, just as scared as you are? But I'm human, Quinn, and I admit it, while you just drift through life pretending to be some sort of robot.

"Well, fine. If that's the way you want to live the rest of your life, I can't stop you. I've offered you everything I have to give because I happen to think you're worth the risk. Now you have to believe that, as well."

He ground his cigarette out in an ashtray on the night-stand—one she'd never seen before, she thought with that strangely detached section of her mind. When the silence had gone on so long that she thought he wasn't going to say anything, she turned to leave, wanting to get back into her own room before the tears began.

He didn't try to stop her as she left the room. She closed her door softly behind her, guiltily hoping she and Quinn hadn't disturbed the entire household during their confrontation, then crossed the room to fall face down on the bed. Remembering the night he'd heard her crying from his room, she shoved her fist against her mouth to hold in the sobs. She wasn't going to let him hear her cry.

As he had that other time, he entered so quietly that she wasn't aware he was in the room until he touched her. "I'm sorry, Laura," he said softly.

She turned her face away from him. "I don't want your apology."

"Well, you're going to get it, anyway. You were right. I was arrogant to assume that I was the only one who's been hurt, who's known what it was like to lose someone to a senseless murder."

"Yes, you were. You were arrogant about a lot of things," she answered, her voice muffled by the pillow and the tears still clogging her throat.

The bed shifted as he sat beside her. "Yeah, I guess. I didn't mean to hurt you."

She sighed and turned back to him. "I know you didn't."

He fumbled at the pocket of his unbuttoned shirt, then stopped with a grumble, his hand falling to lie on his thigh. Laura brushed her hair out of her face and sat up beside him, straightening her robe around her. "Go ahead and smoke, Quinn. You're obviously longing for a cigarette."

"I didn't bring them with me. I don't need one."

She pulled a pillow up behind her and leaned back against the headboard. She didn't know why Quinn had followed her into her room, but he seemed to want to talk and she didn't want to discourage him.

Quinn looked at her, at the tears that had escaped to leave damp paths down her cheeks, at the bruised expression in her brown eyes. His chest tightened. He'd never wanted to do this to her. This was exactly what he'd been trying to avoid. "I was serious about wanting you to go with me to Florida, Laura. It wasn't an impulse. It wasn't an offer I made lightly."

She reached out to touch his arm. "I know it wasn't, Quinn. But surely you understand why I had to turn you down. My life is here. Betty and Renee, Mrs. Elliott, Janet and her baby—there's nowhere else for them to go. I love my job and my home."

He looked down at her hand, so small and delicate against his shirtsleeve. "If—if I had asked you to marry me, would your answer have been a different one?"

She paused so long that he finally turned his head to look at her. "I don't think so," she said at last.

"You're not willing to relocate if you marry? Regardless of the circumstances?"

"I didn't say that," she countered. "Maybe I would consider moving if I thought there was good enough cause. I'd probably take Mrs. Elliott with me, if she wanted to go, and I'd feel it necessary to extend the invitation to Betty and Janet. They depend on me, Quinn, just as if they were members of my family. In fact, that's the way I think of them. I wouldn't abandon family members, and I can't abandon my friends. But you wouldn't like that, would you?"

He swallowed. "No."

"That's what I thought. You want me to go with you to Florida because my friends aren't in Florida."

"You'd be asking a lot of any man to expect him to share you with any stray who comes along needing a home," he muttered.

She nodded. "I know that. I think I even said something to that effect to you once. But it's the way I am; it's what I believe in, Quinn. I love being surrounded by people, though I enjoy my privacy sometimes. I love the feeling of extended family."

"And I want you all to myself," Quinn said quietly, not as an argument but as a statement of fact.

Her fingers tightened on his arm. "I love you, Quinn. You would always come first with me."

"But that's not enough for you. You have to have all these others, too."

"Oh, Quinn, it's not that simple. I could probably be happy with you on a deserted island, content to spend every minute with you. I love being with you. But how could I walk away from these people who depend on me? Could you honestly stand by and watch me put Mrs. Elliott in a nursing home? Send Betty out on the streets with Renee, knowing she's not emotionally strong enough yet to get by on her own? Throw Janet out to fend for herself and her baby?"

He'd never made himself face that decision. He supposed he had just expected her to drop everything and follow him. Because it was so important now, he forced himself to think about what he was asking of her. He pictured Mrs. Elliott in an impersonal nursing home; Renee in a day-care center as Betty tried to make enough for them to get by on; Janet being forced to live on welfare because she didn't have enough education to find a decent job. "Dammit, Laura, you've got yourself so tied to these people that you *can't* break away. Now can you understand why I've chosen to keep to myself?"

"Would it really be so bad if you stayed here?" she asked him in little more than a whisper.

He pushed his hand through his hair. "I just don't know if I can," he admitted. "All these people, all their needs. Mrs. Elliott has already adopted me as some kind of honorary grandson. What about when she dies unexpectedly during the night? Won't that be painful for you?"

"Of course. I love her. And it will happen, eventually. I knew when I asked her to live here that her time was limited."

"And what if Betty decides to move away tomorrow, to take Renee and get a new start somewhere? I know how attached you are to that little girl. How could you let her go?"

"Betty is free to go any time she wants to, of course. But she and I have become friends, Quinn. I don't think she'd just disappear without keeping in touch. I'd miss Renee, of course, but I could let her go if I thought it were best for her. Janet and Larry, too. Janet will want to be on her own as soon as she's financially able."

"And you'll take in some others, let yourself get involved with their lives, their problems."

Since they'd been over that before, Laura didn't bother to answer.

Quinn shook his head. "I've lived for so long without getting close to anyone. Then I met you and I was involved before I could stop myself. But as for all these others, well, I think you're expecting too much from me, Laura. More than I have to give."

"I still think you're underestimating yourself, Quinn. And you're not being realistic. Few people are completely isolated, separate from others. It's true that neither of us have immediate families left—other than your father, of course—but there are still obligations to others. And what about children? Would you be as reluctant to commit yourself to children as you are to other people?"

He cleared his throat. "I've never thought about having kids."

"I have. I'd love to have children."

"God, don't you know what can happen to kids today?" he grated in sudden vehemence. "You work in an intensive care nursery; you watch them die! Or they could be—be—" He shuddered as something horrible hovered in his mind, something he knew he couldn't face. Not yet. He deliberately blanked his mind against it.

"What is it, Quinn? What did you just push away?" Laura demanded much too perceptively. She scooted around to sit on her knees beside him, her hands on his upper arms. "Talk to me."

"Look, it's late. You have to work tomorrow. You need your rest." He shifted to move off the bed, intending to leave the room.

Her fingers tightened on his arms. "Don't go, Quinn. Please stay with me tonight."

"Laura, I don't know what I'm going to do. Maybe—maybe I'll leave tomorrow. Get away by myself and do some thinking about everything."

She flinched as if he'd struck her, but her face remained calm with what he could only assume was a massive effort. "You do whatever you have to do, Quinn. But please stay with me tonight. Just let me have you tonight."

He paused a moment longer, then groaned at the look in her eyes and pulled her roughly into his arms. "Don't let me hurt you anymore, Laura. I can't stand hurting you."

"And I can't bear to see *you* hurting. I want to help you, Quinn, but I can't until you let me."

To avoid answering, he covered her mouth with his. The kiss held all the words he couldn't say, all the confusion he felt, all the desperation at the thought of going back to a life without her in it. Laura clasped her arms around his neck and responded with all the love she'd expressed for him.

He'd intended only to kiss her and then to hold her while she slept. They were both tired. But then she pressed herself against him, her robe parting to press her breasts against his chest bared by his unbuttoned shirt. Groaning on a sudden urge of desire so violent he shuddered in its force, he pressed her down against the bed, his tongue stabbing in her mouth as his hand went to the opening of that robe.

As if his passion ignited her own, Laura's own hands swiftly became demanding, aggressive, stripping the shirt from his shoulders and reaching for the unsnapped waistband of his jeans.

They made love furiously, intensely, as if only by losing themselves in each other could they hold off the pain still facing them. Laura arched beneath him, muffling her cries of pleasure into his shoulder. And then she convulsed with a shattering climax, gasping, "I love you. Oh, Quinn, I love you."

The words echoed over and over in his head as he bowed into his own explosive release. All he could say was her name. "Laura. Ah, Laura."

It seemed to be enough for her. Sighing her contentment, she curled against him and fell deeply asleep. Quinn held her tightly against him, delaying the time when he'd have to withdraw from her, wishing they could stay just the way they were for eternity.

Just the two of them.

Chapter Fourteen

Quinn was sleeping so soundly when Laura woke that she didn't have the heart to wake him. Without disturbing him, she showered and quietly dressed in her uniform. Looking down at the man sleeping in her bed, she hesitated before walking out of the room. He was lying on his stomach, his face turned toward her, the customary frown creasing his brow. Even in his sleep, he was troubled, she thought. She didn't want to leave for work, because she was so afraid he wouldn't be there when she came home.

Risking waking him, she leaned over and dropped the lightest of kisses on his lean cheek. He didn't even stir. He must have been exhausted, she thought sympathetically, wondering how long he'd lain awake after she'd fallen asleep the night before.

Praying this wouldn't be her last look at him, she turned and walked out of the room.

As early as it was, Betty was already working in the kitchen. "Good morning," she greeted Laura with a smile that didn't quite hide the curiosity in her eyes. "Coffee's ready. Want some breakfast?"

"No, I'm not hungry. I'll just have coffee."

"Janet will probably sleep late this morning. The baby fussed on and off during the night."

Laura bit her lower lip. "Did he?" she asked after she'd filled her coffee cup. "I didn't hear him."

"Mmm. Actually, there was quite a bit of noise during the night." Betty leaned against the counter and eyed Laura meaningfully. "Doors slamming, voices raised, that sort of thing."

Flushing, Laura looked into her cup. "I'm sorry. Did we disturb you?"

Betty wiped her hands on her apron and took a step closer to her friend. "Is there anything I can do to help, Laura?"

Fighting back the sudden urge to cry, Laura shook her head. "I don't think so, Betty, but thank you for offering. Quinn is a—difficult man to understand."

"Yes, he is. At first, when I realized the two of you were arguing, it frightened me. I thought back to all the fights Gene and I got into, and I worried about you. And then I realized that, though you might be quite angry with each other, Quinn would never raise a hand to you."

Vaguely shocked, Laura reached out to touch Betty's arm. "No, of course he wouldn't. I'm sorry you had to be reminded of your ordeal with Gene, Betty, but you must realize that most couples quarrel sometimes. Not that Quinn and I can be called a couple, exactly."

"I don't know why not. You're so obviously in love with each other."

Laura sighed and placed her untouched coffee on the counter. "I'm in love with him. He won't allow himself to feel the same way about me."

"Maybe he won't admit it, but he loves you, Laura. I think you both know it."

Laura exhaled shakily. "Okay, so maybe he does. But he doesn't want to love me. He's not willing to take the risk of making it work out between us."

"Laura, is it—would it help if Renee and I found another place to live? I know it must be difficult to conduct a romance with so many people around all the time."

"No." Laura spoke immediately and with full conviction. "I don't want you to leave, Betty. Not until you want to. Quinn has to accept me exactly the way I am, or it's not really me that he wants. Does that make sense?"

Betty nodded. "Yes, it does, and you're right. Any man who would want to change you has to be out of his mind. He'd be a fool not to know what a treasure he's found."

Her cheeks going hot with embarrassment, Laura quickly hugged the other woman. "Thanks. You're pretty nice, yourself, Betty." She pulled away. "Now I have to get to work. Quinn—Quinn may be leaving today. If he does, don't let it upset you. I can handle it."

Her eyes filling with quick, sympathetic tears, Betty cleared her throat and tried to speak lightly. "All right. I won't try to tie him to the porch or anything. I can't make any guarantees for Renee, though."

Laura didn't want to think of Renee's reaction to losing Quinn. The child adored him. Laura knew the feeling. "I'll see you this afternoon, Betty."

The day dragged by with almost unbearable sluggishness. Unused to being so restless while doing her job, Laura chafed against the sensation, trying to concentrate on her duties. But always at the back of her mind was the question of whether Quinn would leave without seeing her again.

Christmas decorations were beginning to go up around the hospital. Laura knew she should be planning for the upcoming holiday, but for one of the few times in her life she wasn't enthusiastic about it. It would be different, of course, if she knew Quinn would be sharing Christmas with her.

She wished she could talk to Sam, but he was out of town for the day at a mental health convention. She couldn't talk to Patricia because she was too afraid she'd break down and cry, something she was determined not to do. Not until she was alone in her room that evening, anyway.

She thought of calling Amos during her lunch break. But what would she say? *Amos, I'm in love with Quinn. If he comes to you, please send him back to me.* She didn't think that would do much good.

She thought of calling home. At least she could find out whether he'd left yet. But she couldn't bring herself to dial the number, deciding she'd never be able to function the rest of the day if she knew for certain that Quinn was gone.

She'd handled the situation the night before all wrong, she decided at some point during the day, wearily filling out a report that was little more than a row of numbers to her. She should have been more tactful in her rejection of his offer for her to live with him in Florida. It was just that he'd taken her so by surprise; she hadn't expected the proposition, and the knowledge that he wanted her to give up everything without a real commitment on his part had been so staggering that she'd overreacted.

She shouldn't have told him in anger about Robbie's death. She should have shared her story with him earlier, when he'd talked about his feelings about losing Michael. Maybe she'd been doing a bit of repressing herself, unwilling to dig up the old wounds of the past. It had hurt to talk about Robbie's death, but it hadn't brought back all the old grief as she'd thought it might. No, she'd accepted her loss, learned to live with it, though she'd never stop regretting the waste of such a promising young life.

Would she ever get over losing Quinn?

She wasn't sure she could.

Quinn wasn't in the den when she got home from work, though everyone else was, with the exception of Betty, who was working in the kitchen. The door to the study stood open. The study lights were off, so she couldn't tell whether his things were gone. Moistening her lips, Laura waited until everyone had greeted her before asking hesitantly, "Is Quinn—did he—?"

"Oh, he's out taking a walk," Janet answered carelessly, unaware of the fear Laura had dealt with all day. "He does love those afternoon walks of his, doesn't he?"

Her knees weakening on a wave of sheer relief, Laura put out a hand to steady herself against the back of a chair. She'd been so sure he would be gone. Now she had to wonder why he'd stayed.

"Laura, dear, are you all right? You look pale," Mrs. Elliott observed in concern.

"I'm fine, Mrs. Elliott."

"Push me on my swing, Aunt 'aura?" Renee asked hopefully, deserting the toy she'd been playing with to bound to her feet and look pleadingly up at Laura.

"I think Aunt Laura's tired, Renee," Mrs. Elliott tried to intercede.

Laura shook her head. "No, it's okay, Mrs. Elliott. I promised Renee I'd play with her for a while this afternoon. Get your coat, Renee, while I change my clothes."

Renee started to run for her room, then paused and looked back at Janet. "Can 'arry go swing wif us?" she asked politely.

Laura joined in as the others laughed, her mood lightening. "I think Larry's a little too young for that," she answered for Janet, who was still laughing. "It won't be much longer, Renee."

Renee sighed as only a bewildered three-year-old can sigh and turned to go after her coat, her braid bobbing behind her.

Ten minutes later Laura stood behind the swing, pushing the little girl in the pink snowsuit who kicked her feet and squealed in delight. Keeping one eye on the path from the woods, Laura chatted with Renee as they played. Renee was pretending to be a circus performer; she'd seen a circus program on television a few days before and had been thoroughly impressed. Laura went along with the pretense, creating a colorful setting for them with her words.

Though she'd prepared herself, Laura still felt her heart skip a beat or two when Quinn walked out of the trees and paused at the sight of her. Their eyes met for a long, tense moment and then he started her way.

Absently giving Renee one last push and reminding the child to hold tightly to the chains, Laura stepped around the swing set to stop only a couple of feet from Quinn. It was all she could do not to throw herself in his arms and cling to him. He was wearing the black and red sweater beneath his parka and, of course, he was hatless, his hair glistening almost gold in the waning sunlight. He looked wonderful. "Hi," she heard herself saying in a surprisingly normal voice.

"Hi." His piercing gray eyes roamed her face. She was sure he could see the ravages of the anxiety she'd been through that day despite the smile she wore for him. "How were things at work today?"

She twisted her fingers behind her. "Fine. They set up the Christmas tree in the lobby this afternoon. The children in the pediatrics ward get a big kick out of that."

He lifted an eyebrow. "I guess it is getting close to Christmas, isn't it?"

She nodded and glanced at Renee, who was pumping her feet vigorously to keep the swing going. "Looks like Santa Claus will be visiting here this year. It'll be fun to have two children in the house at Christmastime, though Larry won't be impressed." *Will you be here, Quinn?* she wanted so badly to ask.

Seeming to grow tired of their carefully polite, studiedly impersonal conversation, Quinn took a step closer. "I didn't hear you leave this morning."

She moistened her lips. "You were sleeping very soundly. I tried not to disturb you."

"I missed you when I woke up," he murmured, his hand going up to toy with a curl at her shoulder.

She couldn't look away from the warmth of his eyes. "I— I was afraid you wouldn't be here when I got home," she told him.

"I thought about leaving today," he admitted, pulling her a few inches closer with a gentle pressure of his hand. "But I didn't want to wake up missing you tomorrow." He lowered his head and kissed her softly.

Her heart swelling with hope, Laura lifted her hand to his cheek. "Oh, Quinn. I'm so glad you're still here."

He rested his forehead on hers, his expression doubtful. "I still don't know what I'm going to do, Laura. I haven't come to terms with this life-style of yours. I just don't know if I can deal with having all these people around all the time."

"You don't have to decide immediately," she offered wistfully. "You could give it some time, try it out for a while."

"I don't know, Laura. I—"

"Quinn! Aunt 'aura! Watch me!" Renee called out suddenly, her voice excited.

Laura and Quinn turned and then gasped simultaneously. Still playing circus, Renee had managed to stand up on the swing, holding onto the chains as she pushed with her feet. Intent on showing off for Quinn, Renee bounced on the swing, the jiggling making her smooth-soled Mary Janes slide off the seat. Quinn and Laura both made a grab for her, but Renee fell backward, landing with a thud on the ground beneath the swing.

Quinn reached the child first. She was lying very still on her back, not even crying. His face white, he looked up at Laura as she knelt beside them. "She's not moving."

Laura ran professional hands over Renee, who was beginning to wriggle and catch her breath in broken sobs. "She just had the breath knocked out of her," she announced after a moment, pulling the little girl into her arms as Renee began to cry in earnest. "She's okay."

The padding provided by the thick snowsuit had protected the child in her fall from the low swing. "She's just scared. It's all right, Renee. You're fine," Laura crooned, patting Renee's back as she hugged her close.

Quinn blew out a deep breath, settling back on his heels in relief. Laura noted in concern that his face was still quite pale. She was surprised at his strong reaction to the relatively minor accident.

"Laura? Is Renee okay?" Betty came running up to them from the house. "I saw her fall, from the window."

At her mother's voice, Renee increased the volume of her sobs and squirmed out of Laura's hold. "Mommy, Mommy. I fell and hurt myself."

"She's fine," Laura assured Betty as the other woman lifted her child into her arms. "I'm sorry, Quinn and I were talking and we didn't see her stand up on the swing."

"Renee, didn't I tell you this morning not to stand up on your swing?" Betty scolded, turning toward the house. "Now you know why I wanted you to be careful."

Laura waited until Betty had carried Renee into the house before turning back to Quinn, who had stood and was staring at the swing set, his expression distant and set. "Quinn?" When he didn't immediately answer, she touched his arm. "Quinn?" she repeated.

He swiveled his head toward her, the vertical line between his brows deeply furrowed. "Yeah?"

"Are you okay?"

He looked surprised that she'd asked. "Sure."

"You look troubled."

"No. I was just a bit concerned about Renee."

"She really will be fine, Quinn. Things like that happen all the time with kids."

"Yeah, they're always getting into...playground accidents," he agreed, his voice fading as his frown deepened even further. Laura stepped closer to him, but before she could speak he seemed to throw off his odd mood and turn to her with his face deliberately cleared of expression. "It's getting dark. And colder. Guess we ought to go in."

Still concerned about him, Laura nodded and accompanied him without pursuing the subject. She knew better than to keep pushing him, but she wondered what it was about playgrounds that was haunting Quinn so.

Quinn stood on the deserted playground, a gun in his hand, his body tensed for action. Somewhere among the play tunnels and swings, picnic tables and merry-go-rounds his quarry was hiding. The man was slime, a drug dealer who'd killed and would kill again if given the chance. Quinn had no intention of allowing anyone else to die at this bastard's hands. "Vargas, it's over!" he called out flatly. "Give it up."

There was no answer. Exhaling impatiently, Quinn started forward, determined to look behind each piece of playground equipment until he found the guy. His partner was around somewhere, calling for backup. Between the two of them, they'd collar this one.

From out of nowhere a child appeared—a little girl in a pink snowsuit, something Quinn found mildly curious since it was August in New York. He caught the child's arm. "Go home," he told her, keeping an eye peeled for Vargas.

"But I want to pway, Quinn," she protested, pulling away from him.

Too concerned for her safety to wonder how she knew his name, he reached for her, but she dodged out of his grasp. And then the playground was filled with children, running and squealing, dodging around him in blissful unconcern as they pursued their innocent games. Damn. He'd have to let Vargas get away. He couldn't risk a confrontation here. Not now.

"Hey, pig!" a voice shouted from somewhere to his left. Quinn spun around to find himself facing Vargas, who was holding a frightened little girl in front of him, a gun pressed to her temple. "Drop the gun. Now."

Going cold, Quinn slowly bent and placed the weapon at his feet, his eyes never leaving the man holding the child. One part of his mind noted the sound of a woman screaming, children crying, but he trained his full concentration on the man. "Let her go, Vargas."

The other man began to walk backward, dragging the crying child with him, his dark eyes narrowed in hatred. "So you can shoot me down? No way. She's going with me."

Quinn tried reasoning with the man, keeping his voice as level and unthreatening as he could. "You'll never get away with it. In two minutes there will be cops swarming all over this place. Make it easy on yourself, man."

Vargas shook his head, causing a limp lock of dirty black hair to fall onto his scarred forehead. "Nah. She's my ticket out of here. Now don't move, you sh—" The word was cut off when Vargas stumbled over a soccer ball behind him, forcing him to scramble for his balance. Taking advantage of his loosened grip, the girl jerked away from him to run away, sobbing loudly.

Vargas steadied himself and crouched, both hands wrapped around the gun as he pointed it at Quinn, who'd dropped to pick up his own weapon. "Vargas, no!" Quinn shouted, desperately waving at the children to get off the playground. "Not here, dammit!"

The answer was a shot that missed him by inches. Quinn flattened himself on the ground, belly-crawling to a nearby merry-go-round, afraid to return the fire for fear of hitting one of the kids. Most of them unaccompanied by adults, the preteenage children were in a panic, too frightened to leave their positions. Out of the corner of his eye, Quinn watched as a woman began to scream at the children to run, her arms waving wildly. And then another shot rang out. Vargas had lost control, was firing wildly in Quinn's direction. Quinn forced himself to take aim, praying he wouldn't hit anyone but his target, terrified that one of the children around him was going to die.

Before Quinn could shoot, a boy of about ten screamed and fell to his knees only a few feet from where Quinn crouched. Blood spread rapidly over his chest as he lay dazed, having fallen directly in line between Quinn and Vargas. Taking a deep breath, Quinn launched himself at the kid, trying to cover him as Vargas fired again. The shot caught Quinn squarely in the shoulder. Fighting to stay conscious against the fiery explosion of pain, Quinn leveled his gun and pulled the trigger.

Vargas fell just as an army of cops swarmed into the playground. The entire incident had taken only a few minutes, though it had seemed like a lifetime. Relieved that it was over, Quinn looked down to check on the little boy he'd pulled down with him—only to find Renee lying there in his place, her little pink snowsuit stained crimson with blood as her big blue eyes stared sightlessly up at him.

"*NO!* Oh, God, no!"

"Quinn! Quinn, it's okay. It was only a dream. Wake up, darling. Please."

Wringing wet, his breathing labored and painful, Quinn fought his way to consciousness, opening his eyes to find Laura leaning over him. She'd turned on the bedside lamp and her face was pale in its light, her eyes locked anxiously with his. Her hands were gentle on his face as she stroked his cheeks, his forehead, wiping away the cold beads of perspiration. "It's all right, Quinn," she murmured again, soothingly. "It was only a dream. It's over."

"Oh, God," he muttered, his eyes closing again before opening to stare up at her. "Laura."

She helped him as he struggled upright, her hand falling to his scarred shoulder when he leaned weakly back against the headboard of her bed. "Can I get you something?" she asked solicitously.

"No." He pulled her into his arms, his face buried in her hair. "Just let me hold you a minute."

"As long as you want," she answered simply, snuggling closer against him, her arms warm around him.

"I remember it, Laura. Everything."

She stilled, then leaned her head back to look at him. "You remember? Do you think it's the same nightmare you've been having all along?"

"Yeah. Only it was no nightmare," he sighed, his head falling back against the wall. "It really happened—at least most of it."

"Do you want to talk about it?"

He ran a hand through his damp hair, disgusted that his fingers were shaking almost uncontrollably. "It happened three years ago, about a year after Michael died," he said after a long pause in which he'd decided he didn't want to talk about it but had to, anyway. "It was a drug bust. A cop wired for sound went into a warehouse for the payoff and he screwed up. He was killed. The rest of us busted in and there was general chaos. In the confusion, this guy Vargas, someone I'd been trying to put away for months, broke loose and ran. My partner and I pursued him through a low-rent housing area behind the warehouses. Before we could stop him, he ran into a playground in the center of the neighborhood. My partner called for backup while I followed Vargas.

"Anyway, he grabbed a little girl and held her hostage until she managed to break away from him, and then he just lost it and started firing. I've never been so scared in my life. All those kids—and there wasn't anything I could do. I was afraid to shoot in case I missed Vargas and hit one of the kids."

"Oh, Quinn."

"He—he shot a little boy. And then he shot me." Quinn rubbed his shoulder almost unconsciously as he spoke, remembered pain causing a dull throb there.

Laura caught her breath. "Did the boy—was he—?"

"He wasn't killed, though I thought he had been at first."

Laura sagged against him. "Oh, thank God."

Suddenly restless, Quinn pushed himself away from her and stood, catching up his jeans and stepping into them. He walked to the window and stared sightlessly out of it, aware that Laura was watching him from the bed. "What I don't understand is why I didn't remember there were kids on that playground?" he asked rawly, leaning his head on cool glass. "As soon as I was out of the hospital and able to work, I accepted a transfer to Florida. The few times I've thought of that incident since then, I remembered the playground being empty, just as I wrote about it. It wasn't. There were maybe twelve, fifteen kids there at the time, most of them about nine or ten years old."

"You blocked it," Laura told him quietly from close behind him. He hadn't realized she'd left the bed as he'd spoken. Her arms, clad in her soft green robe, slipped around his waist.

Laying his hands over hers, Quinn sighed deeply. "Stupid, isn't it? All this time I've been having these nightmares just because I wouldn't let myself remember the way things had really happened."

"You were so frightened for those children. You cared about them, Quinn. You cared very much."

He closed his eyes. "I almost got them killed. If I hadn't chased that guy into a playground in the first place—"

"Quinn, don't blame yourself. No one was killed."

"Vargas was. I shot him myself."

"You didn't have a choice."

"No." He stared outside again. "In the dream, it was Renee lying on the ground beside me, soaked with blood. She was dead."

"Oh, darling, how terrible for you. Her accident on the swing set this afternoon must have triggered your memory. In the dream, you got the two incidents mixed up."

That made twice she'd called him darling. He could get used to hearing the caressing word. He turned and held her close. "The nightmares started almost as soon as I went to work in Miami. I thought they'd stop when I quit, but they didn't."

"You had to face it, Quinn. You had to stop repressing it and start dealing with the unjustified guilt and the terror you'd felt. Now that you've remembered exactly what happened, you can learn to accept that you weren't at fault, that maybe your actions saved those other children from being hurt."

"I told myself I'd stopped caring," he whispered bleakly, his arms tightening around her.

"You never stopped caring," she murmured in response. "You always cared too much."

"Like—" He stopped, unable to complete the sentence.

"Like Michael," she finished for him, reading his mind.

Like Michael. Michael had cared too much and he'd died. "Damn."

"It's not that you didn't feel anything during the past few years, Quinn. It's that you didn't *want* to feel anything," Laura went on relentlessly. "Now it's up to you to decide if you want to keep on that way, or if you want to rejoin the living and get on with your life."

He made no attempt to answer. His head ached and he was tired. So very tired.

Laura gave him a minute, then pulled out of his arms, catching his hand in hers. "Come back to bed, Quinn. You're exhausted."

He nodded. "Yeah."

Stripping back out of his jeans, he climbed under the covers beside her, snapped off the lamp, and turned to pull her into his arms.

Holding her too tightly but unable to loosen his grip, he closed his eyes and allowed himself to savor the feel of her— warm, soft, clinging, caring. He didn't know what he'd done to deserve Laura's love, but it must have been something spectacular, he thought dimly, already drifting toward sleep. Now the question was whether he could prove himself worthy of that love. Because he was beginning to believe that he couldn't live without it.

Laura woke first again the next morning. She lay looking at the man in her bed, the man she loved with all her heart, the man who'd had to face so much in just the few weeks she'd known him. Remembering the things he'd told her in the night, her heart twisted. No wonder he'd tried so hard to repress his feelings. It must have been sheer torture for a man who loved children as much as Quinn did to have to feel responsible for whether the ones on that playground had lived or died.

Knowing that Quinn needed his sleep, she still leaned over him and murmured his name.

His eyes opened immediately. "What is it?"

"I have to get up," she told him quietly. "You can go back to sleep, if you want, but I didn't want you to wake up lonely this morning."

He lay very still for several long moments, his eyes locked with hers, looking as if there were something he wanted to say. Something he didn't know how to say. And then he made an incoherent murmur low in his throat and pulled her head down to his for a long, deeply expressive kiss.

"Will you be here when I come home?" Laura asked when he released her, praying she'd be able to live with his answer.

"I'll be here," he answered after only a moment's pause. "I won't leave today."

No promises for the next day, Laura noted wistfully, but at least he wasn't leaving today.

Chapter Fifteen

Stopping at the tree where he usually paused during his walks for a smoke, Quinn reached under his parka from habit, only to find his shirt pocket empty. He'd forgotten to bring his cigarettes. Mildly surprised to discover that he didn't really want one, anyway, he propped his back against the tree and took a deep breath, noting the crispness of clean winter air even as he wondered at how differently he felt that afternoon. It was as if he'd freed himself of an enormous burden, as if in telling Laura about the nightmare he'd rid himself permanently of its tyranny.

He was still finding it hard to believe that he'd deceived himself for three years about what had really happened in that playground. All this time he's wondered if maybe the nightmares were in some way related to Michael's death, despite his assurances to himself and others to the contrary. And maybe he hadn't completely come to terms with his loss. Maybe grief for his brother had been tied up in some way with his trauma over the playground incident. Somehow he knew that now that he'd faced the worst memories of his recent past, he'd be able to put them behind him. Maybe he'd even start to remember the positive things he'd accomplished during his fourteen years of police service— the lives he and Michael had saved during their careers, the criminals they'd kept off the streets, if only for a short time. Maybe they *had* been fighting forest fires with beach pails, but their combined efforts had doused at least a few destructive flames.

With the past truly behind him, perhaps he could make better use of his future. The only thing he knew for certain was that he wanted Laura to be a part of that future. He never wanted to wake in the night again without having her beside him, never wanted her to shed another tear because of him. If it meant that he was going to have to learn to live with half the homeless population of Colorado, then so be it.

He needed her. Carrying that thought a step further, he finally acknowledged that he loved her. All the time he'd been telling her he was incapable of loving, he'd been falling head over heels in love with her. And had been too stubbornly blind to realize it until he'd wakened from a nightmare that had been too vivid to push away, too painful to face alone. Only Laura could have healed the raw wounds that had been festering inside him for so long.

A line from a poem read at Michael's funeral drifted through his mind:

She glides into his darker musings
with a kind and healing sympathy
that takes away their sharpness
ere he is aware.

The poet, William Cullen Bryant, had been talking about nature, but he could have referred to Laura. With her love and her sweet understanding, she'd eased the sharpness of Quinn's grief. He could only wonder again if he deserved her.

Quinn had spent many years refusing to acknowledge fear, but he freely admitted to himself that he was scared spitless at the thought of asking Laura to share her future with him. What if he let her down? What if he proved himself unworthy of her love? She'd said she wanted children. What kind of a father would he make? What if he failed at that?

He was wasting time worrying about questions he couldn't answer, he decided, glancing at his watch as he started back toward the house. Laura would be home soon. He wanted to be there to greet her when she arrived. He intended to assure her that she didn't have to keep worrying that she'd come home from work and find him gone; it hadn't been fair for her to have to work with that doubt in the back of her mind. Remembering how sweetly she'd awakened him that morning, he quickened his steps.

The house had just come into sight when he heard Janet screaming his name. Something in her voice made him break into a dead run.

She met him in the backyard. "Oh, Quinn, hurry! He's going to hurt them!" she sobbed, her face white as she clutched his arm. "He's trying to take Renee."

Quinn could hear a man's voice yelling from the front yard, followed by what sounded like a cry from Mrs. Elliott. Without pausing to ask her questions, he shook Janet off and sprinted around the side of the house.

Gene Pritchard, Betty's soon-to-be ex-husband, was big—tall with lots of muscle, though some of it was beginning to turn to fat. He was also viciously drunk and intent on taking out his anger on someone who couldn't fight back. While Mrs. Elliott stood helplessly nearby, her lined face wet with frightened tears, Betty was trying to keep herself between her husband and her child. The first thing Quinn noted when he spotted her was the bruise already turning dark on one side of her face.

Just as Quinn was about to make his presence known, the drunken bear of a man pulled back a hand and slapped Betty out of the way, snatching Renee as Betty fell to the ground. Renee screamed a protest and tried to squirm out of her father's arms, but he was already turning toward the battered pickup parked in the driveway, obviously intent on leaving with her. Betty and Mrs. Elliott both moved to stop him, but he shouted at them to leave him alone or he'd kill them.

Going cold on a wave of sheer, deadly fury, Quinn reached the truck just as Pritchard opened the door. "You're not going anywhere with that child," he said flatly, slamming the door closed with one booted foot. "Put her down."

Pritchard narrowed reddened eyes and stared contemptuously at the slightly shorter, pounds-lighter, man. "Who the hell are you?"

"Put her down," Quinn repeated without bothering to answer the question. "Janet, call the police," he added, never taking his eyes off the other man, though he was aware that Janet moved to follow his instructions.

"This is none of your business," Pritchard informed him, tightening his hold on the child crying at his shoulder. "It's my kid and ain't nobody going to stop me from taking her."

"You're wrong. I'm going to stop you."

Pritchard snorted derisively. "Like hell."

"Quinn, he's hurting her," Betty sobbed as Renee cried louder in the brutally tight grasp of one meaty arm.

His eyes still locked with Pritchard's, Quinn nodded curtly. "Come get her, Betty."

"Take one step near me and you'll be on your butt in the dirt again," Pritchard growled immediately, slanting a threatening look at his tearful wife.

"You're pretty tough with women and three-year-olds," Quinn drawled in challenge, shrugging out of his parka and then leaning back against the pickup with his arms crossed over his chest. "How are you in an equal fight?"

Again, Pritchard's snort expressed his scorn. "You think it'd be an equal fight between you and me?"

"No," Quinn replied evenly. "I think you'll be at a disadvantage. But since I'm not particularly concerned about being fair, I'm going to tear your face off, anyway."

Pritchard stiffened at the deliberate insult, his alcohol-fueled temper overcoming any common sense he may normally have possessed. "I'd like to see you try."

"Then stop cowering behind that baby and watch me."

Growling his fury, Pritchard set Renee none too gently on the ground. She instinctively started toward Quinn, but her mother stopped her, catching her into her arms and moving to stand fearfully beside Mrs. Elliott, who was wringing her hands in dread.

"Take Renee in the house. Both of you," Quinn ordered just before Pritchard attacked him with a bellow of rage. He didn't have time to make sure his instructions had been followed.

Pritchard's first blow caught Quinn squarely in the face. It felt as if he'd been hit by a truck. Disregarding the explosion of pain, he kicked out, following the movement with a slash of his hand that connected solidly with the bigger man's neck.

He didn't know how long they fought. Probably not long, though it seemed like hours. There were moments when he wondered if the man would beat him on strength and size alone, but Quinn had the advantage of being several years younger, in better physical condition and sober. The fight ended with Pritchard face down in the dirt, his arm twisted behind his back as Quinn straddled him, his free hand clenched in Pritchard's thinning brown hair.

Ignoring the blood that made warm, sticky paths down the side of his face, Quinn leaned over, twisting the grimacing bully's arm harder. "Have you ever killed anyone, Pritchard?" When the man didn't immediately answer, Quinn pulled his hair to lift his face a bit higher off the ground. "Have you?"

"N-no, of course I haven't killed anyone. Aagh, you're breaking my arm!"

"I've killed, Pritchard. And if you ever come near anyone in this household again, you're a dead man. You got that?"

Whatever Pritchard might have answered—and Quinn was satisfied that the answer would have been yes—was cut off by the wail of a siren as a police car squealed into the driveway. Looking uncertain which man to cuff, the two uniformed cops pulled Quinn off the fallen man.

Rushing to Quinn's side, Betty pointed to Pritchard, babbling an explanation.

"There's a restraining order against him," Quinn added. "You can arrest him for ignoring that, for assault and battery and for attempted kidnapping. The child's mother has full custody."

Minutes later, the police car left, Pritchard in the back seat. Absently swiping at his face with the back of his hand, Quinn watched it go, slowly coming down from the adrenaline rush induced by the sight of Renee in that man's hands.

"Oh, Quinn, your face," Betty murmured in dismay, her hands on his arm.

"Quinn, dear, come into the house," Mrs. Elliott fussed, his parka clutched in her arms. Though pale and still visibly shaken, she hovered over him like a worried hen with a wounded chick, her faded blue eyes taking inventory of his various cuts and bruises.

"Are the two of you okay?" Quinn demanded, touching a gentle finger to Betty's own bruised face before looking in concern at Mrs. Elliott, thinking apprehensively of her weak heart.

"We're fine," Betty assured him, tugging a bit at his arm to start him walking toward the house. "And Janet's inside with Renee, calming her down. Now we have to take care of you. Your nose is bleeding and there's a cut on your eye. Oh, and there's blood at the corner of your mouth."

Mrs. Elliott took his other arm, as if he needed help walking in, Quinn thought, beginning to be wryly amused by their solicitude. He was still trying to assure them that he wasn't quite an invalid when they stepped onto the porch, just as Laura's Subaru pulled up to the house.

"Quinn!" she called out, leaping out of the car. "Oh, my God, what happened? Are you all right?"

Sighing, Quinn assured her, too, that he was fine, but he was wasting his breath. All talking at once as questions were asked and answered, the three women led him into the house and straight to the kitchen, where Laura ordered him into a chair at the table while Mrs. Elliott went to fetch the first-aid kit and Betty prepared an ice pack for his eye. All this attention was flattering, he decided, but rather overwhelming.

"Would the three of you stop hovering over me?" he demanded in exasperation. "Betty, use that ice pack on your own face; it's starting to swell. Dammit, Laura! What the hell are you putting on those cuts—salt?" he added, jerking away from the stinging solution she was applying to his face.

She rolled her eyes at his irritability and, in much the same tone she would have used with Renee, ordered him to be still and stop complaining. And then, gently brushing his hair off his forehead, she kept right on working on his face. Subsiding into disgruntled mutters, Quinn shut up and sat still until she finished.

"There," she said, smoothing the edge of an adhesive strip on his cheek. "All done. Any other injuries?"

Knowing that most of his body would be spotted with bruises, and deciding he'd allow her to check each one of them later, Quinn shook his head. "That's all. Thanks."

Laura's eyes held his for a moment, her expression hard to read. She started to say something but was interrupted by Renee's sudden appearance in the room.

The child ran straight to the chair where Quinn sat, her lip quivering as she studied his battered face. "You hurt, Quinn?" she asked.

He pulled her into his lap and hugged her. "It's only a little hurt, Renee," he assured her. "Aunt Laura took care of it for me."

She wriggled around until she was kneeling on his thighs, her chubby arms around his neck. Planting a wet kiss on his face, she then rubbed her cheek against his. "Better now?"

He cleared his throat of a sudden obstruction. "Yes, it's much better now. Thanks, kid." His eyes met Laura's.

She turned to Mrs. Elliott and Betty, her voice rather husky when she spoke. "We'll have soup and sandwiches for dinner tonight. Betty, I know you want to spend some time with Renee now. Mrs. Elliott, you really should lie down for a while."

Mrs. Elliott nodded. The rosy color was slowly returning to her cheeks, Quinn noted in relief as he got to his feet, setting Renee down beside him. "Yes, I am rather tired," she admitted. She looked up at Quinn. "You're sure you're all right, dear?"

Forcing his bruised mouth into a smile of sorts, Quinn promised her that he was. And then he impulsively leaned over to drop a light kiss on her soft cheek. "Thanks for caring."

Rapidly blinking her eyes, Mrs. Elliott patted his arm and left the room.

"Quinn," Betty began, moistening her pale lips. "I don't know how to thank you for what you did. I'm so sorry you had to be hurt because of me."

"It wasn't your fault, Betty," he told her firmly. "And I really am okay. Believe me, I've been in much worse situations."

"I'm sure you have. But thank you, anyway," she told him, stepping close to hug him quickly. Knowing the move had taken a great deal of courage on the part of the shy, timid woman, Quinn returned the hug. Betty was dabbing at tears when she left the room, holding her daughter's hand.

Janet peeked in for a moment to see for herself that Quinn had survived, then she, too, went off to care for her own child, leaving Laura and Quinn alone in the kitchen.

Very aware of the sudden silence in the room, Laura leaned against the counter and pushed a hand through her hair, drawing a deep breath. It seemed like the first steady breath she'd taken since arriving home to find Quinn on the porch, bloodied and disheveled.

"Would you like some aspirin?" she offered, knowing Quinn must be aching all over.

He shook his head, obviously tired of being a patient. "Need some help with dinner?"

She laughed a bit ruefully and opened a cabinet, pulling out a red-and-white can. "I think I can handle this," she replied, wrinkling her nose in self-derision. "I'm not much of a cook," she admitted, turning to set the can of soup on the counter and reach for a second one.

Quinn's arms closed around her waist, pulling her back against him. "I think I can overlook that," he murmured into her ear, his cheek resting against her hair.

Laura closed her eyes and leaned into his strength, savoring the warmth of him. Her throat tightened with the effort to hold back the words of love she wanted to say to him. She wouldn't, because she wasn't sure he wanted to hear them. He'd been visibly uncomfortable with all the attention he'd been receiving for the past half hour; she wouldn't have been surprised if he'd chosen to lock himself into the study again out of self-defense.

"I haven't kissed you in hours," he told her, turning her to face him. "Kiss me, Laura."

Without even hesitating she rose on tiptoe to follow his instructions, his head lowering to meet her halfway. The kiss was powerful, fueled by the tension they'd both been under earlier. Her knees weakening, Laura clung to his shirt with both hands. He tilted his head and kissed her again, then flinched when the new angle put pressure on the cut on that side of his mouth.

"Damn," he muttered when she pulled back immediately.

Laura swallowed and turned out of his arms, toying with the soup cans. "I guess you were right not to want to get involved with my problems," she said before she could stop herself.

Quinn gripped her arm and turned her back around. "What the hell is that supposed to mean?"

"Well, look at you. You stayed here against your better judgment and as a result you were beaten by the drunken ex-husband of one of my boarders. I wouldn't blame you if you— Quinn, what are you *doing*?" she demanded as she was jerked roughly off her feet and into his arms.

Without bothering to answer, Quinn carried her toward the kitchen door, his expression sternly determined.

"Quinn, you shouldn't—your injuries—" she sputtered, making a grab for his shoulders as he pushed through the swinging door with little regard for her dangling feet.

"Shut up."

Blinking at the fiercely growled command, Laura closed her mouth and wondered what in the world she'd said to precipitate this reaction from him.

Holding an empty baby bottle, Janet paused outside the kitchen door, her eyes widening in surprise as Quinn passed her. "Dinner's going to be late," he announced, not seeming at all disconcerted to be caught carrying Laura through the hallway.

"No problem," Janet called after them, her voice quivering with suppressed laughter. "Take your time."

Groaning her embarrassment, Laura hid her flaming face against Quinn's shirt, hoping Betty and Mrs. Elliott were upstairs in their rooms. Quinn didn't pause until he'd carried her into her room, kicking the door shut behind him before he deposited her on her bed with such force that she bounced. He followed her down, trapping her to the mattress with a hand on either side of her.

"Now listen to me and listen good," he said, his gray eyes holding hers as he leaned over her. "I have been an idiot and a coward. You were right when you said I've been too busy hiding out and licking my wounds to get on with my life. That's exactly what I've been doing for the past two years—hell, maybe even longer than that. But not anymore. I've done a lot of thinking today and I've made some decisions."

Afraid to hope that the decisions were the ones she prayed they were, Laura moistened suddenly dry lips and looked up at him. "What—what decisions?"

"I've decided that only an utter fool would walk away from the home you've offered me here. I may have been an idiot and a coward, but I'm no fool, Laura. You couldn't get rid of me now if you tried."

Beginning to tremble with the force of her emotions, Laura reached up a shaking hand to touch his bandaged cheek. "You—you're staying in Colorado? With me?" she asked in a whisper.

"Damn straight," he answered flatly, and then, a bit less confidently, "if you'll have me."

"If I'll— Oh, Quinn, surely you don't doubt that!" She tugged at him, pulling him down beside her to burrow into his arms. "I never, never want you to leave. But—" she lifted her head to look at him with a worried frown "—what about all the others? Quinn, I love you so much that I'd do almost anything for you, but I can't ask them to leave. I just can't."

"Of course you can't. Neither could I. Nor do I want to." He propped himself on one elbow and pushed his free hand through his hair, seeming to organize his thoughts before speaking again. "When I found Pritchard terrorizing everyone earlier, I was so furious I wanted to kill him. I didn't stop to think about it then, of course, but now I realize that my rage at him had a lot to do with my feelings for the ones he was threatening. Despite my efforts to prevent it, I've come to care for those people; in just a few short weeks they've become almost like a family to me. And Pritchard was hurting the people I cared about."

"So you took up for them."

He shrugged. "I would have taken up for anyone who was being abused by someone bigger and stronger," he admitted, "but in this case I was personally involved because of my feelings for them. It made me realize that I can't stop myself from caring about people just because of the risks that come with getting involved. In spite of the grief I suffered when Michael died, I wouldn't give up one day with him if I had it to do over. The time I had with him, the feelings we shared, were worth the pain in the end. And if he hadn't cared enough about people to stop to help a woman he thought was in trouble—well, he wouldn't have been the man that he was."

Not even trying to hold back the tears streaming down her face, Laura reached out to him. Quinn caught her hand, pressed a kiss in the palm, and held it to his cheek. "Do you know how much I love the way you touch me?" he murmured, his eyes softening. "I don't want to live without having you there to touch my cheek when I'm down, to make me smile when I'm moody, to yell at me when I get too self-absorbed. I don't know if it's enough to offer in return, but I'm willing to give you everything I have, everything I am."

"It's enough," she murmured, her thumb caressing the unbruised corner of his mouth. "More than enough."

"I won't be an easy man to live with," he warned her, and she remembered that he'd used the same words when he'd asked her to move to Florida with him. "I've always been a moody, serious type, and though I'll try to lighten up, I can't guarantee that I'll change all that much."

"I don't want you to change. I love you exactly the way you are."

His eyes closed briefly, then opened again to stare fiercely into hers. "I'll never be able to express my feelings as easily as you do," he grated, his voice raw. "I may never be able to tell you exactly how much I love you. How very much I need you."

"Oh, Quinn." She threw herself in his arms, crying in joy. He rolled to lie beneath her, cradling her against his chest. "I love you so much," she told him thickly, cupping his face in her hands and pressing a kiss to his lips. "I adore you. I'll probably tell you so often that you'll get tired of hearing it."

"Never."

"And I'm not going to be all that easy to live with, myself. I can't cook. I bring my worries home from work with me at night and tear myself up over my babies at the hospital. I can't turn away a stray. And I don't give up on someone I care about, no matter how much she—or he—may push me away."

"Thank God."

She kissed him again. "Think you can accept me under those terms?"

"Under any terms. Are you prepared to marry a man who locks himself up with a computer for hours and makes a living writing books that don't all have happy endings? Are you willing to risk the chance that our kids will turn out to be moody, serious little oddballs just like their father?''

She hadn't thought she could be any happier. "You want to marry me? Start a family with me?"

"Please, Laura."

"Oh, Quinn. Yes. Yes—yes—yes." She punctuated each word with another, longer kiss until their mouths fused in an expression of love that rapidly transformed itself into an explosion of passion.

Quinn rolled to loom over her, his hands going impatiently to the buttons of her wrinkled uniform, his lips roaming feverishly over her face, her throat, the skin he exposed as he released each button. As eager as he to have nothing left between them, Laura struggled with the fastenings of his clothes until she and Quinn were naked, their arms and legs entangled as they tried to get closer than physically possible.

Laura exclaimed in dismay at the bruises revealed when she pulled back to look at him. Her fingers brushed lightly over one particularly nasty contusion at his ribs. "My poor, wounded warrior," she mused aloud, thinking of all the scars he bore—both physical and mental—from his many years of battling for those who couldn't fight for themselves.

He murmured something that sounded like "a kind and healing sympathy."

"What did you say, Quinn?"

"Never mind," he answered, and then stopped all further conversation by sealing her mouth with his, his knee separating her thighs to make a place for him there.

Glorying in his impatience to be one with her, Laura opened for him and arched to receive him when he entered her with one powerful, yet somehow tender, thrust. They moaned in unison at the searing pleasure, made even more glorious by their admissions of love and the lifetime commitment they'd made to each other.

"I love you, Laura," Quinn murmured, holding himself still for a moment to savor the sensations.

Treasuring the words that had been so difficult for him to say, Laura held him closer, her hips moving instinctively.

Her movements shattered Quinn's control. He groaned and kissed her fiercely, his lean, tanned body instigating the smooth, rocking movements that would bring them release from the exquisite tension that held them both in its grasp.

A long time later, Quinn tightened his arms around her, his face buried tightly into the curve of her neck. "Marry me soon. This week," he demanded suddenly.

"As soon as we can arrange it," she promised, smoothing his thick hair, her heart swelling at this further proof of his need for her.

Seeming to find reassurance in her words, he relaxed and kissed her shoulder. "I suppose we really should join the others," he said rather reluctantly.

Laura smiled and trailed her fingers down his sleek back. "There's no hurry," she murmured, pressing closer to him. "They're quite capable of making their own soup and sandwiches."

Quinn grinned, his mustache tilting upward, his rarely seen dimples creasing his cheeks. "In that case—"

And he lowered his head to hers, his hand covering her breast. Murmuring her delight, Laura cooperated wholeheartedly with his efforts to reaffirm their commitment. "I love you, Quinn."

"Laura. My Laura. My wife." He spoke the words savoringly, then added those words that seemed to be easier for him to say each time. "I love you."

Epilogue

Stop him, Quinn! He's got Mike's fire engine!"

Responding to the indignant words, Quinn straightened from beneath the hood of the car he was tinkering with and narrowed his eyes at the overgrown mutt streaking past him—another of Laura's strays, of course. "Drop it, Max!" he ordered sharply.

The dog froze comically, his tattered tail drooping as he sheepishly laid the bright red toy at Quinn's feet and lowered his head, looking up in beseeching apology. The bane of the household—particularly Sabu, who regarded the dog as a personal affront—Max was good-natured, affectionate and hopelessly untrainable, obeying only one member of his adopted family. Quinn. Laura claimed that the wise decision of whom he should obey proved Max wasn't as dumb as he pretended to be.

"Stupid dog," Renee muttered, reclaiming the toy with a moue of distaste at its wetness. "Mike put the truck down for only a minute and Max grabbed it and ran."

"Be sure and wash it before you give it back to Mike," Quinn instructed absently, leaning back under the hood of the car to give one last twist to the clamp on the new radiator hose he'd just installed. The car was Betty's—a used one she'd bought with her savings, to her great pride. It was the first car she'd ever owned by herself; Quinn had helped her pick it out.

"Quinn," Renee protested offendedly. "Of course I'll wash it! Give me a break."

Chuckling, Quinn wiped his hands on a rag and then tugged at her long blond ponytail. "Sorry, kid. I keep forgetting you're seven years old now."

Renee held her haughty pose for only a moment before breaking into the grin that had captivated him from the moment he'd first seen her four years earlier. "Just don't forget it again," she warned flippantly, giving him a quick hug. Unusually mature for her age, Renee had grown into a loving, thoughtful little girl blessedly free of scars from the less than ideal home life she'd had in her first three years.

"Daddy! Max gotted my twuck!" a disgruntled voice complained belatedly as a sturdy little boy appeared from around the side of the house with his hand tucked into Betty's.

"It's okay, Michael. Renee has it," Quinn assured him. "She's going to wash it for you."

A smile spread over his three-year-old son's face. Quinn's throat tightened in a familiar ache as he thought again how very much young Michael resembled the man he'd been named after. Quinn's son was the image of the uncle he'd never known, a resemblance Quinn always noted with pleasure and gratitude.

"Why don't we go inside for a cookie and a glass of milk?" Betty suggested, including both the children in her invitation. She smiled at Quinn when they eagerly accepted, dashing hand in hand for the front porch, Renee shortening her steps to match Michael's. Betty had changed a great deal since Quinn first met her. Her eyes no longer frightened and shadowed with unhappy memories, she'd gained a few much-needed pounds and started wearing more flattering clothing and hairstyles. Though she dated occasionally, she'd expressed no interest in remarrying, claiming to be perfectly happy as housekeeper and cook for this frequently changing, rather unusual household.

"Your car is fixed, Betty. It was just a broken hose."

Betty smiled gratefully. "Thank you, Quinn. Want a cookie and a glass of milk?"

He half smiled. "I think I'll pass. Don't want to spoil my dinner."

"You're only saying that because you know I'm making your favorite dish."

"Could be."

Alone with Quinn, Max sat up and whined, shamelessly begging for attention. Quinn sighed and scratched behind a floppy ear, calling himself a sucker even as he did so. His gaze moved contentedly around the lawn he'd mowed the day before. As beautiful as it was in winter, Colorado was breathtaking in the summertime, he decided. He'd never regretted leaving Florida to move here.

His eyes lingered on the guest cottage. The young woman currently staying there had recently been evicted from her apartment in Greeley. She'd been unable to pay her rent after losing her job for refusing to give in to her employer's sexual harassment. Hearing of Maria's problems, Laura had immediately offered the use of the cottage and found Maria a job at the hospital, as well as finding an attorney who'd offered her services free of charge for the harassment case.

Quinn hadn't minded the latest addition to the clan; after all, he'd recently brought home a stray of his own. Through a friend he'd made in the Greeley Police Department, Quinn had been introduced to a troubled teenager, Brad, who'd lost his mother a couple of years earlier and had been neglected since by his father. Lacking supervision, the sixteen-year-old had drifted in and out of trouble with the local police. Identifying with Brad's untimely loss of his mother and sensing that he only needed guidance from someone who cared enough to give him the proper incentive to stay out of trouble, Quinn had taken the boy under his wing.

Quinn had been a tough guardian, and Brad had tried a time or two to rebel, but Quinn was beginning to see the difference in the young man's attitude. Brad was holding down a job at a fast-food restaurant in Greeley during his summer break from school, hadn't been in trouble with the law since he'd moved in and was starting to respond to the warm acceptance he'd found in this house. Laura, of course, had welcomed him with open arms, and Betty, Renee and Michael were used to sharing their home with others. Quinn had often wished that Mrs. Elliott had lived to meet Brad; she'd have knitted him a sweater and treated him like another favored grandson. He missed Mrs. Elliott, though he was grateful for the two years he'd been blessed by knowing her.

Betty, Renee and Brad now occupied three of the four bedrooms on the second floor, while Quinn and Laura shared what had always been her room and Michael resided in the room that had once been Laura's father's. The house was full, but Quinn had never been happier. He and Laura had even discussed adding a couple of extra rooms to the lower floor in the fall. They'd been talking about giving Michael a baby sister or brother.

Lifting his head at the sound of a car engine, Quinn smiled in welcome as Laura's car turned into the drive. He was already walking toward the car when his wife opened her door and stepped out. After almost four years of marriage, she was still as beautiful as she'd been the day he'd met her, her wheat-colored hair still curling riotously around her porcelain-smooth face, her brown eyes still gazing at him with so much love that he sometimes ached with the pleasure of it.

Nodding greetings to Maria and Brad, who rode home in the afternoons with Laura and were now heading toward their respective houses, Quinn opened his arms to his wife.

Laura smiled and threw herself into Quinn's arms, her own closing around his neck. "Hi," she managed when she emerged from the long, thorough kiss with which he greeted her. "Any major crises today?"

Still holding her, he shook his head, causing the sun to glint off the lighter streaks around his face. Laura never looked at her husband without thinking how very handsome he was, and how fortunate she was to be married to him. She was thinking that again as she waited for his answer to her light question.

"Nothing major," he told her. "Max tried to eat Mike's fire truck."

"Stupid dog. Did you finish chapter four?"

"Yeah. How about you? Everything go okay at work?"

"Yes. I saw Janet today. She said to tell you hello. She and Larry are getting along just fine."

"Good. We'll have to invite her over for dinner soon."

Nodding agreement, Laura turned with him toward the house, their arms linked. Pausing before going inside, she looked up to Quinn, enjoying the moment alone with him before they joined the others. "I love you, Quinn."

He kissed her quickly. "I love you," he told her gruffly, then opened the door for her. Laura knew, as he did, that they would have more to say on that subject later, when they were alone in their bedroom. Much more.

Smiling in anticipation, she stepped inside the door to be noisily welcomed by her son and Renee.

Following closely, Quinn closed the door of their home behind them.

* * * * *

FOUR UNIQUE SERIES
FOR EVERY WOMAN YOU ARE...

Silhouette Romance

Love, at its most tender, provocative,
emotional...in stories that will make you laugh and
cry while bringing you the magic of falling in love.

6 titles per month

Silhouette Special Edition

Sophisticated, substantial and packed with
emotion, these powerful novels of life and love will
capture your imagination and steal your heart.

6 titles per month

Silhouette Desire

Open the door to romance and passion. Humorous,
emotional, compelling—yet always a believable
and sensuous story—Silhouette Desire never
fails to deliver on the promise of love.

6 titles per month

Silhouette Intimate Moments

Enter a world of excitement, of romance
heightened by suspense, adventure and the
passions every woman dreams of. Let us
sweep you away.

4 titles per month

SILG-1R

COMING NEXT MONTH

#499 LOVING JACK—Nora Roberts
Steady Nathan Powell was jolted upon finding impulsive
Jackie MacNamera ensconced in his home. Living with her would
be impossible! But *loving* Jack soon proved all too easy....

#500 COMPROMISING POSITIONS—Carole Halston
Laid-back cabinetmaker Jim Mann definitely wasn't ambitious
Susan Casey's type. So why were his warm brown eyes lulling her
into such a compromising position?

#501 LABOR OF LOVE—Madelyn Dohrn
Alone and pregnant, delicate Kara Reynolds temporarily leaned
on solid John Brickner. But Kara's innocent deception—and
Bric's buried secrets—gave new meaning to "labor of love."

#502 SHADES AND SHADOWS—Victoria Pade
Talented Tyler Welles lived in the shadow of a well-publicized
scandal. Eric Mathias was determined to expose her...until he
discovered the precious secret behind her shady reputation.

#503 A FINE SPRING RAIN—Celeste Hamilton
Haunted by the miraculous and tragic night they'd shared years
ago, Dr. Merry Conrad reappeared in farmer Sam Bartholomew's
life. But could she convince him she belonged there forever?

#504 LIKE STRANGERS—Lynda Trent
Five years ago Lani's husband left on a cargo flying mission—
and never returned. Suddenly Brian was back...but like a
stranger. Could they ever be man and wife once more?

AVAILABLE THIS MONTH:

#493 PROOF POSITIVE
Tracy Sinclair

#494 NAVY WIFE
Debbie Macomber

#495 IN HONOR'S SHADOW
Lisa Jackson

#496 HEALING SYMPATHY
Gina Ferris

#497 DIAMOND MOODS
Maggi Charles

#498 A CHARMED LIFE
Anne Lacey

Silhouette Desire

1989
IS THE YEAR
OF THE MAN!

What makes a romance? A special man, of course, and Silhouette Desire celebrates that fact with *twelve* of them! From Mr. January to Mr. December, every month spotlights the Silhouette Desire hero—our **MAN OF THE MONTH.**

Sexy, macho, charming, irritating...irresistible! Nothing can stop these men from sweeping you away. Created by some of your favorite authors, each man is custom-made for pleasure—*reading* pleasure— so don't miss a single one.

Diana Palmer kicks off the new year, and you can look forward to magnificent men from **Joan Hohl, Jennifer Greene** and many, many more. So get out there and find your man!

Silhouette Desire's

MAN OF THE MONTH...

MAND-1